CROW COURT

Andy Charman

unbound

First published in 2021
This paperback edition first published in 2022

Unbound
Level 1, Devonshire House
One Mayfair Place
London W1J 8AJ

www.unbound.com

A CIP record for this book is available
from the British Library

ISBN 978-1-80018-090-1 (paperback)
ISBN 978-1-78352-910-0 (hardback)
ISBN 978-1-78352-911-7 (ebook)

Designed and typeset in Caslon by Patty Rennie

Printed and bound in Great Britain by
Clays Ltd, Elcograf S.p.A.

1 3 5 7 9 8 6 4 2

For my wife and daughter

With special thanks to
Nigel and Maggie Charman

Contents

CONCERNS FOR HENRY CUFF

~

Wimborne Minster, Dorset, May 1840

Louisa Chilcott is in the dressmaker's by the Corn Market. Taken up residence there, according to her father.

White silk, layered over taffeta and fringed with so many yards of lace that her mother winces each time the dressmaker stretches her arms. Louisa, standing on a stool for access to her hems, has to press her skirts flat to see what is happening on the floor.

'Harriet—darling sister—if you want to touch the silk, please, *please* use your gloves.'

Sisters—three in number—comprise two bridesmaids-to-be and one dearly beloved who looks likely to stand and tremble with envy. They have already argued the virtues of silk over lace and white over colour: another skirmish in a lengthy war of wills, and a barren debate. Louisa has chosen to follow the fashion set by the newly married queen and the cloth is cut; the thread of the conversation has spooled on to a subtle attack on the inspiration for Louisa's choice;

kings, it is suggested, reign more supremely than queens. Louisa defends her monarch, her sex and herself.

'They don't go into battle any more, anyway,' she says. 'King George didn't fight at Waterloo. *Was* it King George, Mama?'

A nod of confirmation from Mama is interrupted in a sister's rush to dispute.

'Well, it doesn't matter now,' claims Miriam, next eldest sister, whose envy will turn to drowned ashes. 'She's married, so the King will take over.'

'Ah, but you are *quite* wrong. He is the Queen's Consort. A mere *Prince* Albert.'

'What's a consort?'

'Like a concubine, but male.'

'Yes, thank you, Louisa!' says her mother, acting umpire for decorum.

'If you could be a-lifting your foot, ma'am?' asks the dressmaker's assistant.

Louisa does so, glancing up at the window in anticipation of the arrival of...

Samuel Portman, the affianced. Proud as a poppy and about the same proportions. Riding into town in a pony and trap. Chin up, reins held high, large-headed and thin as a wheel. Rounding the long slope that arcs down from Furzehill past solemn oaks and Celtic hedgerows. A recent acquirer of superfluous but bountiful knowledge about Queen Victoria's wedding dress, he told his father over breakfast, 'It was adorned with orange blossom, you know.'

'Was it?' came the grumpy answer.

'Indeed it was.'

Has acceded to each and every whim of wedding fashion

as willingly as any young groom might—enlightened by the guiding lamp of adoration. Pony's hooves thump the resounding bricks of Walford Bridge, causing a lift of the head on the parts of both…

Bill Brown and John Street, who stand knee-deep in the waters of the Allen; in braces and waders and under the employ of the Wimborne Corporation; clearing rushes from the river banks with the aim of averting another flood and thereby saving the margins of the Farmer's Fire and Life Insurance Company.

'Proper trimmen crop o' rushes here,' Bill declared on first sight and he has repeated it twice hourly since. Brick walls to the raindrops of intelligence regarding weddings and related articles of clothing. Only very distantly aware of the then Princess Victoria's visit just a few years ago and neither of them sympathetic to the rumoured excesses surrounding her procession through the West Dorset villages. Would be limited to guessing at the meaning of the word 'taffeta'. Some new brand of cattle feed?

The pony draws the trap on. Reined in for safety upon passing the majestic, ivy-covered front of Laing's Hotel, for it would not do to scare one of the women crossing the town square from the Town and Country Bank to the grocer's on the High Street.

Samuel's appearance outside the dressmaker's prompts a flurry of hiding and tidying. Declarations pitched high and a hurried shedding of white silk and lace are a prelude to Louisa's emergence in today's demure striped dress. She blushes causelessly and her eyelids flicker as she climbs the trap to join her future husband. He grins and enquires after the cause of her emotions, but she straightens her expression, along with her skirts, and directs him toward the serious matter ahead.

The trap curls a tight about-turn and steps are retraced, back through the Square, down West Borough until they reach the door of...

Charles Ellis, Samuel's best man; the subject of many muttered terms of admiration, credited with beginning the restoration of his family's fortune following the demise of his violent and intemperate father and held in altogether greater esteem than Matthew Ellis, the choirmaster and his elder half-brother.

If asked, Charles would feign ignorance of the current trends in bridal gowns, and might even raise a single, withering eyebrow in distaste at the question. It would be an errant lie. A good friend to Samuel and Louisa, he has heard more than enough about Chantilly, tulle and gauze to have an opinion. Wouldn't admit it because he considers himself a simple Dorset man along the lines of Bill Brown and John Street.

Presently to be found, as so often, in his accounts room at the back of the family home—once a coach house on West Borough—scratching away at ledgers, shepherding his pennies, but summoned to the front by Samuel's loud and insistent knocking.

A meek appearance around the side of the half-opened door, then a broad smile and greater opening.

'Samuel! Louisa! My, what a welcome surprise! Come in, come in!'

An embarrassed ushering through a bare hall into an ill-decorated parlour; pretensions to simplicity have disappeared now. Charles apologising for the poor surroundings, entreating his guests to be seated and offering a range of refreshments he couldn't possibly supply—tea is beyond him. The offer is waved aside by Samuel and Louisa in unison.

A frowning from the hopeful couple. Charles leaning in, arm pressed on his chair's faded fabric, detecting disquiet but wanting for its cause.

'Something's wrong?' he asks.

'Louisa has concerns for her cousin, Charles.'

Turning to his female guest. 'Your cousin?'

'Henry. Henry Cuff. You met him once, at the fair at Blandford,' Louisa says.

'Blond-haired lad?'

'Yes. Full of life and a delightful smile—at least that's how he used to be. The most beautiful singing voice, so we asked him to perform a solo at our wedding—'

'He broke into tears,' Samuel explains, interrupting his betrothed.

'He did,' she adds, 'but he would not, for all our entreaties, reveal the cause of his distress.'

Charles is concentrating on Louisa's words. She frowns with delicate earnestness.

'It seems to be a problem with either the school or the choir, or perhaps the other boys. He attends Mr Stickland's church school, but rebels against it passionately. Refuses to go in the morning and once there he runs away. Same with the choir.'

At this second mention of the choir, Charles glances away with something sour to his expression. Louisa continues.

'His father, Uncle Thomas, is not a very soft man. Not harsh, I shouldn't say...'

'No, not harsh,' Samuel adds.

'… but not soft either, and the more Henry protests, the more my uncle insists. He must attend school and choir and he's threatened punishment if he runs away again.'

Charles leans back in his chair, running his finger over his lip. 'How can I help?'

Louisa and Samuel exchange a glance. Reflections, perhaps, of an earlier conversation.

'We were rather hoping you might talk to Matthew,' says Louisa, showing that pretty, delicate frown again.

'Talk to my brother?' Charles replies, reacting exactly as he might were he asked to consult the King of Siam.

'We thought… since your brother is choirmaster and helps in the school, maybe he could offer some opinion. Perhaps he sees events we are unaware of?' Samuel says.

'Perhaps,' Charles mutters. 'Might I enquire whether you considered putting your queries to him directly?'

'We did…'

Another glance exchanged, then Samuel speaks for the couple. 'Your brother is, perhaps, not the most approachable of men…'

'Nor is he, indeed. You should understand, it's not that I don't talk to my brother, but he doesn't talk to me. Not in any civil manner at least. He is my half-brother as you know, and while I own to nothing but respect for the dead, I cannot imagine what manner of woman was my father's first wife…'

Charles is halted by the future bride's expression.

'Can you ask, at least?' she says.

He sighs deeply then commences nodding.

'Naturally, Louisa. Naturally. And I shall do so.'

Thanks flow from the happy couple. Their problems solved.

A look in Charles's eye prompted by Louisa resting her hand on her groom's arm. A flickering of his eyelids until his gaze returns to her face.

~

The afternoon has aged. Charles shuffling into the kitchen, dark suit and a cotton shirt hanging from his slender frame. Ruffled hair and tired eyes the visible results of a day's work. Glancing sideways.

'Have you seen that scoundrel of a brother of ours? Did I hear him come in last night?'

Question directed at...

Selina Ellis, weighing flour bags on the kitchen scales. Sixteen years old, dressed to add another decade and behaving accordingly. Only surviving daughter of a deceased mother with consequent concerns already written into her face. Cooking again. Always tidying, washing or cooking.

Her reply: 'You have ink on your nose.'

Charles is provoked into spreading the blot with his thumb. Selina takes charge, wetting a cloth and grasping her brother's face in order to administer her cleansing influence.

'Matthew is not a scoundrel. Our brother has a fine soul. He is a man of God and the Church.'

'He's not a priest, Selina! Granted he has taken residence in the library, but it is not yet clear which god—'

Selina gripping her brother's ear. Clenched, frustrated little fist and a vexed scowl.

'Charles! I will not hear it! Nor will I suffer you to... to...'

Charles surrendering. Holding up his palms to calm his sister, who still has his head suspended.

'Very well. His is a pure and incorruptible soul.'

'Thank you! An example—'

'An example to us all. Yes, yes; where is he?'

Charles released, shaking his head for want of understanding. Selina swallowing, still looking distressed. 'I believe I heard him leave mid-afternoon. He is no doubt attending evensong. You'll surely find him in the library after prayers.'

~

The Chained Library. Close, hot air from a coal-burning stove. Gowns hanging like ghosts, bulking out the wall. Rows of ancient leather-bound books chained, like knowledge enslaved, to their places on the shelves.

Charles, surprised at the door's creak, finds a familiar large-faced man inspecting old, bound papers. The look of haughty superiority is there even before Charles is recognised. His half-brother, presuming.

'Ah. The wanted one. Wanting something, no doubt?'

'I've been asked to speak to you.'

'Naturally. Were it not for that, you would not sully yourself with my presence. And?'

Charles by the door on a stone step, uncertain.

'There's a boy... a boy in the choir. Cuff by name. Do you know him?'

A sigh, carrying with it the weight of the world's sins. Infinite regret.

'Sinners and demons, all.'

'I hardly think you might mistake a ten-year-old child for a demon.'

'Yes, little feather, but that's because you hardly think. Vanity holds otherwise. Vanity and conceit. Nothing else. What is he to you?'

Explaining the connection with the unconcealed impatience of an impotent younger brother. The cousin of Louisa Chilcott, to be married this week; concern for his welfare. Does he know of him? Henry Cuff?

'Henry? The Weeper? Yes, I know him. Youngest of the Cuff brothers. Brimming with pride.'

'Brimming with distress, perhaps. How did you acquire such a faculty for inducing misery?'

A tired, weary, overtaxed leaning backwards.

'It is my duty to reveal the Mystery to young minds more accustomed to pampering and indulgences. Some find the threat of eternal damnation distressing.'

Charles arguing the case for innocence; an exchange that started without warmth growing quickly heated. Old books, leather-wrapped, absorbing the sounds of fraternal confrontation. Echoes of decades of discord, each point and counterpoint raising the pitch. The double-bound tomes imparting nothing. Finally, Charles presents the request: will Matthew have a care for Henry Cuff?

'Have a care for the Weeper? Look out for him.' Spoken like a muttered reminder. 'I am now to be chasing after snotty, squawking choirboys? Their spiritual welfare matters not: I should be wiping their *arses* like a nursemaid!'

Charles turning on his heel, stepping from the room and closing the door, his face impassive. Something—pride, defiance, maybe stubbornness—saves the door from a slamming. After his departure, old insults and resentments still echo silently from the Minster's stones: a feather in the air;

a fart; the boy whose mother lived, whose father never tried to thrash the pretty reminder from his face. All the vanity of men.

Still observed by captive words, a large fist pushing silently against a desk. Pressing. Clenching. Turning slowly. Resenting. Knuckles hard against wood.

~

Sunday-morning service. Children shuffling feet and parents whispering reprimands. Sun through the Minster's windows, casting heavenly white beams upon stone. Dust motes floating ecstatic in the Divine light. Rev Cookesely reading the banns with an unenthusiastic tone. He might be listing the Minster's fittings.

'The third time of asking. If any of you know cause or just impediment...'

Louisa glancing sideways at Samuel. His beaming smile. Her blush and flickering eyelids. Several faces turning their direction until the next couple's names come up and attention is redirected. Only her sighing sisters' gazes dwindle.

A hymn. The church organ moaning out a low and solemn introduction. Joined by the choir's bass and then capped by alto voices.

Louisa's eyes trace the line from the organ-master to the choirmaster to the choir. Leaning in towards Samuel. A frown directs his attention.

What is Samuel prompted to observe? At first nothing untoward, to judge from his expression, but then he too tightens his brow as he reads the expressions on the faces in the choir stand. Children for the most part. Unskilled at hiding their emotions and what they display is easily enough decoded, even from the third row of pews. Anger. Resentment. Hurt. The elder boys towards the back? Spite. Resignation.

When the hymn-singing is done, the Rev Cookesely offers his sermon, preaching the lessons of spring. The lead-in to the Crucifixion. Rebirth must be prepared for. The new life of spring is reliant on 'the shedding of leaves' in the autumn. Sacrifice is not easy or enjoyable—such is its nature. Sacrifice may be considered suffering and certainly the Lord our Shepherd demonstrated this path. Should we expect rebirth if there has been no prior sacrifice? Can a tree bud without first shedding leaves? The question is put as though recited.

Louisa turning towards Samuel. Her earnest frown. Prayers. More hymns. The taking of communion conducted under the considered gaze and intellectual smile of the vicar. Final hymns and prayers and a congregation shuffles towards the church door and blessed fresh air.

Louisa, sisters at discreet giggling distance, walking close by her future husband on the path towards Cook Row and the Corn Market.

'I had never before noticed how oppressive it is. Makes me wish we'd chosen St John's. Poor Henry. He looked utterly miserable.'

Solemn humming noises from Samuel. Agreement and gravity. They meet Charles passing the Oddfellows. Falling in step and looking attentively between the two of them.

'Here's what we shall do,' says Charles. 'We shall go to your uncle and explain. Doctor Firth's classroom is said to be just as good as...'

Both Louisa and Samuel shaking their heads. 'We have spoken with him at length. He demands an objection of substance. Did you gain anything from Matthew?'

Charles's head is bowed as it shakes. Confessional. 'Louisa, my brother...' A sigh. Thoughts of his sister's solicitations. The choosing of words. 'My brother, I'm afraid, may yet prove to be a source of your cousin's distress. Are you sure we cannot reason with the boy's father?'

The couple concede that it might be possible, but their expressions offer less hope. Charles offers to talk to the schoolmaster—and then, almost as an aside, to enquire of John Street. 'John was never able to tolerate Matthew. Maybe he'll provide me with his reasons.'

Louisa suggests that old Mr Cuff might be approached once the additional enquiries have been completed; that they could be offered as further information. A parting completed in agreement and with renewed purpose.

~

Monday morning. John Street out in Walford Meadows, the town's northern boundary, where the terraced dwellings of East Borough stop and the hills rise up above the Allen. Knee-deep in reeds when Charles finds him.

'Morning, John!'

'Mornin', Charlie!'

Spoken quietly. Deep tone from a large frame. Hands white and puffy from the water.

'No Bill today?' Charles asks.

'A-diggin' graves for the vicar, then he's goin' up carter's vor to fetch the raves.'

'For this?' Pointing at the heap of reeds.

'Cassn't leave it there—cattle'll have it and it'll send em skent.'

Charles nodding, regarding the pile of wet reeds with new respect.

A cheeky smile on John's face. 'You joinin' us a-labourin'?'

Charles shaking his head. 'Need to ask you a question, John.'

'Well you ax away. Axin's free.'

John always loathed Charles's brother. Never did say why, but refused his company outright; even the prospect of it turned him away. What was the reason? That's what Charles wants to know.

John staring back at him. Smile withered. Face dark as a gathering storm. Has his reasons. That's all.

'When was it, John? Sunday school? Or Bible classes?'

A reddening of the face but no answer. Charles imploring, explaining his motives—the safety of the boys. Care of one in particular. Justifying self-revelation.

John chewing on these new demands of him: looks up, looks away, looks awkward. Finally, while surveying the green-leaved ash trees that screen the back of the workhouse, settles on a renewed refusal.

'Best ax the lad hisself, Charlie. Or one o' they boys of the choir.'

'Well I could, but I'm asking you, John. Why can you not suffer my brother's company?'

'Oh, Lor', Charlie.' Shaking his head, looking up at Charles uncomfortably. Brows raised. 'For fear... most part. Fear of bein' hanged for a murderer. I keep vrom his company, Charlie, to save myself vrom bein' hanged for en.'

Two men staring at each other. And their eyes are laced

with meaning. John looks away first. A sideways glance, then: 'Here; I'll tell you. Find out what they calls en. Ax about the name they kids has vor your brother. That'll tell all.'

~

A town about its business on a Thursday morning. The domain of housekeepers and good wives of Dorset, broad-skirted and bonnet-topped. Supported by the moustache-bearing tradesmen in braces and smart aprons. A proud little centre. The Square is smart without being boastful. A broad-fronted bank and two welcoming hotels, but no pompous civic hall nor other signs of vainglorious mayoral indulgences. A place of work. Builders toiling away just off the Square in Luke's Lane, and Wilkinson's the boot-maker's all closed up with a notice in the window citing bereavement. The butcher standing in his doorway greeting passers-by and customers alike.

Charles Ellis climbing the steps to the school hall. Inside, a greeting. The tall, pinched frame of Donald Stickland. Glasses removed and cleaned while Charles poses his ques-tions. And in answer, a shaking of the head. Once, and then again more emphatically.

In the long schoolroom, lit only from one end, Stickland is darkness and light, casting a spindly shadow halfway down the hall. The dark side of his face is cast into mystery by his presupposing nose. His eyes are content to lurk deep under cavernous brows, looking out with nervous suspicion.

He offers a judgement on young Cuff: a difficult child. Such is the explanation, prompting Charles to seek confir-mation that Henry Cuff is the subject at hand. Confirmation of understanding; taught his brothers before him but they were better disciplined. And then that phrase again. Vain and proud. In need, evidently, of correction.

Charles tightening. An imperceptible withdrawal. A dismissive tone, disbelieving and a little contemptuous. Stickland reciprocating, withdrawing into his schoolroom, further into the shade, like a spider between bricks. Further words exchanged, but only as a means of hardening positions.

A handle rattled as a door is opened. An empty-handed retreat.

Charles calls upon Samuel. The groom hears relayed conversations with increasing concern. Charles is exasperated.

'They are quite unconscionable. He thinks Henry a mouldering nest of sin. I mean... Henry! And I fear my brother may be at the very heart of the boy's torment. He's as bad as Stickland. They both see children as corrupted demons in need of taming.'

'So now?'

'I'll talk to his parents. There's nowhere else to go.'

~

Late in the afternoon. Indeed, the Minster's bell has struck five and Charles Ellis, walking north along East Borough, checks his pocket watch. Watch and clock concur. Surprisingly bright for the time of day. Martins curling through the warm afternoon air like fanciful decorations.

Warm by the time he reaches Walford Mill. Dabs at his forehead with his handkerchief to clear the sweat away before venturing through the small gate to Mill House.

Hand-pull for the doorbell. A greeting to the housekeeper, Elizabeth Goode. Asking after her family—her sister. 'How's Jane?'

'Oh she's a-missin' her girls, Charlie. Entered service, up Cranborne. Miles away. Please…'

A lengthy, cool corridor, presided over by a stately long-case clock that is gently sounding its observations. An emergence into a long, angular drawing room. Windows out onto the lush green gardens. Muttered excuses and Miss Goode withdrawing.

Outside—well-tended lawns host a flock of starlings. Two weeping willows sweep the surface of the River Allen as it approaches Walford Bridge.

Inside—an oak desk; bookshelves fronted with leaded windows, populated by shapely volumes; the gentle, melodic rhythm of the hallway clock. A fire in the grate that looks to have been burning all morning and a tall-sided armchair, back to the room, facing the garden. A question is lit: is the armchair occupied?

The doors opening and Elizabeth Goode ushering in the lady of the house, Mrs Cuff. A flurry of skirts, an out-stretched hand and serviceable smile offered for no longer than politeness requires.

'You've met my husband?'

Charles's uncertain frown. A tutting and further rus-tling of skirts. Relocation to the far side of the armchair and suspicions are confirmed. It is occupied and has been since Charles entered the room.

'Thomas! A visitor!'

'I know!' comes the self-satisfied answer. Spoken by the occupant of the chair. Charles, moving to stand by the window that he might see and be seen, stops himself from looking between man and wife. A clear and discernible age difference. The appearance of the man himself: a pointed nose and lengthy chin; small spectacles; a bald head that is not compensated by uncontrolled eyebrows, rampant nasal hair and beds of hair flowering in the man's ears.

'Mr Ellis, isn't it? I knew your father.'

A high-pitched voice, collapsing into a squeak in moments of emphasis.

An invitation to be seated. An exchange of familiarities. Charles apologetic. Thomas condescending; his wife demure and silent. Charles leading on to the business at hand: an issue raised by Mr Cuff's niece—shortly to be wed—the welfare of the couple's youngest son. Old man Cuff taking up the topic with earnestness and learned self-confidence. A mini-sermon on the most efficacious methods of child-rearing; the importance of unyielding firmness and consistent application of judicious discipline. Mrs Cuff enduring the lecture with a straight face and the same from Charles. The father undermining his own authority by seeking confirmation that Henry is, indeed, their youngest.

Charles offering compliments on the father's wisdom and a sidestep. Might some questions be directed to the boy himself? The raising of prodigious eyebrows, surprised by the audacious question. Nonetheless, Mr and Mrs Cuff are accommodating and after the summoning of Elizabeth, the boy is sent for and is soon stood among them. Directed by his aged father to be upstanding, he nonetheless maintains a bearing of dejection. A mother's frowning.

Charles's question: 'Henry, I have a young nephew who may be coming to live with me. If he does so, I shall have to choose between the schoolroom of Doctor Firth and that of Mr Stickland. He is a somewhat gentle-mannered, studious boy, not accustomed to rough play or harsh punishment. Which school would best suit him, do you think?'

A quick, compulsive answer. 'Why, the other one, sir!'

A frowning of adults. 'The other?'

Explanations, justifications and excuses follow. Mr Stickland's strictness described. Roughness abounds. Punishments are harsh. Exceedingly harsh. A pleading tone not far from distress.

Stickland's defender is found in Thomas Cuff. 'Misdemeanours are punished in all schools, are they not, boy? A schoolmaster must be strict.'

The flickering of eyelids. Like a wincing. 'They are, sir. But Mr Stickland is exceedingly strict, sir. Sometimes without cause...'

'And what of the choir, Henry? Should my nephew join—'

'Oh no, sir! Do not suffer him to attend the choir, Mr Ellis. Please!'

A moment's pause among the elders of the family. Charles lowering the pitch of his voice. Softening. Consoling.

'Why not the choir, Henry? What happens there?'

Hesitation, and eyes flicking between parents. Checking the ice he walks upon, lest he falls through.

'Don't send him to the choir, sir.'

'My brother is choirmaster, isn't he? What nickname do the boys have for him? Can you tell me?'

A widening of eyes and the answer is clear. To tell would be a fate. Charles sighing, ready to retreat from the ineffable, but Cuff senior intercedes.

'Come now, answer this, Henry. What is this name?'

A moment's panic. 'I shall not say, sir!' Distress edged

with tears. But a father's authority has been brought into question.

'You would deny me?'

'No, no, sir!'

Charles offers a saving hand. 'No doubt you forget…?'

But the boy's honesty is his undoing. 'Why no, sir. I recall it, but—'

'But what? Come, come, out with it!' Thomas Cuff demands.

But Henry remains entrapped by his own morals. Hands behind his back, head lowered so his head of shaggy blond hair hides his face as he sobs defiantly. He will not speak. Tears drop onto the rug.

A mother's compassion overrides and Mrs Cuff gets to her feet.

'Maybe, Henry…'

Charles splutters, raising a hand to beg indulgence.

'One last question, Henry. How should my nephew be at Mr Stickland's and the choir?'

The boy's head rising. Eyes drowning. Cheeks blotchy and flushed.

'He should be the most miserable of boys, sir.'

'Thank you, Henry. You've been very helpful.'

The boy withdrawing. The mother ready to guard his retreat. The father open-mouthed, missing his right to dismissal. Charles picking his careful path.

'Mr Cuff, pardon me, please. If you would ask me what manner of man is my brother…?'

'Hm? What say you?'

'My brother, the choirmaster. He is a villain, sir. I would not submit a dog to his care, much less a nephew.'

'Your nephew is fictional?'

'A ruse. No more. You'll forgive me, but consider the situation if our roles were reversed. Were you arriving in Wimborne seeking a school for your son, how might you respond to young Henry's opinions?'

A deepening frown. Considering. Charles appeals to other authorities.

'Mrs Cuff, would you...?'

'Mrs Cuff's opinion concurs entirely with that of her husband,' Cuff snaps.

'Of course.'

A moment's silence while the gathering gives due consideration. Cuff expresses his reservations.

'Doctor Firth is a dandy. A vain man who will make a virtue of vanity.'

Charles momentarily closing his eyes. 'There are worse sins,' he says, with quiet conviction. 'My brother's flaws are better hidden. I fear they may be far more insidious.'

A slow and thoughtful walk home, watching the crows hopping around horse-dung cairns in the road.

∼

Charles's office. Nestled, cuckoo-like, in the outbuildings behind West Borough. The interior is ordered, but in a manner known only to him. Hurricane lamps burning bright enough to show the thin, sloping marks on a hundred slips of paper in dozens of stacks that cover every surface.

Charles's nib floating over places and dates, deliveries and consignments—Halifax, Swanage, Okeford Fitzpaine, 3rd, 25th. Ships, wagons, captains and cargoes moving with the gentle swaying of the lamplight. Charles, failing to concentrate on his work—his gaze wandering around the room, following thoughts rather than figures.

The knock on the door makes him jump—perhaps all the more for it being a timid, uncertain little tapping. One sheet of paper is pulled back to cover another. Chair scrapes over floor. Latch clicks. Door creaks. Light rises upon a familiar face.

'Cornelius!'

A shadowed expression glancing along the house, reluctant to be witnessed. Charles standing aside to allow entrance.

An alarmed, uncertain entry.

'I was with Bill, sir. My brother. We were taking a glass of ale with John Street. Said you'd been asking about the choir, Bible classes, poor Henry Cuff, sir.'

'Yes, yes, sit down. Tell me.'

'Begging your pardon, sir...'

More regret. Concern on his brow.

'Cornelius, I've asked and asked. No one will tell me anything. Please.'

'They do hard by him, sir. Most hard.'

'Who does? Who are they?'

'Well...'

A nervous glance, checking the reception his words might receive.

'The schoolmaster, Stickland, he was always strict and has his way of setting the older boys to punish the younger ones. And the older boys can be dreadful cruel, Mr Ellis.'

He looks up again nervously and licks his lips like a guilty hound.

'But your brother, Mr Ellis, he... um...'

'Half-brother. He's my half-brother. They have a name for him, do they do not? A nickname?'

'Nickname? Yes... I suppose... yes they do.'

'Tell me.'

A hint of a frown. As if confused.

'They don't call him the choirmaster, sir. He's Buggermaster. Begging your pardon. That's what they call him. Some find it funny. Others not.'

Charles assessing the news.

'Buggermaster?'

'He is terrible harsh with the boys, sir. Terrible. He is poor Cuff's principal tormentor.'

Silent. Cornelius blinking. Charles frowning. 'Buggermaster?'

A nodding.

'Dear God.'

And more nodding.

'He makes the lad a target for the older boys too. Vicar does nothing, nor the schoolmaster. They all know, though. They know what he is called.'

Staring. Eventually, a deep draught of breath. A turning away, momentarily, before return.

'Very well. Thank you. We'll sort it out.'

'You'll... you'll not mention me?'

'No. You can rely on that.'

'I felt I had to tell you, Mr Ellis.'

'And I'm very glad you did.'

~

Cotton rags for bandages. Knuckles cleansed with witch hazel. Selina the nurse. Charles Ellis the patient.

'I thought you were going to kill him!' she says, leaning sideways to stop herself from treading on the cat rubbing against her ankles.

Charles still dark-eyed and white-faced.

'I could have.'

'Charles, don't say such things. It's a mortal sin!'

'There are worse sins, Selina. Do you know what your brother—'

'No! And I do not wish to know!'

Charles's sudden urgent grip on Selina's wrist.

'Selina! You cannot blind yourself—'

His urgency trumped by her thin, stiff determination, wrenching her hand away.

'Stop it!' she hisses. 'We have lost Mother and we have lost Father. All I have left are my brothers. You cannot—you *must* not—betray me with a feud. You might argue, but I will never forgive you, Charles, if you force me to take your side against his. I shall not denounce my brother nor speak ill of him. He is a virtuous man.'

Charles staring at her, nostrils flaring. Her hand gently lowering his to the table where she can work on it again. Wrapping the cotton over raw knuckles.

'You might also think of the impact, Charles, if you seek to destroy our brother's reputation. Think! What should the world say of me if he is disgraced? What have I, if I have not my name?'

Charles, holding his little sister's hand. Staring at flagstones.

'He'll not hit you again,' he says. Quieter.

'What makes you think—'

'I know he did. But I've never bested him before. That

will have given him a shock. He will not dare. Not after that.'

'He is a man of virtue, Charles.'

'Yes, Selina. Of course he is.'

~

A bright young morning. Samuel in his wedding suit walking towards Charles across Minster Green. A day for a wedding. Blue skies decorated with smart white clouds and Samuel looking as fine as a pin. He grins at first, but then turns to seriousness and nods back at the Minster.

'Is Henry in the choir? His sisters say he has not been seen since last evening and it would be a great relief for Louisa if she knew where he was.'

Charles, best man, reliable lieutenant.

'I'll ask.'

He excuses himself through the gathering guests. Anxiety for Henry largely abated since he is confident now that Cuff senior will move him to the other schoolroom. Into the church, cool, dark and quiet. Footsteps on the flag-stones echo from the tall arches. The organist frowns, but Charles finds Cornelius Brown among the gathering chor-isters. Eyebrows employed for a beckoning.

'We're concerned for Henry Cuff. Is he here yet?'

Looking over Cornelius's shoulder, checking the faces.

'Thought I saw him earlier,' says Cornelius. 'I'll look out for him.'

Charles returns to the green. Catches Samuel's eye.

The guests look—in heightened pitch—towards the High Street, towards the clattering sound of coaches arriving.

~

Walford Meadows are scented from the grass and decorated with insects and wind-carried pollen. Over the river itself, dragonflies hover and small clouds of midges drift. If there is something portentous in the air, it cannot be seen—and John Street is insensible to it.

He leaves Bill—equally innocent—sorting his boots on the river bank and wades into the waters of the Allen, humming 'I Loved a Shepherd Girl'. A grip on his string and sickle, swinging his shoulders purposefully. The watching crow is but a bird to him.

~

Queen Victoria seething with envy at Wimborne's latest bride. Louisa, at least, thinks it possible. As she steps from the carriage, awash with white silk and lace, an involuntary gasp of admiration escapes the onlooking crowd. Louisa is taken by her father's hand through the church gates. Peering through her veil at grinning faces as though looking out from a painting. She's oil on canvas.

Charles ought to be with Samuel but he wants to finish his errand. Louisa sees him—reaches out a delicate arm with an enquiry on her lips. Charles taking the lightest of grips on her hand.

'Cornelius says he saw him in the choir. He's fine.'

'Oh, thank heavens. Will he sing?'

'I think not, but he is safe.'

Releasing her.

Louisa floating from face to face across the green. Then passing under the arch, through the portico. The light dims and her skin shivers as she passes from the warm summer air outside to the cool of the church.

So many faces. Her uncle down from Warminster, her mother's seamstress, her many cousins, school friends and companions—her French teacher back from Salisbury. Mouthing greetings, advice, good wishes.

At the end, stood before the altar, Samuel. Grinning broadly, proudly.

And when the walk is done, she is standing with him. His presence. Her husband. She wants to take his hands, though her father has her arm. A smile at the priest. A hush descending.

She looks beyond the priest at the long lines of choirboys. No sign.

Louisa draws a deep breath and sighs it out again. She shall rely on Charles's reassurance. Satisfaction. Preparedness. Her future within easy reach.

~

When John sees the fabric floating among the reeds, he merely thinks it strange that someone well-to-do should misplace their linen in the river. Even a recognition of the chorister's gown leads him to wonder why a choirboy would not remove his clothes before going for a swim.

Then he stops wading, stands still, and takes it all in: the one hand floating; the knuckles breaking the surface; the other arm obscured from view; the sheen on the fabric from the soaked-in water and the dreaminess of the boy's gown where it wafts around in an underwater billow. He takes a slow step forwards, frowning, causing breaks in the stream as he does so. The weeds, the gown and the body move with gentle waves, back and forth, to acknowledge his approach. He watches the body's open mouth as water drifts in and out like ocean waves among the ribs of a shipwrecked hulk.

He knows the boy. He recognises the head of curly blond hair, even though it is spread out, sullied with weed and specks of grain from the mill.

John, standing midstream, water pushing against his legs, turns, without moving his feet. He is looking—looking back over the fields for someone to bring help, someone to absolve him from the scene—to witness his innocence—someone to make it right. But there is no one. He thinks that maybe Bill Brown would be by the bridge and he even shouts for him.

'Bi-ill!'

And while Bill calls back asking what the matter is, John has not the words with which to answer. He looks again at the body and his eye catches the crow that has been watching him. Black-feathered and cold-eyed, the crow seems to sense a threat, lifts its wings and pulls itself into the air. It arcs up and across the field in a great long curl, allowing the wind to take it.

John mutters to himself. 'Oh Lor'.'

~

Charles Ellis sitting alone in his front room. Staring at the empty fireplace where coals have not burned since March. Is he imagining the fire? He is not. Although figures blaze in his fantasies and enflame his emotions.

Here flickers the portent on the face of John Street, approaching the wedding party trailing wet footprints on the flagstones. There the image of old man Cuff, brow crumpled first in confusion, and then in disbelief. And Mrs Cuff, failing in her understanding. And then the crumpling. In the centre, burning brightest, Louisa's face reacting to the words: *A body in the river... Henry.* Her hand over her mouth; sisters stepping in beside her; the congregation falling silent save for two voices that linger, until they too fade in recognition of the inexplicable quiet.

In the corner, older recollections: his brother in the library... *wiping their arses, like a nursemaid?* Outside, through the window, John once more, his eyes meeting Charles's and the echo of words spoken over the flowing of the river, slow and wide.

I keep vrom his company, Charlie, to save myself vrom bein' hanged for en.

And again.

... to save myself vrom bein' hanged for en.

And the river curls around Walford Meadows, burly and snake-like, onwards, deep into the heart of the town.

CROW COURT

~

Wimborne Minster, Dorset, May 1840

'I'll be just one minute,' the Reverend Giles Cookesely said.

He did not look up. Indeed, he maintained his concentration on searching through the Psalms—searching, as it so happened, for passages that might be consoling in the upcoming remembrance service. He found few that appealed. Most passages caught his eye only because they carried references to judgement. *Behold he travaileth with iniquity and hath conceived mischief, and brought forth falsehood. He made a pit and digged it, and is falled into the ditch which he made.*

Apposite, one might say.

The intent in ignoring the choirmaster was to induce in him some disquiet, although it might have been predicted that a man such as Matthew Ellis would remain uncowed.

Annoyingly, rather than waiting meekly in the chair by the desk, he took up a position by the window, clasped his hands behind his back and looked out over King Street with his feet firmly apart.

Giles gave up the charade. He flicked his inkpot closed and could only sigh with petty frustration when a small spot of ink was cast onto the open page of his notebook.

'So then,' he said.

The choirmaster grunted a response but remained motionless. The man was immovable. Was it not an act of hyperephania to fill the room while occupying no more than its edge?

'Have a seat. We need to address the matter of Master Cuff.'

'God rest his soul,' Matthew answered as he turned.

'Amen.'

He was a large man, this choirmaster—large, with large features. His mottled face was broad and recently bruised around the eye, while his calloused fingers were so thick and powerful it was a wonder he could hold something so delicate as a sheet of music. Nor did his being seated reduce the imposing effect of his bulk, not least because the wicker chair he occupied was not equal to his proportions. He was in many ways ill-fitted. Nonetheless, he was before the Reverend Giles Cookesely and needed to be addressed.

'He'll need special arrangements, no doubt,' said the choirmaster, seemingly oblivious to the far more distressing aspects of the choirboy's demise.

'No doubt he will, but... that is not what I wish to discuss, Matthew. As a matter of fact, I wish to talk about your involvement in his er... in his death.'

'My involvement? What involvement is this, then?'

Giles knew he had not the gravity of advanced years.

Nor was he a man of much physical bearing, whereas the choirmaster, it appeared, had the capacity to project a threat through the merest sneer. On the other hand, the vicar was endowed with the might of righteousness and had a sturdy oak desk in front of him.

'I'm sure you're aware of the accusations and rumours that are discussed in the town,' Giles said, withholding the hesitation from his voice.

'I am not,' answered the choirmaster. 'I do not concern myself with tittle-tattle.'

'People believe that Henry Cuff did not drown by accident; that he took his own life.'

'Suicide is a sin,' the choirmaster said. 'Life is our Lord's to give, and our Lord's to take away.'

'Yes, yes; you might assume, Matthew, that I am sufficiently familiar with the theology of the situation. The point being that there are those who believe his suicide was the result of your actions.'

When the choirmaster raised his eyebrows, his overlarge ears moved in response. The effect would have been comical were the man less sinister.

'Well, that is clearly ridiculous, Reverend. Suicide can only be the result of *his* actions. If they were my actions, it would be murder.'

Giles felt his face redden as he looked down, driven from the wherewithal to look the man in the eye. And when he regained the capacity to speak, his voice was so strained with enforced calmness, it came out so strangled he had to repeat himself.

'If you were... if you were accused of murder, we should not be discussing the matter at our ease! They accuse you—for heaven's sake, *I* accuse you—of tormenting the boys in your charge! It seems to all the world that your cruelty has grown to such excess that it has driven one of God's children to take his own life.'

And yet the choirmaster still scowled back, without so much as a nod toward the need for an answer.

'So? What do you say to this charge?' Giles demanded, provoking nothing more concessionary than a shrug.

'I'd say I have to doubt the wisdom of reacting to town gossip.'

'Town…? Matthew, I was quite clear that *I* accuse you!'

'We have long disagreed on my methods. You hold I am too harsh on the boys and I see the threat to their mortal souls if they are not taught—'

'No, this is not a debate about methods. One of the boys is dead!'

'The Lord giveth and—'

'Do not quote Scriptures at me!' the vicar demanded, his voice rising to such a crescendo that his body rose inelegantly from the chair to accompany it. 'Do you know they accuse you of unnatural relations with the boys?'

'Oh, please!'

'You deny it, then?'

'Do you not see how weak these people are? Their feckless progeny are damned from the moment they see light and they do nothing but mollycoddle the brats. They whisper accusations when they should be thanking me!'

'So you don't deny it?'

'Gossiping wives of the town should follow me a little more and slander me—'

'Never mind the townswomen.'

'Well, am I to address their accusations or not? I should sooner pay them no heed, for they are flea-minded and spiteful.'

'But the way you treat the boys...!'

'Reverend, I do what is needed. I ward the boys from evil deeds and sinful thoughts.'

'Choirboys? What "evil deeds"?'

'Oh! All their myriad acts of vanity. Vanity above all. Pride and wilfulness. Answer me this: when did sinfulness not complain about virtue? When did those petty-coated demons ever act to protect the mortal souls of their own offspring? They languish in their complacent world of ease while accusations of immorality are directed at me?'

'Indeed they are. And I would have you address them!'

'Oh really! So I bugger the odd choirboy to shatter his pride?'

'You confess it?'

'I confess to nothing. I bring their consciousness back to the eternal.'

'And you... you think this an act of Christianity?'

'I think it necessary!'

'It is a sin against God and nature.'

'No greater sin than they commit!'

'Wanton cruelty!'

'They deserve it!'

'Dear God, man, you should be horsewhipped!' the vicar exclaimed, but, having been standing himself, he now found he raised the defensive anger of the choirmaster, who joined him—abruptly and with a sudden dark anger, sending the wicker chair backwards onto the floor. Their faces drew close over the now inadequate-seeming desk.

For a moment, nothing was said. And then the choir-master spoke, with a low and growling voice.

'So now who would do that *whipping*, Reverend? Eh? Would it be you?'

Giles shook his head very quickly as the choirmaster loomed over him.

'Not you, then? Not the priest who takes God's name in vain, nor the schoolteacher who drinks himself to sleep each night, nor the philandering organist, or the adulterous wardens…'

Giles raised his hands, palms up, to the choirmaster, shocked, defensive and imploring him to stop. But the choirmaster was not yet done.

'Cowards and sinners, every single one. All revelling in the vanities of man and steeped in pride. Like the brats in the choir, their painted, whoring mothers and cuckolded fathers, all of whom are damned to hell, Reverend, because you do *nothing* to save them. Your sermons are ineffective and as weak as your congregation. So they accuse me! Let them! They can indulge in all the tittle-tattle they like. It shall not budge me one inch!'

And having delivered this speech, he turned, snatched up his hat and marched towards the door.

With renewed and sudden courage, Giles called after him, 'Think of what you owe unto God!'

But the ferocity in the eyes of the choirmaster when he turned his head—it was awful. He spat his parting words.

'I cannot! My mind is full to bursting with raging memories of what *He* owes *me*!'

And then he was gone.

The housekeeper appeared in the vicar's study a moment

or two after the choirmaster had slammed the front door. She watched for a second, and they both glanced at Giles's trembling hands.

'That man!' he complained. 'Utterly, utterly, utterly unanswerable! Despicable. I am beyond words, Mrs Kelly, quite beyond words.'

He backed away from the door, not wishing to turn his back on Mrs Kelly directly, but taking necessary steps toward the dresser. His hands were shaking so violently that when he took the brandy bottle, he could not stop it from rattling against the glass. He downed a good draught before pouring a second while Mrs Kelly opened and closed her mouth before speaking.

'He is… very poorly thought of among the congregation.'

'Poorly thought of!? He should be hanged! He should be whipped! He should be whipped and then hanged, and I'll tell you, I should gladly undertake either with my own hand.'

'Perhaps the bishop will advise…'

'The bishop? The bishop! Oh, I wish it were so, I really do. How many times have I spoken out? He tells me, Mrs Kelly, he tells me to practise forgiveness—forgiveness! We are to keep the good standing of the Church uppermost in our minds. That's what he says. While that man…! That man commits sins against God and humanity—crimes that he could swing for, mark you!—yet we are to consider the standing of the Church, and I am supposed to forgive his… his abominations!'

Mrs Kelly remained mute. Perhaps she agreed with the bishop. Maybe she agreed with the choirmaster. There really was no telling. But she glanced down at the note she had been holding all the time, while the vicar refused to allow its interruption. She should, surely, feel some sympathy for his position. He emptied the second glass and wiped his mouth before speaking again.

'Do you know, Mrs Kelly, the bishop actually forbade me from dismissing the man? Can you imagine? My own church? It tests my faith, it really does. I'm not one for the Old Testament, but in these circumstances, I wonder where is the justice of the Lord, that He can smite the Sodomites and the Canaanites, while his own bishop refuses me the right even to dismiss that ogre of a choirmaster?'

Any sympathy Mrs Kelly might have felt passed by her face without influence. She flicked the note in her hands to make it harder still for him to ignore. He glanced at it with a deep reluctance.

'And now I suppose we have some new matter to attend to?'

'With some urgency, Reverend. David Eyers is dying, poor man.'

'Eyers? David Eyers? That's sudden news; I saw him only last week.'

Mrs Kelly raised the note as evidence. 'Taken gravely ill and not likely to see out the evening, I'm a-feared to say. Mrs Eyers says he has been asking most earnestly for a priest.'

Giles put down his glass and leaned forwards, as if he was taking on a burden with this news, then took the note.

'He does not *need* a priest, Mrs Kelly. We are not papists!' he said, flicking open the envelope.

But Mrs Kelly's consequent scowl was reprimand enough to revitalise his sense of duty. He scanned the handwritten words to confirm her information and then reassured her. 'Of course, I shall go if he seeks solace. Remind me, Mrs Kelly. The Eyers…'

'On Furzehill. The little cottage just beyond the brow.'

'Ah, yes, Furzehill. Is my mother awake?'

'The last I looked, she was, sir, yes.'

So Giles climbed the stairs to his mother's room, trying to calm himself and rid the agitation from his own soul. He found her where she had been for some weeks now, sitting up in bed supported by a broad array of pillows, white in the face and so heavy-lidded she looked asleep. All else paled.

'Giles, Giles is that you? Is there some trouble? I heard raised voices.'

Giles, guilt-struck, hurried to his mother's side. He was making soothing noises even as he took her hand.

'No, no. Nothing amiss, Mother. The choirmaster was here. A little disagreement. Nothing more.'

'Oh dear. How regrettable.'

'It's over now, Mother.'

Mrs Cookesely closed her eyes and allowed her head to sink slightly to one side. Then she spoke without moving, as if talking in her sleep.

'No. Not over at all. Giles is troubled. My little man of God is angered and agitated.'

She knew him, of course, better than he knew himself.

'Well yes, that is true enough.'

'We all must suffer,' she murmured quietly.

'Also true.'

''Til death's release.'

'You just rest now, Mother,' Giles said, stroking the back of her hand. His mother remained motionless. He uprooted the sticky medicine bottle from the bedside table and held it to the light to judge how full it was.

Not nearly as full as it might have been. He looked again upon his mother's quiet face, then withdrew from the room.

Mrs Kelly was waiting with his hat at the bottom of the stairs.

'Is she taking too much laudanum?' he asked. Mrs Kelly winced.

'She suffers such pain without it. I cannot know what is right, sir.'

Giles felt such a wave of sympathy for his mother's housekeeper in that moment. She endured so much, and offered such unselfish service, he could not have thought of words enough to praise her. It was unthinkable that she might reproach herself.

'Dear Mrs Kelly,' Giles said, 'you cannot but do right. Your patience and your virtue are a true blessing.' And then they stood a little distance from each other, doing nothing somewhat awkwardly, and Giles felt certain he had spoken out of turn. At length, he held out his hand and Mrs Kelly gave him his hat and opened the door.

'At the top of the hill?'

'Just over the brow.'

~

He cut through the narrow lane past the smithy. There was, he knew, little hope that his mother might recover. And little point in praying for her deliverance, since such prayers moved the universe not one jot.

'"'Til all be fulfilled..."' he muttered to himself as he emerged into West Row. The thought brought some solace, but he could not banish from his heart a *tittle* of resentment that His plan should be so obscure and so painful.

By the time he had skirted the Square, resurgent thoughts of Matthew Ellis had plunged him anew into a growling mood. Passers-by greeted him on the streets, retrieving him from his thoughts at each raised hat, but by the time he was stretching his legs on the long march of West Borough, all the greetings were done.

He was left with the cool spring afternoon—grey in the sky—and a paucity of options to consider, each of which was a torment. Should he do as advised by the bishop? The bishop who preached forgiveness for no better reason than to prevent the scandal that would accompany the prosecution of an abominable choirmaster. How could he? How could he employ forgiveness when they should have cut off the hand that offended them? And cast it away.

A crow passed him as he approached Walford Bridge. It flew in the direction Giles was walking and he thought its dark cloak and the long, ominous curl to its wings a perfect accompaniment for his mood.

Could he defy the bishop? And risk his own good standing? And should he suffer himself because of that scoundrel Ellis? It was beyond enduring. Could the man not trip at the top of the tower stairs and be found lifeless at the bottom the next morning? Could he not slip in front of a coal cart? Might a fishbone not stick in his gullet?

Another dark bird passed over him just past the Crown and Anchor and several more by the turning to Burt's Hill as he was imagining bundling his unconscious choirmaster into a barrel, sealing it and rolling him off Poole Harbour and onto the deck of a ship bound for Africa or Australia. Yet more crows passed him as he climbed the rise past Walford Farm, so he looked up, squinting at the brightness. The sky was blotted with crows—all flying the same direction and in such gathering numbers that they arrested his attention.

From the vantage point of the rise further up the hill he could see more of his surroundings, and the view showed birds flying in from every quarter. Crows, all of them—or rooks maybe. Singly, or in twos and threes, they were converging on a field beyond the hedgerow, where the road dipped before climbing up Furzehill.

There must have been some special feed there. Perhaps a farmer had left out a sack of seeds, or maybe there was some more morbid attraction—crows being what they were. Whatever the lure, it certainly appeared compelling. They were arriving in such numbers that they spiralled around each other before coming to ground, curling in a miniature storm of birds, like animated paisley patterning the sky.

Giles forgot himself. So puzzled was he by the massing crows, he let go of his concerns, and all that was left was the mesmeric effect of the spiralling birds. He became peculiarly concerned to discover the object of their attention: what was in the field they were attracted to?

He hurried down the slope, searching ahead to find a stretch of hedgerow clear enough of brambles that he might climb it. He thought of his brother up in Oxford, wondering whether they might soon be locked in correspondence about some newly observed avian behaviour.

And as he came close, the sky emptied of birds. Only three more arrived while he searched the hedge for a vantage point to see the field beyond. A great number of crows had gathered—that was evident from the cacophonous cawing coming from the field. So many voices combined that it merged into a single, steady sound, like a great tearing noise that went on, unending.

Keen that he should not miss the sight of the gathered birds, he became careless of the brambles and stones in the hedgerow, took hold of a thicker branch and hauled himself up the side of the bank. Thorns and twigs plucked at his coat, but he took no heed—not once he was up; he was too astonished by the sight that greeted him.

The field had not a crop—it was obscured by a vast flickering of black-feathered birds. In the distance, perhaps, there were fresh, bright green shoots lining the ploughed furrows, but the ground in front of him was utterly black.

He shook his head at the sight—there were so many of them. All clustered into such a small space they shouldn't all have been able to spread their wings. Beady eyes, big beaks all flickering and calling and twitching. It was a swarm, an infestation, a plague of crows.

But it was not merely a spectacle of scale. Nearby, in the corner of the field where the birds were so densely packed the ground itself seemed to be black and feathered, there was a bare circle—a ring where the soil was naked but for a solitary specimen of their species standing at the circle's centre. A crow alone amid a multitude of crows.

The impression of the scene was unavoidable, and yet it could not possibly have been as it appeared. It looked as though the crows had congregated to encircle the one individual, but for what further purpose?

The birds continued to stand where they were, filling the air with their raucous squawking while the forlorn-looking individual isolated in the middle stepped from foot to foot.

None of them seemed intent on doing anything, but there was a lot of flapping and flicking of heads, so the scene looked like a black clockwork sea with waves of motion coming in sudden mechanical order.

And then, as if responding to a signal only they could see, the birds fell silent. It was the most alarming thing. They continued to move as before, twitching their heads to and fro, but the squawking ceased, making way for the far more delicate twitter of smaller songbirds. It gave him the most uncanny sensation, an impression that made a shiver run down his spine in anticipation of whatever might come next; the certain impression that some drama was nigh, but wanting for the merest hint at what it might be.

And so, when the motion to his right caught his eye, Giles looked towards it with completely open anticipation. A single, large crow had left the ground. With the broad, confident sweep of its wings, it lifted itself up, ten, twenty feet above the scene, then turned suddenly and, wings out wide, came gliding down, looming larger and larger. Its final flapping was right in front of him—above the hedge. Its wings seemed to almost encircle Giles's head as it came in. He flinched, pulling back from the onslaught. But then the crow had come to alight on the hedge, and it folded its wings neatly like a tall aristocrat stowing his umbrella.

The bird turned its head to the left, then turned back to the right and finally came to point its beak in Giles's direction. It was no more than a few feet away, the same height as his head. He could have reached out and grabbed it, if the hedge had been lower. As it happened, the crow was the one to lean forwards. It opened its beak and emitted a loud, violent, rasping squawk.

So alarming was the noise and the sight of the bird's sharp little tongue that Giles took a step backwards, but he missed his footing and his leg slipped down the bank. His grip on the hedge wasn't firm enough to hold him so he stumbled backwards, slipped more and actually fell—watched by the merciless crow—back onto the road.

Whether it was frightened by his fall or dislodged by the sudden movement of the hedge, Giles couldn't tell, but when he next looked up, the crow was flapping its wings, lifting itself away from the hedge and flying back to the field.

He sat in the dusty road for a moment, astonished by everything he had just witnessed. Had he really just been frightened off by a bird?

He regained his feet, spent a while dusting off his trousers and his jacket and repairing the harm done to his hat before he remembered that David Eyers was reported to be ill and dying and calling for his ministrations.

With the loud squawk of the crow still ringing in his ears, he set off up the hill, periodically noticing and beating new patches of dust from his trousers. What days were these, he wondered, when he should be bullied first by a chorister and next by a bird?

He slowed his pace a little when the incline of Furzehill became more acute, and then stopped altogether when he heard the sudden recommencement of a great cawing sound. The crows, it seemed, had gone back to their calling. He looked down the hill but there was no view of the field from where he stood, so, greatly unnerved, he continued. He stopped to look back twice more, but without ever being able to see the field and its occupants.

When he finally reached the cottage of the Eyers couple,

he was angered by the choirmaster, unsettled by the birds and overly heated from the exertion of climbing the hill—not really a fitting state for comforting a dying man, so he took a few minutes before the garden gate, composing himself.

At last, he put all other thoughts aside, intent on bringing comfort to David Eyers, stepped up to the cottage door and knocked three times; an announcement, not a summons.

The day, however, was not yet done with him and the door was opened by none other than David Eyers himself. A thickset man, short of stature and with an unusually square face. It was the healthy-looking face of a man whose considerable distance from death's door was evidenced by proximity to his own.

'David?' Giles said. The man frowned—quite reasonably, since no one should have been surprised to see him open his own front door.

'Vicar.'

'You're quite well, then?'

The farmer shrugged, holding on to the door.

'Cothe come on I yesterday. Passed the eve abed, but t'were naught.'

'Well, I hope to see you fully recovered soon, David. Your wife's note?'

He held up the smaller letter and Eyers took it, scowling, unfolded it and took in its contents with a glance. A pained expression of disappointment crossed his face.

'Ugh! Dor slommock!' he grumbled, then he leaned his head back into the cottage and called out loud, 'Dreen!' which Giles assumed was an abbreviation of the woman's name.

Mrs Eyers came to the door with a pair of shearing

scissors in her hand, her apron covered with fluff, no doubt the side effect of her labours.

'Oh, 'ello, Vicar!' she said, as if his visit was a surprise.

'Good afternoon to you, Mrs Eyers. I have come in response to your note.'

She suddenly frowned as if the mistake was Giles's.

'Oh no! No need now. He's quite recovered!'

'So I see,' he said. They regarded each other for a silent moment. 'Madam, what am I? Am I a man?'

Her face shrank further back, and her husband intervened before Giles could really vent his anger fully, which was, most likely, a fortunate initiative.

'Beggin' your pardon, Vicar,' he said. 'She's the most doughbeaked bird at times. That zaid, she don't mean no harm. But we do beg your pardon, Vicar, most humbly. Come. Step inside. We've bread and cheese… a bit an' drap, perhaps?'

Giles thanked him and declined his invitation to eat. He wasn't able to imagine the fare being especially good, and he would only have remained angry with the Eyers woman. So he surrendered up his forgiveness, bade the pair of them good afternoon, and set about the walk back.

But was he not a man? Truly? Walking down the hill he had so recently climbed, he wondered how it might be that he was treated so cheaply—by men, women and even the birds. Was he not a man? Was he not—though he scarce ever angled it to his advantage—a priest withal?

When he reached the stretch of road beside the field where the crows had been, everything seemed peaceful. The only birdsong came from a few blackbirds and a lark. Still Giles was too curious to simply walk on past. Would there be no sign at all of the birds having visited? He couldn't believe it would be so and he was fortunate to find the same branch in the hedge with which he had pulled himself up previously.

He mounted the bank a second time with a tremor of anticipation—he couldn't be sure the crows were not still waiting silently.

As it turned out, the scene was almost empty. The crop looked unimpressed by the hundreds of crow feet that had trampled it. But where the circle had been, in its centre, precisely where the single crow had stood—there remained a solitary bird. It was dead. Not merely dead, but a mangled mess of feathers.

Giles stared, creasing his face in disgust and pulling his head back. It was a particularly repellent sight because the only conclusion he could accept, going from the feathers, the marks in the soil and the mutilated bird's corpse, was that they had pecked one of their own number to death.

Was this credible? Would birds truly treat their own kind in this fashion? And how might he ever come to understand the way they had fallen silent in his presence?

He was turning over these troubled thoughts, still taking in the scene, when he realised there was movement in the hedge not far away. A crow squawked loudly at him and Giles recoiled from it with a little grunt of loathing, then waved at the bird with his arms.

'Get away! Be gone!'

The bird remained in its position, turning its head first to the left and then to the right. In the end, it was Giles who went. He slid back down the bank and scowled at the dark-cloaked crow, whose demeanour now seemed insufferably arrogant.

He covered the ground back to Wimborne with a hurried, scuttling pace, glancing back on occasion, and not slowing until he reached Walford Bridge. Once within the town's boundaries, he walked with his head high, defying circumstance. The greetings of passers-by began to distract him and with his calmness came his wondering—whether the whole episode wasn't dyed with meaning.

~

His mother was asleep when he returned to her room. Giles sat in the wicker chair by the window and watched her. His fingers grasped at each other and his mouth chewed at nothing while he watched the fine hairs by her mouth wavering back and forth with each of her wheezing breaths. He had been called out of town for no purpose, it seemed, and yet he had witnessed something none other had seen. A phenomenon so unlikely, so contrary to nature, he was bound to consider its provenance.

He didn't lift himself from the seat until it began to grow dark—by which time he had thought events over several times. Then, at last, he crept over the creaking floorboards and found his way downstairs in the dark.

On a shelf in the pantry there was a plate of food protected with muslin and when Giles uncovered it on the kitchen table, the lamplight showed it to be some ham, cheese and bread.

He blessed Mrs Kelly and sat in the semi-darkness eating alone and staring into the gloom. Then, once he had brushed the crumbs from his hands, he took a lamp through to the study.

He snorted a sort of derogatory laugh as he pulled the

Bible from the shelf. He hadn't done this in so many years now and it was childish to think of it. But then, when he recalled that dead crow in the centre of the circle, and the other fellow on the hedge, watching him, he wondered how it could be otherwise.

He sat at his desk and closed his eyes. His lips barely moved with his prayers. 'Dear Lord...'

Wasn't it a foolish thing to do? The vain habit of a child tempting God. He stared into the darkness. What else should he think of the message from the crows? What else?

He gripped the cover of the book, and closed his eyes once more. 'Dear Lord, guide my hand...' he whispered.

Then he reached to take hold of the pages and pull the book open. And when the pages were flat, he stuck out his index finger and placed it on the page. It was done. He drew the lamp close to complete his discovery. *Blessed are those servants, whom the Lord when he cometh shall find watching: verily I say unto you, that he shall gird himself and make them to sit down to meat, and will come forth and serve them.*

He had picked upon Luke 12:36. For a moment he was excited, thinking the birds to have been watching, but there was nothing else to cling to. He read on, trying to make the words fit the moment: *Be ye therefore ready also: for the Son of man cometh at an hour when ye think not.*

He rearranged the puzzle several times but quickly came to accept that he could have made those words fit any circumstance he chose.

It was in the act of closing the book that the words on the opposite page caught his eye, so he stopped himself and laid the book flat again.

Ravens.

That was what had arrested his attention. Had they been ravens? He had thought them crows but would have been hard pressed to tell the difference. Perhaps they were rooks?

Consider the ravens: for they neither sow nor reap; which neither have store house nor barn; and God feedeth them: how much more are ye better than the fowls? And which of you with taking thought can add to his stature one cubit?

He stared at the lines for few moments more, then scanned back, reading the verses that came before.

And I say unto you my friends, Be not afraid of them that kill the body, and after that have no more that they can do. But I will forewarn you whom ye shall fear: Fear him, which after he hath killed hath power to cast into hell; yea, I say unto you, Fear him.

He pushed the book away across the table and sat back in his chair, but then with another sudden thought, pulled it close again, rereading his first selection, the passage that his finger had fallen on, without guidance or intention on his part, when he first opened the book. *Consider the ravens: for they neither sow nor reap; which neither have storehouse nor barn; and God feedeth them: how much more are ye better than the fowls?*

And he stroked his chin with thoughts tumbling, rushed and muddled, and realised that all he really needed to read was that single line. *Consider the ravens.*

A GROOM'S FLIGHT

~

Wimborne Minster, Dorset,
May 1840

'Give en up to the magistrates, let's zee the bugger swing!'

That's what Bill says. Cornelius's own brother. And there's no lack of feeling in the saying of it, neither. Let's see the *bugger* swing. A real dark-eyed black cap.

Cornelius has so much to say in answer, he can't choose a word. He's left sitting there on the bench by the back wall of the Rising Sun, pint mug in hand, mute as a mole. All those thoughts rippling through his head.

What stops his tongue more than anything else is wondering whether Bill would say the same if he and Oswald were revealed. *Let's see the buggers swing?* He hardly dares think it. Not the same, of course. The choirmaster's frenzied tyranny is a vile and cruel thing, and everyone is talking about how Henry Cuff did himself in on account of it. Him and Oswald? The way Cornelius sees it, it's perfectly natural. But that's just him, and who's to say what goes on in others' heads? There's no way of knowing how much Bill has understood, or guessed, or been told. So Cornelius gapes at his brother but keeps his tongue still.

It is Charles Ellis who responds, commandeering the moment. 'What would they hang him for, Bill?'

'Buggery,' Bill answers plainly, leaving the words undecorated.

Cornelius's stomach churns.

'That takes two,' Charles responds, 'so who would we name as the second?'

Bill looks around the table, back straight, elbows out, beer mug held like a ceremonial weapon. John Street's there too, sitting beside Charles. None of his bright face this evening; he's grim as a judge, staring at the table edge, his jaw clenched closed. Bill looks on the verge of asking, but looks to think better of it, and turns back to Charles.

'Well... he done it to all o' em, didn't he? Near all.'

Weren't so. Cornelius could explain how it was. He doesn't, though. He stays quiet for the same reason as John. They both attended Stickland's school and saw Buggermaster take lessons. They know very well what the choirmaster did, and by Cornelius's estimation, John will blow up like a wounded bull if anyone's fool enough to remind him.

Perhaps John was one of the boys whose faults warranted the choirmaster's sneering attention. Hard to imagine now, but perhaps he was hesitant, or stumbling, had a lisp or a stutter. Or maybe he was brave enough to stand up to the choirmaster but not strong enough to fight off his retribution. Cornelius knows what went on. He knows how the choirmaster dealt with those few he selected; those who he said needed thrashing back into grace.

'What do you think would happen, Bill, if we said the

choirmaster had been interfering with half the town's children?' Charles asks. Bill has no answer, so Charles explains. 'He'd deny everything, and the schoolmaster would back him up. So would the vicar. Cookesely would want to protect his church, so he'd get the bishop involved. And who do you say the magistrates would support?'

Bill nods his head sideways, like an uncertain calf, reluctantly conceding the point. Charles is pointing his finger at him now. 'You know Cookesely as well as anyone here,' he says, forcing the point.

'Aye, well… yes,' says Bill, 'he's not zo bad…'

Charles seems to accept that as a concession. Bill has been gravedigging for the vicar. It's not work he's proud of, and Cornelius isn't sure the others even knew he was doing it. Not what you'd call a seat at the top table, but it puts him closer to the vicar than the rest of them.

'*All* the children is no one at all,' Charles continues. 'We need two or three witnesses, maybe just one.'

'We'll name Cuff, then!' comes back Bill's immediate answer, and it is so insensitive to the boy's suffering that each man at the table looks sharply at him.

'I think that family has suffered enough,' says Charles.

'But they knows the truth of the matter! As good as murdered the lad. You don't think they wants somewhat done about it?'

His brother's obduracy gets the better of Cornelius and he can't help but blurt out his objections.

'He's dead, Bill! Can't say nothing in court, can he? There's no one to say what Buggermaster done.'

'But everyone knows!' Bill protests.

'Bain't enough!'

He can't remember when his brother became so dull, but it's frustrating. He always thought of Bill as being quicker with his wits.

His beer's warm and staling, but sipping it keeps him from talking, and as he lowers his gaze, he notices how Charles's fingers are rapping on the table. The man's face and voice might be calm, but the drumming signals stronger emotions out of sight. Charles then proves that he has the courage to enquire where Cornelius would not. He looks along the table to ask John his thoughts.

John speaks without the slightest movement. 'Well, geldin's too good for en,' he says, all matter-of-fact. 'Zo I suppose we should do the hangin' ourselves.'

Wouldn't do to laugh at Charles's reaction—it's funny, though. His eyelids bat like a shy bride. He doesn't know what to say. Shouldn't have put his question if he didn't want an answer. He stammers a little, mouth opening and closing, then carries on heedless.

It is unlikely, he explains, they'll achieve anything via the magistrates or the law. Bill argues with this, of course. The magistrates should know, and should act on it, and if they don't, it shows what little use they are. No one disagrees because there's not much point in arguing. You may as well rail at God.

'I think John is right in this: whatever we do, we must do ourselves,' Charles tells them, bringing the table to silence. They're staring at him, like obedient sheepdogs waiting for his direction. 'There's only one thing we can do,' he says.

~

'He'll laugh you to blazes!' Oswald snorts.

It is the next day and, under bright sunlight, Cornelius is buckling up an old black harness in preparation for Oswald's morning ride. It's good leather, but Oswald left it out and Cornelius had thought it lost. They're by the brick pigsty—him sitting on the wall, working the leather, and Oswald leaning against it, his leg close to Cornelius's.

'Well, perhaps he will. But that won't stop us. We have plans,' he says.

The harness was dirty and shrivelled from rain and sun by the time he found it. That was the day before the wedding, the day before they found poor Henry Cuff's body. He's been waxing it for days now. Working life back into it. And he's got it ready to be used again, once the fastenings are adjusted properly.

'And what sage strategies have you concocted?' Oswald asks.

Cornelius doesn't know the expression. He's thinking of the herb.

'Sage?'

'Doesn't matter. What did they decide?'

He swallows his pride again because Oswald always does that to him, treating him a fool when he could just explain his meaning. That was their difference—Oswald had his schooling from a tutor in the farmhouse, not Stickland's schoolroom. But even he admits that doesn't make him better, or smarter.

'Charles says the choirmaster's more sensitive to opinion than he shows. Maybe he'll budge straight away. If not, Charles says, we'll make his life so difficult he'll move on for relief from it.'

'Oh yes, and how will you do that, my pretty?' Oswald asks. Knees touching.

Cornelius smirks.

'I'm not your fuckin'"pretty"!'

Oswald smiles back at him with a sober, controlled expression, and pokes his arm. 'Oh, but you are, though!'

Cornelius laughs off the tease, shaking his head. 'Ar, you say. I ain't no one's nothing.'

'Are you sure? Well... what are you in this plan to be rid of the choirmaster? What will they have you doing for them, Cornelius?'

It seems lopsided to hear Oswald being suspicious of his friends. Oswald is the one who's always ordering him about—not the others.

'Charles says we'll think of different things...'

'Charles says so, does he? Charles says this, Charles says that. Who is this Charles?'

'Charles Ellis. The wine mer—'

'Ellis? He's the choirmaster's brother!'

'Half-brother. He says it don't matter none—'

'I'll bet he does. He's the youngest, isn't he? Old man Ellis recently deceased and now he wants his brother harried out of town. Oh, Cornelius!'

Oswald shakes his head. He even looks Cornelius up and down, as if he is a child caught in an orchard.

'You know what this is about?'

'It's about—'

'Inheritance. That's what. It's about money, Cornelius. Money. Same as always. You must have nothing to do with it.'

Cornelius can't believe this version. Charles is simply not

that type of man and he explains as much, knowing full well that Oswald won't budge in his view. They're still arguing about it while he puts the harness on the bay stallion.

Oswald mounts the horse, looking irked by the conversation. 'Things are not the same for you as the others. Remember that. You know what they'd have done to Bankes if he hadn't run off to Venice?'

Cornelius has to think for a moment. Bankes? Oswald moves in different circles. He's talking about the old man of Kingston House. Owns most of the farmland around Wimborne. No doubt Oswald's family think of the Bankeses as neighbours. Everyone heard about it. Him and a guardsman caught with their breeches round their ankles in the bushes of a London park. For a moment, Cornelius hesitates to wonder whether Oswald thinks their circumstances similar. Would that make himself the guardsman?

'You remember?' Oswald asks. 'They'd have hanged him, Cornelius, that's what! Strung him up!'

The stallion is getting restless now and Cornelius is having to hold the bridle, letting his arm jerk up and down.

'But they didn't though, did they? He done a bunk.'

'Skin of his teeth.'

'What happened to the other fellow, anyhow?' he asks.

'Which other fellow?'

'The guardsman.'

'Oh, for God's sake, no one cares about the bloody guardsman. The point is, if this thing with the choirmaster goes queer, he'll look for someone to pick on. He knows your face and he knows my face. He's no fool. So you must have *nothing to do with it*!'

With that Oswald yanks on the reins, trusting Cornelius

to release the bridle, then he rides off. The thudding of hooves moves off around the copse as Cornelius wanders back to the stable.

His chest is tight with suppressed indignation. Oswald cares for himself and nothing else, that much is clear. But Cornelius was not hired by Oswald Guthrie, he was hired by Squire Guthrie himself, so Cornelius can do as he chooses and if he chooses to follow Charles's lead, then so he shall. *Charles says this, Charles says that.* Cornelius wouldn't be at all surprised if Oswald wasn't just plain jealous. Ridiculous.

~

The last thing Bill says before they set out through the night for the Minster is, 'Come on then, let's set to it!'

His words are still echoing in Cornelius's head when they reach the door in the transept. *Let's set to it!* The little door is hidden in the dark shadow of the churchyard's yew trees, built in an age of lesser men. They all four of them duck to step through it. Bill has a set of keys and takes the lead, while Cornelius takes the rear, still hearing Oswald telling him to have nothing to do with it.

They halt just inside the door as Charles lights a lantern and, so the light shan't be seen, Cornelius pushes the door closed. Then Charles turns up the wick and shadows are sent skittering around the sandstone.

His pulse is already thumping and insistent when Charles nods toward the stairwell and whispers, 'This way.' A meek voice, but enough to send his heart racing and his thoughts chasing circles.

Have nothing to do with it!

Let's set to it!

This way.

The stone staircase is steep, and it spirals tightly so they can only ascend in slow single file. Cornelius is at the back, following John Street, and the light is thin two turns behind the lamp. The echoed rattling of the lamp handle seems stronger. He focuses on John's hobnail boots just ahead of him, scratching the stones with each step. The stone-damp air tickles his nose.

He's near the top when they come to a sudden halt. Up ahead something is wrong. Noises break out like bats from a cave; Charles calls out in alarm. There's another voice, saying, 'Yeomen.' A scattering noise. Metal on stone. Cornelius is pushing forwards trying to see past John, wondering who would call for 'yeomen' in a moment of distress, but whatever is going on is out of his sight. Shadows dart around the stones, moving the whole world as Charles swings his lamp, then he hears, 'Oh Lor'!'

He pushes up, pressing into the space behind John, but Cornelius is still partway down the stairs, so he still can't see what the matter is. On the other side of the dark, windowless landing, the tiny arched door to the library is open, letting candlelight spill on the stone walls. But everyone is looking at the floor, so Cornelius pushes himself onto the top step and peers over John's shoulder.

So much at once. The body clothed in a dark shirt and a waistcoat. The knife on the stones. Bill and Charles staring down at the motionless form, both with their palms upturned. Skin stained with blood. The darkening pool looming out from under the corpse.

'You killed him?' Cornelius hisses.

Bill and Charles turn his direction instantly. They say, 'No!' at once. Then they tell him the same thing, garbled and in unison.

Bill: 'He comes out; we catches en.'

Charles: 'He came out with the knife… He must have…'

And then they all stare down at the body. The utter absence of motion is somehow exaggerated by the pooling blood that is creeping its way between the flagstones. Cornelius tears his eyes from it to look at the others.

Their expressions—not easy to read in the flickering light—look regretful and resigned. Charles has not moved.

Have nothing to do with it. Things are not the same for you.

'They'll say we killed him,' Cornelius mutters.

Bill and Charles look towards him. But John, whose back Cornelius was leaning against, steps forwards and kneels by the body. There is something strange in his movement. Cornelius is puzzled. John looks curious, but purposeful. They are all motionless as John raises his arm, forms a fist and smashes it down into the dead man's face. They go rigid when he lifts his arm again, and finally leap forward as he hits the face over and over with a sudden, manic fury.

It is an unearthly reaction. John is saying nothing, just punching the corpse, and carries on punching at thin air when Charles and Bill get a good enough grip to pull him back.

'John! John!' Charles says, 'Calm! It's all right. He's dead already.'

If he wasn't dead before he certainly is now. John's fist is cut and bloodied and Buggermaster's face is mangled.

'Well that's a-smattered that then,' Bill mutters. Charles

looks shaken—wide-eyed and frightened. John is just staring at the body, nostrils flaring like a raging bull, all ready to set to it again.

'Now what?' Charles asks.

Bill scratches his nose and looks down at the problem.

'I'll fetch me cart. We'll bury en. I dug a fresh one this av'ernoon—that cobbler's wife—zo we can just... we'll have to get en down they stairs virst.'

Charles starts nodding. 'Yes. Yes, that's right. John, go fetch a tar sheet.'

John looks up and there is still rage in his eyes, but he shakes his damaged hand and pushes past Cornelius to descend the stairwell. He smells of sour sweat and sweet blood. Charles looks up, directly at Cornelius.

'It's best if you just go home. Say nothing to anyone.'

Cornelius nods, turns and backs away, feels Charles grab his arm.

'Better still, if anyone asks, say... say we came to talk to him, but there was no one here. We all went home. Just that!'

Then he's hurried out, but he takes a last glance at the lump of a body on the stone floor. Blood has gathered by the man's leg in a puddle a quarter-inch deep.

Cornelius doesn't go home. Couldn't. He passes the Oddfellows thinking it more likely to find Oswald in the George or the Albion. But he's there, playing shove ha'penny with two of the gasworks lads. Peering through the window, he catches his eye then withdraws back into the street. Oswald is out of the pub like a racing hound.

'What's wrong? You look like you've seen a ghost.'

'Might do yet. Buggermaster's dead. Knife in the gut.'

'Oh, good God! You went with them! Fool. I told you to keep clear of it!'

Cornelius hushes him, waving his arm as they walk towards the Square, but then Oswald stops to think.

'Wait. I'll fetch my coat. Stay here!'

So Cornelius has to stand around like a servant by the corner of the Square, looking away down West Borough. When Oswald returns, he finds himself grabbed by the arm and propelled towards the dimness of West Street.

'Tell me what happened. What did they do?'

Cornelius recounts events as he remembers them while they walk past the hotel. He went with the others to confront the choirmaster, just as they'd been planning. They were to tell him to leave town while he was still able. Four of them. Charles, John, Bill and him. He was at the back, his brother at the front, and when they got to the top of the stairs, he couldn't see. Bill said the choirmaster came out already stuck with the knife. 'He must have done himself as we was a-coming up the stairs,' he concludes.

He feels himself pulled close as Oswald wraps an arm around his shoulder, still marching him along the roadside.

'And you, sweet idiot, you believe that?'

Cornelius stares at the shadowed face of his friend. Oswald knows nothing. Hasn't heard them denying it in unison.

'Yes. I believe them,' he says.

'Then you're a bigger fool than I thought. They killed him. Of course they did. And you'll swing with the rest.'

Cornelius feels himself pulled round as Oswald stops them in the street. A hand on his chin pulling his face into the light of the gas lamp. And Oswald's face looking down, like they were going to kiss, but sinister in its stead.

'Unless… they mean for you to take the drop *for* everyone else,' he says, and his eyes narrow with the last word.

Cornelius pushes himself free, shaking his head.

'This ain't a lark!' he says.

'Deadly serious,' Oswald says, but before Cornelius can reply further, Oswald is marching on, calling back orders.

'Come on, look lively. We have to get you away.'

'Wait. What? No. Stop. That's my own brother!'

'Who led the assault!' Oswald says, barely turning back.

Cornelius sighs, eyes momentarily closed with impatience but aware it's a pointless gesture with no one to see it. He's no choice but to hurry after Oswald, who's still talking to him.

'What?'

'I said… that you said… you saw nothing of what happened.'

They're turning out of West Street's dog-leg, emerging from Wimborne's narrows, and light from the houses is growing weaker.

It takes a march to keep pace with Oswald. 'What do you mean by "get me away"?'

Oswald seems untested by the pace and answers with ease. 'You've no choice. If we're lucky, there'll be no one waiting for you at the farm. But you have to get away immediately, before they come. Beaucroft might be an idea. You can ride there directly. My cousin will shelter you tonight. I'll come tomorrow morning, first thing.'

'What? Why?'

Finally, he has said something to get Oswald to stop.

A firm hand grips his shoulder. The grip is insistent, proprietorial and therefore strangely intimate.

'Because, my pretty, if they take you by this evening, or the morning, you'll be hanged by the week's end.'

Oswald's breath is beery.

'Ain't your pretty,' Cornelius mutters.

'You certainly won't be with a lifeless, purple tongue lolling from your gob. You ever seen a hanging?'

'No.'

'They piss themselves.'

Cornelius is left with this ringing in his ears as they continue up St Margaret's Hill. *They piss themselves.*

As soon as they reach the farm, the barking starts. Cornelius calms the dogs, skirts the stables and climbs the wooden steps to his room while Oswald goes to the house.

He was pleased with this space when he was first offered it. Stable boy. Room of his own. Had a ring to it. The sound has dulled and these days he hears it for what it means. Stable boy in the stables—barely a grade above the stalls.

Oswald has already told him to bundle up everything he wants to take, but when it comes to it there's not much choosing. There's the razor Bill gave him that he rarely uses, his Sunday-best shirt and breeches and the small leather-bound prayer book his ma bade him read each night and which he hasn't opened since. But the whole escapade seems a little silly. Overblown. Running off when he has done nothing is a folly. Like some young maid making a haystack from someone's casual enquiry. Except, of course, Buggermaster's dead. Lying a quarter-inch deep in blood.

There's a quiet rapping on his door. He opens it to find Oswald holding up a letter. He starts protesting, 'D'you really think I need to—' but Oswald talks right over him, pushing the paper into his hands.

'When you get to Beaucroft, go to the front door. If you go to the back, the servants will just turn you away as too much trouble. See that this letter reaches my cousin.'

Before he can protest further, they are taking a lamp into the stables then Oswald starts saddling the young mare, Penny. Cornelius can't stop himself from smirking at the thought of Oswald saddling a horse for his benefit.

'Can't take the bay, then?' he jokes. Oswald's look calls him a fool.

'You know your way to Beaucroft?'

He shrugs. In the dark, maybe not. Likely the young mare will be skittish in the night and won't like having her sleep disturbed, but Oswald won't want to incur his elder brother's anger at having one of the working horses missing in the morning. The dogs stay quiet as they leave the stables, not even reacting to the sound of hooves on the cobbles. Almost like they know. At the gate Oswald takes the lamp and its light casts his face into ghostly shadows.

'You'll not run off somewhere?' he says.

'Course not... how would I?' Cornelius complains. It seems an unreasonable suspicion.

Oswald takes a grip on his arm, which grows tighter until finally he pulls them together. He kisses him, holds him close, then—typical Oswald—slaps his back and pushes him towards the mare.

'Get on then. I'll be with you by dawn. Take care, my pretty.'

'Not your fuckin' pretty.'

*

He mounts the young mare and Oswald swings the gate open, and it provokes another smirk to find himself looking down on his master. But beyond the gate there is darkness and the silhouette of trees and he makes a mess of his departure by hesitating to choose the direction.

The quickest route to Beaucroft would be clear through town, but he might meet someone who should ask why he's out by night on one of Squire Guthrie's horses.

'That way!' hisses Oswald, pointing up the hill. It makes him feel gawky and Penny gets nervous as he turns her nose. She's thumping the ground with her front legs, so when he urges her up the hill she surges forward blindly. There's nothing before them but darkness and he reins her in quickly.

'Whoa, whoa, whoa! Slowly, slowly, Penny! We can't see nothing!'

Oswald is already gone. Retreated back into the farm or obscured by the darkness, so they walk carefully up to the corner, then descend the narrows of Stone Lane.

This road: he's walked it a thousand times, but he knows it best by the memories it serves up—John Street's cousin kept a pony down by the brickworks that would bite anyone it could, and he and the Stout boys used to dare each other to run through the field defying the old nag. And it was this very hill he walked up, one bright summer morning five years gone, to take his lodgings in the stables at Stone Farm, excited at the thought of the Squire's dashing younger brother, who'd winked at him the morning they tried him with the horses.

At the end of each summer a fair will gather on the green at the bottom of the hill by Blind Lane. First time they went, Oswald showed off by shying three coconuts from their stands and then won a game of Aunt Sally with only two batons.

But the memories don't help him see his path, and it is awful dark. The young mare slows as the roadsides melt into darkness, slows again when the small lights from Walford Mill are obscured, and when they're feeling their way between the hedges of Mill Lane, she'll barely take a step without Cornelius's urging. 'C'mon, get on now, get on now...'

But it is as nothing to the dark once they have crossed Walford Bridge. It is the edge of town, that bridge. Just the Crown and Anchor close by the other side and then nothing but open countryside, sliced by narrow lanes with towering hedgerows.

Only a little distance up Burt's Hill, the horse refuses. She slows and stops, and no amount of rein-flicking or flank-kicking will induce her to go further into the darkness and Cornelius doesn't blame her neither. He holds up his hand and can barely see his fingers; there's not the tiniest sprig of light to see by. Climbing off her back feels like an act of bravery. He's feeling for the ground before his foot finds it. Unsighted, he gets his trailing foot wedged in the stirrup and has to stand, one knee by his chest, and free himself by hand, at peril of toppling over backwards. The mare snorts, but Cornelius ignores her. Not taking criticism from no horse. Barely more than a foal.

Once his boot is freed, he takes the reins and stands close by her.

'No, no, c'mon, Penny,' he says as she tries to edge backwards.

But it only takes two steps before he realises how slow this will be. His two steps, four from the horse. Dull thuds on the earth. His hand is out front but he's far from sure of himself. He can't be far wrong—there's a dog that's been barking since they passed the Crown and Anchor. He hardly took notice of it until now, but it must be over near Onslow, and it gives him a steer. Three barks at a time, then a pause, then three more. Ro-ro-ro. Away to his right.

And the trees above him rustle in the breeze. They're thicker on the left of the road. Just enough so he has a sense of them. Rustling like stars a-twinkle. The bark to his right. Ro-ro-ro. Rustling to his left.

He tries walking slowly and steadily forward, acting confident, but it's an awkward pace for the mare, who would far rather not move at all. He doesn't dare think of much else. The day's events aren't far from his thoughts, but his mind's fixed on the road's sides. He doesn't want to spook poor Penny by walking her into a face-full of branches.

All the same, he keeps hearing Oswald saying they must get him away and has odd wonderings what that could mean. Shall he wind up in France, like Bonnie Prince Charlie? There's a Frenchman that works in Laing's Hotel. Funny-looking fellow, with a twirled moustache similar to Tom Dowding, the butcher, except the Frenchman's is more fussy.

When his foot sinks into something soft, he knows it to be horse dung. Almost certain, because there's very little else it could be. He can smell it besides, and he'll have to clean his boot before he climbs the steps to Beaucroft. He's trodden on dead animals before and it doesn't feel like that. Nor stink like that.

Wanting to be sure again where the side of the road is, he stops and lets out the rein so he can edge across the road and find the bank. Penny won't let him get a step away, though. Each time he edges sideways she takes a step with him. No fool, this mare. Doesn't want to be left alone by night. He can see it, almost, this dark black mass that is the hedge-row. But each time he reaches out expecting brambles or branches, it seems another step away. Of course, when he finally gets his hand to it, he finds a clutch of nettles.

Annoyed at the sting, he turns, but bumps his head against the horse's head because she was close by, and she yanks her chin up, pulling against the reins, rattling the tackle, and he has to calm her again.

'Easy, easy, easy!'

He worries about her treading on his foot. It's easily done.

He strokes her muzzle to calm her, then turns and looks up the hill at the dark task ahead.

'C'mon,' he says, 'we're just going to have to be brave.'

He leads on, eyes boggling into the darkness, straining for the barest outlines. The sound of the barking dog fades and some other creature starts calling from over to their left. It's an eerie sort of screaming cry. Could be a bird, could be a demon. Penny doesn't like it, whatever it is, and she can't stay close enough to him. She'd have her muzzle by his ear and would tread on his heels if he didn't hold her away with the reins.

The ground is levelling at the top of the hill, and that's when the sky clears. The clouds open for only a moment, but the break is enough to cast a cool thin starlight on the trees, allowing him to recognise the corner. It's not far now until he'll cut around by the brickworks and head downhill for Beaucroft.

Craning his head back, he notices the wispy puffs of his breath in the cool night air, then his focus switches a million miles into the sky and falls on a distant star. Framed by simmering clouds, it is a tiny, bright, God-like light that must have been shining down on these fields since the days of Jesus. It will still be there, shining down, when Cornelius and Penny are both dead and gone.

The clouds close. The stars disappear behind the curtain, the light is withdrawn from the trees and the dark path leads ahead. Penny tugs on the reins and gives an ominous, nickering sigh. He doesn't remember having stopped, but there they are, in the middle of the darkened road. And he is alone. Events of the day come back to him in a flood.

His brother Bill in the Rising Sun, thick forearms resting on the varnished wooden bench: *Let's zee the bugger swing!*

Oswald standing close by him in the bright sunlight: *Have nothing to do with it!*

Charles standing back from the still-bleeding body: *He came out with the knife… he must have…*

Oswald striding up St Margaret's Hill: *We have to get you away.*

He pushes his arm out again, keeping the horse from treading on him, and sets off into the darkness. 'Who d'you think it were, then, Penny? Hmm? Who did for old Buggermaster?'

Penny snickers. Almost as if she knows.

It comes as a surprise when he recognises the gateway to Beaucroft. He had thought there was still some way to go down the hill, but the tall gateposts are distinctive and clear and he feels a fool for having walked Penny the best part of the journey. Still, he pats Penny's muzzle. 'Soon have you home,' he lies.

He cleans his boots in the grass by the gate, then starts the long walk up the gravel drive. Pain in the neck, that. Some poor garden hand no doubt has to rake the entire length of it. But it shows a lighter path to the door, so he is glad of it. Go to the front door, Oswald told him. See that his cousin gets the letter.

They'd joked about that just recently—him and Bill. 'Zee that these apples don' rot!' Bill complained. 'An' how the blazes am I supposed to do that then? Zee that the mud don't dirty your tunic. Zee that the sky don't vall on our heads! I tell 'e, Corny, I could get em to zee a few things, no mistake.'

His heart's in his mouth as he ties Penny to the post then climbs the five steps up to the front door. Calling uninvited in the night's darkness. They'll likely shoot him. He pulls out Oswald's letter. It is the only defence he has, so he holds it in front of his chest as he tugs on the bell pull.

He has to endure only a few seconds' waiting before a light flickers behind the glass—which is good, because it means he has woken no one. But still, when the door creaks open to reveal a butler in full livery, Cornelius feels his heart trembling. He holds out the letter.

'I beg your pardon,' he says, as correctly as ever he might. And feels it too; he's begging.

Beaucroft Lodge is an ill-lit, tumbledown old ruin of a place ruled by Oswald's cousin. He's a short man, Oswald's senior by many years, and he directs his servants with curt abruptness. After a short display of discontentment and irritation, he accepts the responsibility foisted on him by the letter and Cornelius is given an awkward little room in the servants' quarters.

It is not a room for restful sleep. There is a window behind Cornelius's head and although it's a calm evening, there is an almost constant draught ruffling his hair and keeping the room cool, so he spends most of the night lying on his back, staring up at his future.

They piss themselves. Quite suddenly, lying in a strange bed, he shudders with horror at the thought of pissing himself with his purple tongue a-lolling. And it's not just that he doesn't want to go that way. He doesn't want to die at all. And how long has he got? Another sixty years? Less? Far less if Oswald is right and they come looking to blame him for Buggermaster's murder. It shudders through him as an overwhelming fear and he has to physically shake his head to get rid of it. He turns on his side, wraps his blankets closer and tries to quieten his thoughts—but he couldn't feel more alone.

~

Cornelius knows he'll not sleep again when he is woken by a blackbird whistling at the morning. Light starts creeping through the window and it seems like he can almost hear his future waiting for him.

The world is different this side of the night. He has to think his brother will be angry. Running off without a word. And he was to have visited his ma and pa on the Sunday and

unless Bill makes the journey, they will be all day expecting him, not knowing he's gone away. And there is no way
of knowing when he might see them again; not if Oswald's
plan is borne out.

Oswald's plan. And why does he do as Oswald says?
Because he can't refuse the man a thing, that's why. But how
wounding to think this might be the last they'll see of each
other.

God forbid that Oswald recognises the finality of the
moment. He'll attempt to say something soft, achieve only
a belittling farewell, and that will be the last of it. Cornelius
will be sent off into the unknown. It'd be a comfort if he
thought there was some measure of concern for his welfare
in all of Oswald's energetic arrangements, but any compassion that might be noticed is entirely obscured by Oswald's
passion for self-protection.

With dawn come and gone, he gets himself out of the
bed he was given and pulls on his breeches and shirt. There's
not a squeak from elsewhere in the house. His own floorboards croak like a pond of frogs, so he can only imagine the
silence shows there's no one else moving. He perches on the
side of the bed and bides time. Perhaps someone will come
for him. He would surely rather risk waiting too long than
attempt to find his way around the servants' corridors of an
old and unknown house. No gain to be had being mistaken
for a burglar by a sleepy maid.

The question that he settles on is whether the Minster
floor by the library was brick or stone. He tries to picture
the flagstones, to remember the feel of them. If they were
Purbeck stone, or something like it, then Charles and John
might have washed the blood away—with plenty of water

and a good deal of soap. Cornelius has had a hand in the slaughter of pigs, and he knows what it's like trying to clean dried blood. If it is sandstone, like the older parts of the building, they shan't budge it.

And if they get the blood away and have the body off to the grave Bill had ready dug, will it not come round that the Buggermaster's disappeared? It'll be for Charles to say where he is, should anyone ask, but then, who will? The Rev Cookesely? If no one else, he'll surely feel the choirmaster's absence. Will it trouble him enough to make enquiries? What then?

He'll be sooner missed himself. Squire Guthrie will miss his stable boy. Likely he'll miss his young chestnut mare first, but it won't escape him either way. His parents will miss their son and his pa always said that a man does not run from an ordeal. Bill will miss his brother. Only Oswald will know what has happened, and all matters considered, running away doesn't seem right. After all, it was he who told Charles about Buggermaster when Charles was ignorant of the cause of poor Cuff's distress.

The house stays silent. The sun warms the eastern fields. Why should he run? He did nothing. And he is not Oswald's pretty nor is he anyone's anything. He is his own man and his home is in Wimborne.

His thoughts have drifted further still by the time he hears footsteps in the corridor. He's thinking of the railways and the speed they travel and whether he might one day see London when the door bursts open.

'Right! Come on, Brown! We're off to India!'

Oswald has planted himself halfway into the room, with

his feet firmly apart and his fists on his hips. He is grinning with excitement.

'India?' Cornelius laughs.

'India! We're going to join the army. Make a man of you. Been thinking about it for ages anyway. I'm going to purchase a majority and you'll be my batman. What d'you think? "Major Guthrie". I shall cut a dashing figure in a uniform, shan't I?'

Cornelius laughs again as Oswald strikes a martial pose, but all he really feels is a delighted form of relief washing through his senses.

'So you're coming with me?'

'Don't be ridiculous, Brown. You're coming with *me*!'

MRS WILKINSON'S GRAVE

~

Wimborne Minster, Dorset, June 1840

Waking is a painful transition. It has him leave hold of a world of mingled impressions: his concern for the boots to be made, the scent of cotton, and of Lily's hair, the comfort of her quiet giggles and the fear of what she's giggling about. It makes him writhe, that fear.

What *is* she giggling about? And who is that beside her?

Then it grows cold, and colder still, until it is no longer a credible chill for the bedroom and at last Sidney becomes sensible to the world.

It is not the bedroom at all. He is outside. He is here, in the graveyard, at the day's dawning, wearing pyjamas and his gown; he has been sleepwalking.

This vivid reality beyond his dreams is overwhelming. The thin wetness soaking his pyjamas is a shock, and the vast openness of air is an affront, brushing his skin while yawning up into the broad open reach of a sky that is pink with the dying night. But none of this, not even the pinching cold in his toes and fingers, remains in his awareness when he recalls that his Lily is dead and gone.

The memory assaults him anew each morning. Usually it comes with the warmth of his bed and the need to descend the stairs to the leather and the last, but the difference is pitiable—bed or none. She is gone. Taken in an agony of labour. Their first never-born taken with her and no dream or detail has more claim on his senses.

He turns, alert to the significance of the mound he is lying on, to look at the tombstone.

'Oh… no.'

LILY WILKINSON, 1816–1840

WITH THEE, O LORD, FOR EVER.

Nausea regains its grip on his stomach. This is the message he had to trim to fit the stone-carver's fee. It is carved into the bright, fresh, clean stone, newly laid.

He pushes himself off his wife's grave, hands collecting cold dew from the grass, and looks around at the others. In comparison, Lily's grave is grotesquely oversized, rising a foot or more from the ground, making the earth seem pregnant with the deceased.

He studies the size of it for a moment, screws his brow into a deep, wounded frown, then states plainly the realisation his dreams were trying to wake in him: 'There's someone else in there!'

There's still mist in the spring air as Sidney Wilkinson shuffles home down St Margaret's Hill; a bitterly weak, unbounded glow in the sky over Julian's Brewery; most likely the sun, but it is mean with its precious warmth and offers no comfort through the damp folds of Sidney's dressing gown.

He weaves his way through the town, avoiding the midwife's cottage, cutting behind the undertakers, preferring the longer route until he reaches his own place. And he stands on the pavement, sighing with dissatisfaction at the shop door. It is wide open. As open as the sky.

~

Later in the morning, after he has taken time to wash and shave and feed himself, Sidney is addressing the backlog of boots when the shop door rattles. He looks up from his pin hammer to see David Woolcott, turning, already closing the door and removing his cap. This is a rare visit. David's too idle to leave his own shop; he waits for folks to come to him. There must have been talk of Sid's sleepwalking. He focuses on the boot.

'Morning, Sid! What you been up to, then?' David asks.

Sewing a sole is one of the more rewarding stages of bootmaking. The combination of upper and sole being so thick, each stitch must be hammered through, each blow struck with precision to save the needle from being bent useless.

David Woolcott ceases to exist for a moment. Then the thread is punched cleanly and Sid draws it out on the underside. David approaches the bench—it seems he does not intend to be ignored. 'Been sleepwalking? Is that it?'

It won't do to deny something put so directly, but Sidney shuffles his shoulders, reluctant to reveal his guilt.

'Ah... well, I woke up on Lily's grave. So... is that sleep-walking?'

''Less you flew there?' David jokes. It almost makes Sid wince. David draws his chin in, looking abashed.

'Just had Bill Brown in,' David explains. 'Says he seen you walking down St Margaret's Hill, bare-headed in your nightgown.'

'I were in a dressing gown. I wouldn't ha' thought him the sort for tittle-tattle.'

David lowers his voice at this. He even leans a little closer. 'Nor is he, Sid. Just concerned for your welfare, that's all.'

'Hm. Well, I don't recall seeing him. What's he up to?'

'Filling in for his brother, looking after the stables up Stone Farm. He were just in the shop after harness rings. Axed me to see you were all right. And that's someone looking out for you, not gossiping.'

Sidney gives up work on the boot for a moment and rests his hands on the bench. David is still standing awkwardly in front of the workbench.

'They say sleepwalking's a sign of a troubled mind.'

'Well... I've reason to be troubled, ha'n't I?'

'You've lost your wife, Sidney...'

He has. He has lost his wife. But that's not it. He is harbouring the most unreasoned of suspicions and can't shake a resentment that it might be David ensconced with his wife in her grave, even though the man is standing before him. That can't be, but if not David, who? There's someone in there. Someone recently deceased.

David cocks his head to one side. 'Sid?'

'Who else died?' Sidney asks.

'Eh?'

'Someone else must have died, disappeared or somewhat.'

David's face wrinkles up. 'Someone else?' he asks, so Sid explains his dream and the size of the mound on top of his wife's grave.

'I thought it were shallow when they… when they lowered her in,' he says, his throat suddenly tightening. 'But if it were just shallow, the mound should be the same, see? Enough for a coffin. But it's more than that, Davie. It's enough for two. There's someone else in there.'

It is clear from David's wrinkled brow that he is unconvinced.

'You were ever a jealous husband, but this…'

'That's true, I confess, but…'

He wasn't thinking of telling anyone else, but having done so he can't suffer being doubted. 'You'll have to see for yourself,' he says.

'Will I?'

'This afternoon. Shut up shop sharpish. Come with me. I'll show you.'

~

It's still light when they get there, although their shadows are long, spreading across the neatly kept grass that borders the graveyard plots. David has his hands in his pockets, which causes Sid a hint of discomfort as they stand and survey the mound.

'Lord almighty,' David says.

'You see?'

'I do. That's huge. It's like… it's like a double grave.'

'My point! My point exactly.'

As they walk back down St Margaret's Hill, it pleases Sid to think what a good friend he has in David. He never should doubt him.

'What can I do, Davie? I'm lost. This isn't my sort of business...'

'No, well I don't suppose it's anyone's. No one normal. I'll tell you what you've to do: you've to go see the bailiff's men, that's what. If there's a body involved, it's a matter for the law. You want Rawlins' offices.'

'Rawlins...' Sid mutters. It would give the matter real weight to take it to an official. 'You think there'll be an inquiry?' he asks.

David shrugs. 'Can't know, can we?'

'No,' Sid agrees. And when they have walked a little further, he asks, 'Who d'you think is in there?'

What he really wants to know is whether Davie thinks it is her lover, except he doesn't dare say so.

'Could be anyone, couldn't it?' David answers. And that's true enough, except Sid can think of lots of people it couldn't be.

'They'd have to be dead,' he says.

David looks at him sideways.

~

Next morning, Sid is woken by his own shivering. It's like he has shaken himself from his slumber, and he firmly resents his first moment of consciousness, jolting awake with a scowl and a reproach on his lips.

But then he looks at the mound of turf he is lying on, at Lily's gravestone, at the graveyard around him and at the grey dawning sky above his head.

'Oh Lor',' he mutters. He's so cold he feels sick. He wraps his dressing gown tighter, puts his slippers back on (which someone—it must have been him—had placed at the foot of Lily's grave), and with a last look back at her headstone, sets off back into town. The familiar aching loss doesn't reach him until his shivering has stopped.

~

That afternoon, he digs out the sign he had to hang on the shop window when Lily went into confinement. *Closed due to Unexpected Circumstances.* Even Lily joked about how well 'expected' the circumstances were, but Sid couldn't think of another way to phrase it. He fiddles the string onto the hook at the top of the door, then pulls down the blind. Then he takes off his leather apron and his shop coat, hangs them on the peg by the shoe-shine stand and dons his waistcoat, watch chain, jacket and best bowler. So prepared, he steps outside and locks the shop door.

At Rawlins' offices, he is met by a clerk in his shirtsleeves. Sid stammers, not quite knowing what to say, but the clerk smiles on him. 'You're here for Mr Rawlins?'

Sid grabs his hat in an act of unnecessary deference. 'Yes, yes…'

He is waved into a broad hallway with mustard-yellow walls and gilt-framed paintings. 'You've an appointment?' the clerk asks.

'Er… why no, I've not. May I…?'

'No matter. The afternoon has been easy. Won't you please take a seat? Mr Rawlins will see you shortly.'

So Sid sits, according to the clerk's gesture, on a silk-upholstered chair beneath a broad oil painting. He watches the comings and goings for some minutes. Clerks walk directly across the hallway and they walk back again, always carrying papers. One of them approaches and asks if he is there on insurance business and Sidney has to think about it before deciding not.

Eventually the clerk who first met him comes back. 'Mr Wilkinson?' he asks, even though he took his name not twenty minutes earlier. Sidney nods. 'If you'll please follow me...' So Sid trails behind him up the carpeted stairs to the first floor, noticing the split in the heel-seam in the clerk's brogues.

He is shown into an office at the front of the building. It stretches the width of the building, hosting five desks, all but one of which are occupied by men hard at work. It is well lit by large windows that look out over West Borough and has been slightly overheated by two coal fires. There's a threadbare red rug on the floor, trapped in place by the heavy desks, and the clerk warns Sid to mind the fold as he leads him to the largest of the desks at the end of the room.

'Mr Rawlins? This is Sidney Wilkinson.'

Very promptly, the bald man behind the desk looks up from his papers.

'Wilkinson... Sidney... the cordwainer? Is it... the High Street? It is. I'm afraid that condolences are in order, are they not? I am indeed very, *very* sorry that they are necessary, Mr Wilkinson. Please have a seat. Sit yourself down. Just there. That's fine. And now tell me your business, Mr Wilkinson: it is not a question of insurance, is it? Does it concern the late Mrs Wilkinson's estate?'

His face becomes serious with this question and he holds

on to his enquiring expression, lips pursed, head slightly tilted to one side.

'Well, no, not as such. It is question of her grave, see.'

A frown. 'Of her grave?'

It seems ridiculous suddenly. Sidney has no real reason to suspect there's anyone else in Lily's grave—none except his own foolish jealousy prompted by his night-time ramblings. Yet here he is: having started to make a fool of himself, he is condemned to complete the act.

'I believe...' he says, finding sudden confidence in the serious tone he has stumbled upon, 'I believe... that her grave...' but faltering now for the lack of an ending.

'What do you believe about your wife's grave, Mr Wilkinson?' Rawlins prompts.

Sid gives up trying to sound important and states the matter plainly. 'There's someone else in there!' he says.

At this, Rawlins frowns and the clerk looks up sharply.

'Someone else...?' Rawlins says.

'With her. In her grave,' Sid answers, nodding firmly.

Rawlins looks perplexed. 'Ah. A legal question, that would be a matter of...?'

The clerk jumps into action. 'Er... registry of births and deaths... consecrated ground? Proper burials, maybe?' Then he shrugs.

Rawlins looks back at Sid. 'Do you have any notion as to who it might be? This... interloper?'

'Well, no. No idea,' Sid answers, holding back his irrational suspicions. 'Someone who's died. That's for sure.'

Rawlins smiles. 'Yes. Of that, I think, we may be confident. Graves making very bad dwelling places for the living.'

'But I don't know no one else who's died, you see,' Sid explains.

'You don't? Other than your wife. Of course you don't. And now you…?'

'Now I've come here to enquire whether you know of someone. Someone who's died but not been buried proper. Is there someone?'

Now Rawlins understands. His eyes narrow and his face seems to stiffen. It makes his ears move back slightly.

'Er… no. There have been no… no unexplained deaths or misplaced corpses. That would be—'

'There's Mr Ellis though?' the clerk says.

Rawlins doesn't seem to appreciate this intervention. His face tightens further, and he swallows as he turns to his clerk—as though an unpleasant taste has assailed him.

'Mr Ellis… he isn't known to be dead…'

'Ellis?' Sid asks.

It's the clerk who explains. 'Matthew Ellis. He has not been seen since shortly after the death of the choirboy.'

Sidney has heard about the choirboy. But he was buried properly—he remembers seeing the ceremony emerge through the Minster gate.

Rawlins looks serious now. Not at all the welcoming figure when Sid first walked in. 'There is to be an inquiry into the death of Master Cuff. This coming Friday. If you have any relevant information…'

To Rawlins' apparent displeasure, the clerk is rifling through his ledgers.

'When was your wife's funeral, Mr Wilkinson?'

Sid grits his teeth for a moment to shield himself from the memory.

'Buried her on a Tuesday. In the av'ernoon.'

'Last Tuesday? The first?'

Sid nods. That would be right. The clerk turns towards Rawlins, eyes wide and unblinking—full of portent. 'The information we have been given, Mr Rawlins, indicates that Matthew Ellis has not been seen since Monday the thirty-first of May.'

'Does it indeed...'

Looking from one of them to the other, Sidney can't make sense of their interaction. The clerk, appearing enlivened by his discovery, looks expectantly at his employer, but Rawlins' face is dark.

'So is it en, then? In my wife's grave?' Sidney asks.

'We can have no possible way of knowing, Mr Wilkinson. If you have information that relates to the death of Henry Cuff, you should bring it to the coroner's inquiry on Friday in court at the White Hart.'

'And this Ellis? Is there to be an inquiry about en?'

'That would be a matter for the magistrates.'

'So how shall I know, then, whether it's en that's in there?'

Rawlins is leaning on his elbows on the table and has formed a bridge with his fingers.

'The only way you can discover what is in your late wife's grave, Mr Wilkinson—and you'll excuse me for the distasteful suggestion, but the only means by which you can learn its contents is by opening it up and emptying it.'

It is a vile suggestion, and so shocking that Sidney's throat suddenly tightens. Just the thought. He knows she is still in her coffin but momentarily he imagines her clothed body lying on the wormy soil—a result of emptying 'the contents'. He has to grind his teeth and focus on the blotter on Rawlins' desk to dismiss the image from his mind.

Everyone in the room is staring at him now, and his problem is clear. There is no other way of knowing for sure. Finally, he looks directly at Rawlins.

'Can I do that?'

'I… I know of no reason why not, although really, it would be a question for the church. Church land: a religious matter. You'll have to ask the vicar.'

The vicar. The man who towered over the head of Lily's grave, committing her mortal remains to the ground, who prayed over her interment with his droning monotone, his face unmoved—as if Lily's death was a common occurrence.

'However,' Rawlins continues, 'a disinterment is a serious matter. You should think very carefully about whether you want to take such an action, or whether you wouldn't rather leave your wife in peace.'

'A serious matter. Yes. No doubt it is. Thank you for your time, Mr Rawlins,' Sid says. This provokes Rawlins to look darkly toward his clerk and Sid has to wonder if he has said or done something amiss.

'Oh, should I… er…'

'No, no. There's no fee, Mr Wilkinson. I'm glad to have been of service.'

'Ah. Well, I'll take my leave then.'

Sid stands and withdraws, assuring the lawyer that he is exceedingly grateful.

He doesn't head straight home, but crosses the Square under the long evening shadow of Laing's Hotel and heads up Mill Lane to an old tumbledown shack of a building under the sign of a weather-beaten horse saddle. Wilkinson's saddlery.

The old door still sticks—it has been on a promise for decades. It's silly because the edges of the door have rotted away so the only place where its old planks meet the frame is the one spot where it sticks. Sidney puts his shoulder to it and barges it open and steps inside. The old familiar odour of leather embraces him. It is the mingled scent of hide and polish and tanning and oil and he knows it like a brother.

He finds his ma in the dark little kitchen at the rear of the workshop. She's not lit a lamp and the room is a dim golden colour from the late sunlight coming over the town roofs.

'Oh, Sidney...' she says. She greets him with a sympathetic hand half-cupping his face. Her fingers are cold, despite the warmth in the room, and her face is soft and plaintive—at first. After a moment, she frowns.

'Who's minding your shop, then?'

'Closed up early, Ma. I had business to attend to.'

She scowls. 'You've been haunting the graveyard, I hear.'

Sidney slumps onto a small chair by the low table. There is a half-cut loaf on the table and crumbs scattered all over it. There's nowhere to put his hat.

'I've been a-sleepwalking, Ma. Can't stop myself.'

'And now you're all got up in your Sunday best?'

'Been to see Rawlins.'

He's about to explain the reason for his visit to the bailiff's offices when the outer workshop door rattles.

'Look who's here, Pa!' his mother calls.

'That my Sidney?' comes the muffled answer from beyond the kitchen door.

Then the door opens, and Sid's pa is there, smiling into the room. He looks very pleased to see Sidney and only slowly realises his happy grin does not suit the mood of the room.

Soon they all have tea and are sitting around the small table in the workshop's kitchen. Sid has explained how he found himself on Lily's grave and his ma has explained how she heard as much from the seamstress in the Corn Market. Then Sid relates the conversation he had with Rawlins.

'Ellis? The choirmaster?' his ma repeats. 'Huz-bird. Bad from the day he was born.'

Sid's surprised to see his mother so venomous. She doesn't normally speak ill of people. 'Never knowed the man,' he explains.

'You wouldn't ha' wanted to, Sid,' says his pa. 'He were...'

'A huz-bird,' his ma mutters again.

It leaves Sid with what feels like a responsibility. Without wanting to, it seems he has a duty now to determine who is in his wife's grave. His pa disagrees.

'You don't want to be doing that, Sidney. Leave well alone.'

'Course I don't want to, Pa. But there's someone else in there!'

The old man turns away. That's his way when he disagrees. He downs his tea and goes back to his workshop to find some small leather harness to fettle.

Sid stays with his ma for a few minutes. She advises him to think of how he would be seen and thought of. He'd be known forever more as that cordwainer who opened up his wife's grave. It is a consideration Sid had not thought of previously.

Then she tells him about his brother in Blandford—all the proud successes that sound like a reproach. Even his little sister, married away in Stur, seems to have made more of her life. Sid finishes his tea, kisses good evening to his ma and takes his hat out into the workshop.

Sidney's pa has always been a large man. Lean, not fat, and broad-shouldered, with a chest like a barrel. He has taken a large hide from its rack and is laying out a pattern on the cutting table—a significant task that requires care and concentration. It was always his way to remove himself from conversation with tasks in the workshop. Taking on something so involved puts up the biggest barrier to interruption.

Sid heads straight for the door to the street.

'G'night, Pa,' he says. He expects a grunted reply, but there is a thump from behind him. Something solid. Sid turns and sees his pa removing his spectacles. He has interrupted himself.

'When a man buries something,' he says, and he rubs the bridge of his nose as he speaks, 'he don't dig it up again for to check upon it.'

'I know,' Sid says, 'I should let be. Believe me, Pa, I should like to. But I keep a-wakin' up on her grave. And every time I see it, I think the same thing.'

'Think what?'

'That she's with someone.'

Old man Wilkinson scowls at this. 'With someone?' he says. He looks around at the sawdust on the floor for a moment and then he turns back to Sid and he says, 'Course she's with someone.'

That's a shock. And the shock lingers until he explains what he means.

'She certainly ain't buried alone, is she? You've two brothers an' three sisters in that graveyard, none o' em saw five year.'

Sidney rarely hears mention of the siblings that died. His mother used to pray for them every Sunday. He can't recall his pa ever mentioning them before. He can't think of anything to say, so they stand in silence for a moment before his pa resumes.

'She ain't alone, zon. Under the earth is all our forefathers and their forefathers and every living thing that ever died and weren't someone's supper. She ain't alone. She's with her own mother and her own father. Her cousin, John, he's buried up St Margaret's and all. A mound or two larger or smaller don't make no difference. They'm all up there under the earth an' their souls abide in Heaven. And now, you...'

He points a workman's finger at Sid. 'You've to be a man about it. Em that's dead is dead, zon. And em that's dead and buried is gone. And you cassn't go diggin' em up to check on em.'Cause it ain't right.'

There's no arguing with that. It ain't right. His pa mumbles a few other comments about giving up this sleep-walking, but Sid ignores that.

As he walks home down the High Street, he hears the simple truth of it echoing in his head. *It ain't right.* It makes up his mind. He'll let it be, that's what he'll do.

He still wakes up in the graveyard, though. He goes to bed that evening determined to let the matter be, but wakes with a sudden jolt and knows, before he's even looked to check, that he's lying on her grave. The grief has two parts now, like a demonic harmony of emotions. The sudden lurching recollection of loss comes with the fear and despair at realising he is out of control. There's still a part of him that won't let go, and it won't listen to reason.

He tells that to David Woolcott in the Rising Sun that evening. Two of them at the bar and barely another soul in the place because they have their ale just after shutting up shop when most others are at the supper table.

'There's a part of me that just won't listen to reason, Davie.'

'A part?' David says. He gives a little scoffing laugh and drinks from his glass. 'Remember that time you got it in your head she was seeing the butcher.'

Sidney remembers it well. He remembers, particularly, the butcher's grinning face—those ruddy cheeks—and the insistent sense that his laughter was mocking.

'I had to stand around with you watching wives come out o' that shop for close on three hours afore you'd accept he joked with all of em. Remember?'

Of course he remembers. 'I remember all right.'

'I'll bet. Was Lily ever madder with you?'

'No, never. Most of all 'cause I'd paired her up with the butcher! She said if I's to be jealous of someone, better make it someone worthwhile! Wanted me to be jealous of a count or a duke or somewhat.'

David chuckles a little more, raising his glass to his face and Sid stares at the floor remembering how chastened he felt—how foolish and unworthy for ever having doubted her. He should probably feel the same way now but for his waking every morning by her tombstone.

When he asks about Ellis, David Woolcott knows nothing. 'Don't suppose they need much ironmongery in the choir,' is his explanation for his ignorance. They turn to the barman instead.

'Of course,' he says. 'Talk of the town, that.'

'What do they say, then? What happened?' Sid asks.

The barman gives him one of those sideways glances he has seen so often these days. It is a check. A question whether one so recently bereaved is strong enough to hear tell of such things. Then the barman stops wiping the glass to tell the story.

'Well. Everyone knows about the Cuff boy. And most reckon he done himself in on account of Ellis.'

'Why's that, then?'

'Well, Ellis… he was a bugger, weren't he?'

'What? With the choirboys?'

'So they say. Anyhow, everyone blames him for Cuff and after last Sunday's service he just ups and disappears. Not seen since. And that night Squire Guthrie's brother—the younger one—he takes off for India with his groom in tow. So… stands to reason, doesn't it? Guthrie done for the choirmaster and then takes his groom and scarpers, sharpish.'

'Groom? Who's this groom?' David asks.

'Young Bill Brown's brother. Stable boy at Stone Farm. Cornelius, was it?'

'And what of the choirmaster, then?' Sid asks. 'They find his body?'

'Body?' says the barman. He resumes wiping the glass and shakes his head. 'Not so far as I heard. Far's I know, he vanished into thin air.'

Sid turns to David just as David turns to him. Neither of them says anything because neither of them needs to.

~

He thought perhaps that a couple or three pints at the Rising Sun might cause him to sleep so soundly he'd wake up in his own bed. It doesn't, though—he wakes on Lily's grave again. The only difference is that he wakes earlier. It is barely light, so he walks home without being observed. He has time to shave and wash and make himself breakfast before dressing for Sunday morning service.

He joins his parents in the common pews, near the back where it is their habit to sit. Some folk he's not seen since before the funeral pass by to offer their condolences.

Sid is grateful for their concern, but as soon as the noise dies down and the service starts, he is set to wondering what he should do.

He doesn't really decide until the very end of the service. His parents are leading out of the pew and, without looking up—almost to prevent anyone else from noticing—he tells them to go ahead. He'll catch them up at home. Then he lingers until he's last out of the door.

The vicar, Rev Cookesely, is there passing blessings on everyone who leaves, exchanging a few words here and there, and Sid's throat tightens again as he approaches.

'A word, Vicar?'

'Of course, Mr Wilkinson, tell me the matter.'

'It's about my wife's grave, see.'

At the vicar's invitation, Sid explains what happened the first morning he woke on his wife's grave. As he talks, Cookesely draws him back into the empty church.

The vicar blinks a great deal, that's what Sidney notices. When he explains the conversation with Rawlins and the suspicion that his wife's grave might be distended by the body of the choirmaster, Cookesely blinks like a guttering candle.

The verger comes over and the priest waves him away—as he does with every other churchman that comes to him with some or other question until by and by the church is deserted, and they are alone.

They are seated on the pews by the church door by the time Sid has finished telling him everything. And he surprises himself with how much he explains—from his father's advice to his thoughts about Lily's companion.

When the priest sits back on the pew, Sid finds himself uncomfortable under his gaze. Cookesely's expression looks more than just thoughtful; Sid feels like he's being appraised. Then the priest leans forward again.

'Do you remember the day you were married, Sidney? I reminded you that you were brought together into the sanctity of marriage under the eyes of God, do you recall?'

Sidney does not recall those words exactly. He remembers that he nearly ran away from it all for thinking he wasn't good enough and that Lily told him he was a marvel. Those were her words: 'You're a marvel, Sid.' That stuck in his memory.

'Well, in much the same fashion as the blessing of marriage, Mr Wilkinson, life is a Divine gift. In short, it is our Lord's to give, and our Lord's to take away.'

Sid nods, not knowing how to respond. Cookesely continues. 'Your wife was not taken from you by man's hand, was she? She was stricken by an ailment visited upon her by Divine Providence.'

This is not something Sid could have imagined. Who would ever think of a God so cruel he would first tease Sid with such a wife as Lily and then take her and their child from him at the moment of birth. The cold-heartedness is horrific. He struggles to keep his emotions in check, shifting in his seat, sniffing heartily, rolling his head around to look high into the yawning arches of the Minster's roof.

Cookesely stammers for a moment; he even sounds a little irritated. 'These are matters we cannot hope to fully understand, Mr Wilkinson. You see that, I hope? We must submit ourselves to the will of the Almighty, d'you see?'

Sid bites his lip and nods. The vicar is pointing to emphasise his comments—not directly at Sid, just past him towards the church door.

'Your wife was committed to the earth in a holy sacrament and her immortal soul is with God. To reverse —to even attempt to reverse—this process goes against the natural order, you see.'

'Yes, I understand…'

'So then, for you, Mr Wilkinson, you… you must come to accept God's will. Surrender yourself… to the power and the will of the Almighty.'

Struggling as he is to control his emotions, Sidney can't help but frown at this and then the tone of the vicar's advice changes.

'You must submit yourself… to the mystery… the Divine mystery of His plan.'

Sid nods because at last the vicar has said something he can make sense of. Submit himself to the mystery. He is small, but the plan is huge around him. That is the best of the advice on offer. He carries on talking, but only to repeat himself, and Sidney is soon nodding anxiously, keen to get away. He reaches for his hat on the pew beside him, suddenly concerned to remember to take it, and he nods again solemnly.

'So, I've to let it be, then,' he says.

Cookesely agrees wholeheartedly. 'I think that is very much for the best,' he says.

'Right.'

~

Sidney says nothing of this to his ma and pa over Sunday dinner. His ma talks of his brother in Blandford and his sister out in Sturminster, repeating the news she told him two days ago, and then complains about the mill owner, who has let the place go to rack and ruin.

In the evening he crosses town to the Rising Sun, where he knows he'll find David.

'Thought you'd be here,' he says, taking a stool at the bar. Davie frowns at him.

'I don't often miss a Sunday evening.'

'And you're too bone idle to try any place else.'

David raises his glass to toast his own insouciance.

'You still waking up over St Margaret's?' he asks.

'Every morning. Can't help myself.'

'Ah, well, in that case you'd best wear your boots to bed tonight.'

'How's that then?'

'It'll rain tomorrow. Gertie says so. Now Gertie don't know much—barely dress himself if we're honest—but he knows the weather all right.'

The prospect of wearing his boots to bed is surprisingly depressing.

'Vicar reckons I have to submit myself to the will of God,' he grumbles.

'Well he would, wouldn't he? Question is, did he tell you what the will of God might be?'

For a moment Sidney sees a great opening of freedom; the vicar has no better idea of God's will than anyone else. Then he remembers.

'Well… it was God's will that we were married, then God's will that she… you know… that she was taken…'

'So is it God's will that you find yourself up St Margaret's every morning?'

'Certainly feels like it.' Sid sighs and sips his beer. 'I just have to get a-hold of myself, that's all.'

'Is that all?'

~

It feels stupid to be wearing pyjamas and a pair of boots. He sits on the edge of the bed and stares at his bedroom door, wondering what else he might do. If it is really going to rain, he might be wise to sleep in his coat, but he can hardly claim to be getting hold of himself if he's actually planning his sleepwalk in advance.

He decides to take both approaches. He dresses in his trousers and his overcoat, and laces up his boots. Then he locks the bedroom door and hides the key in his waistcoat, which he tucks into the chest of drawers. Then he clears everything off the bedroom chair and wedges it under the drawer handle, thinking it highly unlikely that he could overcome such an obstacle course without coming to his senses.

With all this in place, he's ready to get into his bed. He can't, though. He can't bring himself to. Lily might be dead, but she doesn't seem to be gone and certainly isn't forgotten and would under no circumstances allow him to sully her white cotton sheets with his boots. She'd have batted him around the ears.

He has to remake the bed, pulling the sheets and blankets aside so his feet can rest on an old rug. Then, at last, he can lie down. He hears the Minster clock chime twice before he finally falls asleep.

~

He wakes in the rain, of course. The double sense of loss swamps him, and he feels his bedroom key in his hand, rain pattering on his coat and wet grass tickling his cheek. And there's someone standing nearby.

Sid lifts his head to look and the figure steps back quickly. 'Oh blimey! You give me a fright! Thought you was just a tar sheet!'

Sid can't determine who it is standing over him: the sky is still dim and the man wears a broad-brimmed hat. He sits up, water drains off his coat and the mud underneath him makes a sucking noise.

'How long you been here, Sid?' the man asks. The voice is familiar.

'I dunno,' Sid grumbles. 'How long have you been here?'

'I just come across. Got a load on today; need to get ahead, see.'

Sid has to get onto his knees before he can stand up. His bones ache with cold. The man standing by him has a spade in his hands and that's how he realises who it is. It's Bill Brown.

He feels a fool to be standing before Bill, covered in mud and dripping rainwater.

'Lor', look at you,' Bill says. 'You do need to get yourself home, Sidney. Get yourself dry. You'll catch your death.'

Feels to Sid like he already has: he's shivering cold. But Bill looks a sight standing in his oilskin in the rain and it strikes Sid that it's not quite normal.

'Mighty early to be digging graves, Bill.'

'Mighty early for anythin',' Bill replies, 'but I got a load on today, like I said. An' this weather bain't going to help none neither.'

Sid grunts agreement. His back feels like old, dried-stiff leather. He sneezes suddenly and violently.

'Get yourself home,' Bill repeats. 'You should stop a-comin' up 'ere.'

Sid starts moving. He can't manage more than a shuffle, he feels so stiff.

'If I knew how to stop myself, I surely would, Bill,' he says. Then he turns towards the path back to the road. But something will not allow him to leave. He looks back at Bill as a question comes to him.

'Who died?' he asks.

'Eh?'

'Whose grave are you digging?'

'Oh, that. Don't know her name. Ol' maid vrom the poorhouse, God rest en.'

Sid grunts and looks back toward the distant gateway. Rainwater is dribbling from his brow and running down his eyebrows. He turns back again, suddenly realising the question he needs to ask.

'Who else is in there?' he demands, pointing at Lily's grave.

Bill is standing with his feet apart, one hand on the spade, like he doesn't plan to move.

'What's that?'

Sid goes back to him, close enough to see Bill's face.

Because suddenly it is obvious. Bill's the person to ask because he's the one who'll know.

'Look at her grave, Bill! Look at the size of it. Never was right. Not from the first day. There's someone else in there.'

Bill looks back at him and his face is full of fear. He's stammering.

'Well, it's...'

'Who is it, Bill?'

Bill is shaking his head. 'You know, Sidney, I did hear it said that you were a jealous husband...'

'No, no! I've been through that. Yes, at first I feared it were her lover, but that's not it, is it, Bill? You work for Squire Guthrie now, 'cause Cornelius done a bunk with Oswald. And you're left here. So who is it?'

The change in Bill's face is ghostly. He goes pale. His eyes widen and he just stares back. And that's when Sidney knows for sure.

'Oh, Bill. What have you done?'

Bill starts by shaking his head. 'Ha'n't done nothing, though.'

'Who is it?' Sidney demands, pointing at the grave again.

'Buggermaster,' Bill says abruptly.

'Who?'

'The choirmaster! En that was buggering the choirboys, and that did kill young Cuff.'

Sid looks at the grave and then back at Bill.

'In my Lily's grave?'

'Ah, well. Sorry 'bout that. We'd no place else to put en.'

He stares Bill in the face. He makes it sound so simple and everyday. Like he'd left a handcart in Sid's yard.

'You *killed* him?'

But Bill shakes his head vehemently. 'No. Didn't touch en. I's there with Charlie, John behind us. But he were already dead when we found en.'

Sid doesn't understand this. And the rain is still dripping from his brow. 'What of Cornelius, then?'

Bill shrugs. 'Nothing to do with it.'

'So why'd he take off?'

'No reason. Just bad luck. They just left that night. I know the whole world thinks Guthrie had a hand in it, but I don't know that he did.'

Sid wipes his brow and looks back at the sodden ground around his wife's tombstone and he sighs deeply.

'So how come you buried him, Bill? Why didn't you just tell someone you found him?'

'Well, because he'd a knife in his belly, ha'n't he? Someone done him in. You know they magistrates. We was there. With no one else to blame, so they'd ha' hung us and had done with it.'

They stare at each other. 'They still might if you tell em any of this,' Bill adds.

'Is that it, then? I've to keep your secret?'

Bill shrugs. 'That or watch me hang…'

Sid lets out a long, heavy breath, shaking his head.

'S'a turk of a business,' Bill says.

'It is that,' Sid agrees.

'It was me and John Street that found Cuff in the river. Poor lad—a-floating in the reeds in his choir gown. You know that?'

'No.'

'We all knew that he done hisself in on account o' the

Buggermaster. So we decided to have it out with en. Tell en to piss off out of it. Leave Wimborne and ne'er come back. Except when we come upon en, he's there, on the floor with thik knife in his guts. Course we're all a-feared to be blamed for it. That's when I recalled there were a grave open.'

Sid receives Bill's earnest looks, not knowing what is coming.

'I's sorry it were Lily's, Sid. Truly.'

Sid nods.

'Zo...' Bill mutters, looking sideways at the mound. 'Zo it is. He's at the bottom o' Lily's grave.'

They both stare at the grave for a moment and then look back up at each other.

'I'll be getting home,' Sid says. He moves towards the path that leads out of the graveyard and he claps Bill on the shoulder as he passes.

'You'll not tell no one?' Bills asks.

'No, Bill,' Sid says, 'I don't suppose I shall.'

∼

The front door of the shop is wide open and the rain has soaked the floorboards inside the door—but it will dry quick enough. Sid is more concerned to get himself warm. He changes out of his wet clothes and piles coal into the grate to stoke up a warming fire.

While the coal catches, pouring thick smoke up the chimney, he pulls out a blanket from the closet beside the door. Lily kept them all neatly folded in there, so it is hard to remove one because he's not sure he'll ever get it back so tidily.

He takes himself to the other side of the room and sits by the hearth. The first flames are curling up from the grate and some of the coals must be damp because there's spitting and an acrid smell of coal smoke.

But that gets swept away when he wraps the blanket around himself. It can't be two weeks since Lily folded that blanket and put it in the closet. It doesn't smell just of her rosemary perfume. It smells, also, of her skin. Of her. And Sid can't stop himself from closing his eyes, and for a moment she's there again. Arms wrapped around him, telling him he's a marvel.

'You're a marvel, Sid.'

THE THIRD PERSON

~

Part I: You

It is the 29th of August 1841. A blue-skied Friday evening.

You're a twenty-six-year-old Englishman—a wine merchant by profession, living and working in the market town of Wimborne Minster, Dorset. At this instant, you're hot and irritable, riding in a hired carriage up the hill towards a house on Rowlands Hill for the inauguration of Mrs Harris's Annual St Cuthburga Memorial Dinner.

You're dressed in stiff, formal clothes, irritated by a high collar that rubs against skin already sore from a late-afternoon shave. The smell of wax from your polished shoes is mingling with the dingy odour of the old leather upholstery. This carriage is not used more than twice a year and has the musty air of the barn it is stored in.

Your sister, Selina, is seated beside you, repeating advice she had from her Aunt Louisa about men and their ways. Selina is scornful, knowing full well that Aunt Louisa is neither a blood relative nor fully seasoned when it comes to men, judging them all by the yardstick of her husband,

Samuel, who, Selina argues, is gentler, kinder and wholly more intelligent than is typical. You don't bother to defend your sex.

Instead, you hold the carriage straps and wonder how you will endure the evening without appearing sullen and whether the barn smell will carry onto your clothes, causing people to look down on you. You bear a mild resentment towards the whole event, having been forced to hire your childhood friend, Bill Brown, to drive the coach. And you feel nothing but scorn for the Harrises' arrogance in misappropriating Wimborne's patron saint's name for a dinner that cannot possibly be both inaugural and annual at the same time.

Your sister prods you as the carriage turns a corner and the Harrises' house comes into view.

'Isn't it lovely? Oh, Charles, please cheer up, you'll give us a reputation for dourness.'

No. The sight of the Harrises' house does not cheer you. It is spectacular, no doubt about that; the entrance is lit by the new gas lamps and they shine with an unusual brightness. It reminds you of the theatres in London, where the lamps were truly brilliant, and for a moment you are transported back to the dream of a midsummer's night and the astonishing sight of a man with an ass's head, but the house is such a display of disquietingly effortless wealth, it gives you no joy.

When the carriage finally pulls up in front of the doors, you hear Bill jump from his seat with a lively bound, then he appears by your door, holding it open with a mocking bow.

'Mr Ellis, sir.'

You try and joke with him, demanding to know 'What

took you so long, you scoundrel?' but there's no real humour in it. He opens Selina's door, calling her 'm'lady' and warning her about the horse dung at her feet. She mutters, 'You two...' as a reproach.

~

You have Selina on your arm. She's your baby sister. A tough little sparrow who has endured the loss of her mother, the expectations of a self-centred father, then his loss, then bullying from your brother until his disappearance. She's a doughty spirit with unequalled self-reliance. Sometimes she speaks a little sharply, and not everyone favours that side of her character, but you admire her determination. You are proud and protective as you walk into the Harrises' entrance hall.

You know what Selina's thinking from the hold she has on your arm as she cranes her neck to look around. She tightens her grip slightly when she looks at the crystal chandelier hanging high over the hall, at the broad staircase and the lead-lighted window, and again when she looks down at the diamond-patterned black-and-white floor tiles. The house is like a miniaturised mansion.

The hall is thick with guests and you nod at each familiar face, passing greetings here and there, trying to ignore the irritation from your collar. Dr Packman bids you good evening, scowling at your head, and you realise you have forgotten to remove your hat. You whip it from sight and avoid looking at Selina so she may not reproach you.

Repeat it to yourself: You're as good as any man here.

You may believe it for a moment too, just until you recognise the figure on the landing, reviewing the gathering crowd like a critical general. That's Sir Richard Glyn, the head of a family so august and venerable they were already established in Gaunts House when St Cuthburga was still considered *parvenu*. Under his gaze you feel as rustic as an old farm gate.

Your sister is drawn into a conversation with Mrs Rawlins, the solicitor's wife, and you find yourself talking to Thomas Rawlins himself. You know him from a coroner's inquest a year ago, but it is your good fortune that he is more interested in talking about wine.

'Laing told me about your Bordeaux last Friday evening. The Brillard, I believe. He seemed very satisfied with it.'

'Very kind of him to mention it. A fine wine. A small chateau. Often the way.' It never does any harm to illustrate knowledge of your trade.

Rawlins raises his ample chin, looking surprised.

'Small vineyards?'

'The size of the chateau is, I'm afraid, more of an indicator.'

'You intrigue me, Mr Ellis. An indicator of what?'

'A longer tradition of vintnery. Not always the case, but the larger chateaux proved more of a target during the Terror, I'm afraid to say. Families of the smaller, less ostentatious chateaux tended to survive and so retained their traditions. A most unfortunate fact, but there it is.'

Rawlins does not look impressed, and mutters something scornful about Jacobins.

Recognition is a singular experience. You are at first aware only of having seen something you know. As if you were scanning a page of typeset text and happened upon your own name; something personal and familiar.

When your head turns back for a second look, you fix upon a woman's neck and the back of her head—her face being obscured from your view. It is her. You are sure of it. It is impossible to be so certain from such a limited view, and yet you are.

There are a great many women in the room with hair gathered into a tidy bun on the crown of their heads—it is something of a fashion—but none are quite as delicate or as elegant as hers. There is an exquisite refinement to the curve of her neck as it rises proudly to her hairline and you are enchanted by the grace of her shoulders and the delicacy of her white lace collar. A few wisps of hair curling like exquisite decorative rolls catch the lamplight and you are enthralled. You want to keel your neck over to see her again, but Rawlins still holds you in conversation.

She turns towards you—just as you are asked whether the vineyards suffered the same fate in the Loire.

Did she sense you staring? It seems that way. She looks at you directly. And you recognise with a great, bounding leap of the heart that you were right. You know that perfect oval face—those beautiful brown eyes.

Remember Rawlins!

'Worse,' you answer, catching his eye a moment before he detects your distraction, 'they worked their way along the river. Chateau to chateau.'

The solicitor is frowning—perhaps he is imagining a Dorset Revolutionary Guard swarming up the Stour Valley.

Looking back, the woman in the white lace collar has disappeared into the crowd. Mrs Harris is raising her voice, persuading her guests to take their seats in the dining room, and as a consequence the gathering is pressing into the narrow doorway and you can see only the back sides of heads. But you may calm yourself, because this time she shall not disappear so completely.

You chanced on that face before, at the county fair in Blandford. It was a momentary encounter—she was profusely apologetic when her parasol caught your cheek—but you were wonder-struck, enchanted, but wordlessly incapable of preventing her from fading away into the fairground throng. And since that moment she has commanded your daydreams even though you surrendered hope of ever meeting her again. And yet, at last, here she is.

So, again: calm yourself.

Mrs Harris is standing just inside the dining-room door, ushering her guests into the room with a melodious and ready laugh, and you see the object of your dreams on the far side of the table, so, with gentle, firm guidance you lead Selina close by your hostess and make a discreet enquiry.

'The young lady on the other side of the table? I'm sure I know her from somewhere. Church maybe?'

'Anne Frampton? She's a regular at St John's. You go to the Minster, don't you, Charles?'

'Yes…' you answer, 'usually…' but you are deeply distracted by the realisation that for all this time she has been so close by.

Anne Frampton. A local name, Frampton. There's a family in Witchampton.

Then, as you approach the long table, you see the card with Selina's name on it; a small white card with writing in a near perfect hand. It is a strange mix of excitement and fear to find your own card only two seats removed from Miss Frampton—on the opposite side of the table.

You take your seat, glance around to check the correctness of your behaviour and do your best to avoid staring at her, but you can't deny yourself a glance in her direction every now and then.

Still, you bide your time. You have to deal with the manners of the meal and the challenges of a soup starter. You keep a constant eye on your neighbours and check the accuracy of Selina's cutlery choices, while for her part, your sister comments a little unkindly on the motives for the meal.

'The St Cuthburga Memorial Dinner is a child of the gas lamp,' she says, nodding at the wall fittings. And it's clear, from the hum of appreciation, how right she is. Newly installed, the bright, clean and odourless lamps are flooding the room with brilliant light. It shines on the tall and buxom silver candlesticks that bleat their weak candle glow from the middle of the table; it winks from the silver cutlery and the crystal glasses, and defines the fine fabric of the tablecloth.

Across the table the gas light gives artistic definition to the slender contours of Anne Frampton's chin; it adds shine to her hair, and, as she smiles in sympathy with the conversation around her, she seems already accustomed to the light's flattering effect. She is an established part of the new gaslit world. All others remain outside—admirers. And they leave no light-related superlative unuttered before the soup terrines are carried away.

You start to resent such easy wealth; such nonchalant ostentation. Your home is lit only by candles and you can't imagine yourself being equal to either the funds or the presumptions required to install gas lamps.

Face it: you're a farmer's son. A bumpkin. You have a finger-hold in commerce selling overpriced wines, but you only make a living out of that by sneaking half your stock into the country to avoid the excise duty. Your family was crude and misbegotten. Both mother and stepmother deceased; your father was an alcoholic, your missing brother a defiler of choirboys.

If you want Anne Frampton, you will have to become someone you are not.

Over the fish, Selina engages in an earnest conversation with young Barnes. He stutters nervously in the face of your sister's metallic opinions, but they are talking about novels, and since she is rarely without a fiction to hand, it is a well-matched conversation. Effeminate on his part, but that is Barnes for you. That your sister has a taste for French novels is forgivable—she has precious few hours to herself and can be excused her own style of indulgence, but a man like Barnes should have more serious matters to attend to. He has insect's fingers and bulging, insistent eyes and whenever you have spoken to him in the past, he has always solicited agreement by hectoring. *You do agree, Mr Ellis, don't you? You agree, surely?* You trust that he is a match for conversation and no more. Selina will undoubtedly find him too ugly.

On the other side of the table—opposite Selina—Henry Jacobs is discussing the corn price with Farringdon, the insurance man. Jacobs, red-faced as a bawdy house, actually cares about the matter, since the yield of his many acres swings from it. Farringdon is failing to disguise his Sturminster accent while pretending corn prices matter as much to him.

Then, as you parade the room with your eye, you start to suspect that everyone has some level of pretence. From the Harrises' claim to St Cuthburga to Farringdon's false accent, there is not a person at the table who is simply, wholly themselves. There are a few faces you don't know, but each is betrayed by an excessive gesture or a forced laugh. Even the servants are false; hired in for the day, no doubt—grass plucked from their hair and stuffed into a uniform.

So as the plates are cleared, your confidence recovers. What is there to stop you from gaining the attention of someone like Anne Frampton? Or—a glance in her direction—of Anne Frampton herself? Your last shipment of claret hid several crates of brandy. All told, you cleared thirty guineas. If you could manage that four or five times a season, you'd see 150 a year. And what else is needed? A little Latin and a knowledge of cutlery?

You stare at Gerald Harris, who sits at the top of the table, laughing with his arms spread wide. What would he say to 150 a year? It seems like a lot to you, but perhaps he'd laugh at it. You will have to learn. You'll have to know what Miss Frampton might expect.

While staring towards her end of the table, you become gradually aware of the conversation Miss Frampton is engaged in. It's ranging around the railways and there are several opinions. The aged-looking fellow seated to her right has no time for them, since there are too many lines and they scare the cattle. The young man seated opposite you believes that one day every village will have its own station, while Mrs Evans, on your left, has it from a physician of Geneva that travelling at ever greater speeds is both unnatural and unhealthy. Only Miss Frampton—of course—has the modesty to ask a simple question. She wonders how long it might take to travel to London. The enquiry goes unanswered.

You know. You have taken the journey twice since the

station opened. But the exchange of opinions continues, and no one appears to heed her. The chance seems gone—until she asks again. You open your mouth and plunge into the opportunity.

'One must change at Southampton before travelling on to Waterloo Station, Miss Frampton. It terminates there at half-past five in the afternoon.'

She looks at you with slight surprise. A smile on her lips.

'I'm sorry, you have me at a disadvantage...'

'Oh. Ellis! I'm Charles Ellis. I've had reason to make the journey several times just lately—wines coming in from Bordeaux.'

The faces surrounding Miss Frampton turn to you with dark eyes. Miss Frampton is not so severe, however. She raises an eyebrow—just as you might.

'Is it very uncomfortable to be in one of those carriages for such a long time, Mr Ellis?'

'Why, Miss Frampton, that very much depends on the company.'

She smiles. She takes your meaning. The old man beside her understands you just as well and scowls disapprovingly, looking for others to support him, but you do not much care. Anne Frampton lifts another morsel of lamb to her mouth and looks sideways at you, still smiling. And your future aims are—as far as they may be—clear.

At the end of the evening it is Selina who wants to be at the front of the throng trying to reach the carriages. You are content to remain beneath the well-lit chandelier, discussing your experiences of France with Miss Frampton. You have twice agreed to visit her guardian and talk him through the wines you have available and you are happily convinced that Miss Frampton told you about her guardian's enthusiasm for wine purely to entice you into offering to visit. You are quite prepared for him to be utterly bored by the topic and a committed drinker of ale.

You stand with your hands behind your back, rocking on your feet, describing the approach down the Gironde and the *jardin botanique* by the docks of Lormont. You deliberately deny that there was any glamour to your visit.

'I'm afraid the docks of Bordeaux are no more pleasing to the senses than docks in any other town. Broader than our own in Poole, busier indeed, but alas no prettier.'

Anne Frampton is smiling constantly through your conversation; grinning almost.

'I daresay you are right, Mr Ellis, but it sounds divine, and to see places one has read about is, for a provincial girl such as myself, something to be envied.'

You could happily stay and talk for hours, but Selina turns from the crowd by the door and calls to you. Your carriage has reached the front of the queue. You nod gallantly to Miss Frampton—you have never done that before in your life—and repeat again the date when you'll bring wines to her guardian. And you leave.

The air outside the house is cool and fresh, and a brilliant Milky Way arches over the oaks at the front of the Harrises' property.

Bill is standing with the carriage door open and you wait while Selina climbs in.

'A good evening?' he asks.

'Yes. Thank you, Bill. A very good evening indeed.'

He nods, looking thoughtful, and holds the door for you.

Part II: Her

I remember the Harrises' St Cuthburga dinner. It was the evening I met my husband, Charles. He is not the first man that comes to mind, though. Not when I think of that dinner.

There was a waiter. He was actually dressed up like a footman, which was ridiculous because the Harrises very evidently could not afford to maintain footmen and also because he was so very coarse. Hands like paws. They had him in white serving gloves, but I already knew his hands.

The previous autumn, Aunt Harriet had taken me to Cranborne Chase. She had wanted to visit a cousin there and we arrived in the middle of harvest. I was young and still very sheltered, but mischievous like you wouldn't believe. I wanted to know everything and to experience all. So, since the talk was of the harvest, and everyone there was working on it, I wanted to join in. Harriet had no interest, but she sent me off into the fields with a farm girl she knew—Lizzie her name was, about the same age as me and just recently married.

Most of the corn was already brought in, which was fine because the big event was the haymaking on the common. Lizzie told me the time was ripe, everyone knew the weather would hold for a couple more nights—long enough for the cut hay to dry. When she introduced me to the others several people said the same thing. 'Oh, you'll rear the weather!' but they laughed immediately, so I took it as superstition that none had much faith in. They had names for every stage and every part of the process. In the evening, they cut the grass and they raked it into long lines called rollers. Then they decided there would likely be a dew in morning, so they raked all the lines into heaps.

The heaps were called cocks and at first Lizzie wouldn't use the word in my presence, she just giggled a lot and told me about rollers. The cocks were to be turned in the morning to ensure all the hay was dried—so that was our first task. Before long someone was talking about tossing the cocks and they were all falling about with laughter, glancing my way and saying, 'Begging your pardon, miss.'

I must have seemed like a spoilt child to them; I was exhausted by lunchtime but they, being more accustomed to labour, seemed able to carry on working and chatting without fatigue. The time for gathering the hay into more bunches—they were called wales—was the early evening, and by suppertime we were working into the dusk and it grew dark.

They forgot themselves after a few hours, and the ribaldry was astounding. Witty—they were quick with a play on words or sharp comment. But bawdy—my guardians would have fainted.

Throughout the whole day, there'd been one reaper who had seemed unable to take his eyes off me. He was tall, quite slender to look at and cheeky with his smile. All the maids joked with him, then they followed his gaze towards me. I'll confess I blushed several times.

I don't really know how the notion got into my mind. The supper was very simple—cheese and bread and some fruit and someone brought some cider. And there was a violin.

A fiddle. So before long we were dancing in these fields. It was night-time and whenever I came round to the reaper, I could feel his big hands on my waist and his eyes boring into me and, when it got truly dark, I just led him away.

It was part of that impulse—wanting to experience everything. And also, quite simply, it seemed like the most perfectly natural thing to do.

So, on the night of the St Cuthburga dinner, I was there in my finest evening gown—it had a lace collar that I admired particularly and that Harriet insisted suited me like no other—so I was feeling very much the elegant English gentlewoman. Then I looked up and saw my reaper standing in footman's uniform on the other side of the dining table. And the moment I saw him, I had the most vivid memory of his nakedness and firmness. An irresistible recollection that did not feel at all appropriate, given my company. There were Mr Farringdon and Mr Jacobs seated to my left and right and the impulse to giggle like a child was hard to resist.

Of course, it struck me very quickly that my circumstances had suddenly become pungent with danger. This reaper-waiter recognised me as quickly as I knew him. His face coloured, from his neck to his brow—a violent, vivid red—and he struggled to know where to look. And while I had been initially very selfishly concerned for my own reputation, I quickly understood how his was the more perilous position. A disgraced woman is unmarriageable, but a disgraced servant will surely starve.

So, even though I desperately wanted to see his face, I dared not look up again for the duration of the evening. I forced myself to engage with the conversation, terrified— and simultaneously amused—by the presence of my reaper.

So, Charles was a sort of godsend. At first he was someone to distract me, but then I realised how attentive he was. He was trying so hard to impress without being *seen* to be trying, and he was really very charming and, in all honesty, very handsome.

I do not know what sort of person it makes me that I am not ashamed of this episode, or of my actions during the harvest. No doubt I should be mortified and wracked by guilt—but the fact of the matter is that I am not. I have never mentioned it to anyone, and I have never repeated it. Nor shall I.

Charles brings half his wines into the country without paying the duty. He is clever and thinks I am ignorant of it, but I've known since before we were married. The reaper, on the other hand, will remain for ever my secret.

Part III: Him

Walt. Walter Pugh his full name. His pa is Art, short for Arthur. Art marries Jane Goode and they takes a cottage up Dogdean.

They've two daughters, two zons, they have. Walt's the youngest, zo he gets the scraps. Art does work the farms —hired hand, like—and zoon enough young Walt's doin' the same.

Oh, he's a good-lookin' lad, Walt. Everyone zays zo. Grave for the most part, but he do have this twinkle in his eye—like his ma. By time he's half-grown the maids are already a-talking about Walt, and they do giggle—Lord, they do giggle when Walt's around.

Well, it ne'er were easy. When winter comes there's next to nothin' to be done on the farms and the family has to move—the whole kit o' em. They moves from village to village, lookin' for work, stayin' with kin, however distant. They's four or five families to a cottage. Ten somewhen. Volks are kind, though. They'd share their last crust o' bread, they would, without a bird's notion of where the next one's a-comin' from. So the Pugh family survives.

By time he's sixteen, Walt's been workin' for eight years and 'e's a strappin' lad. He does work the harvest around Cranborne each zummer, beens that's where his sisters are in zervice and he likes to see em—if only for a few hours each year. Then his eldest brother, Ed, gets made gardener up Gaunts House.

Everyone makes like he's zettled, but he weren't, though. He's a farmer not a gardener, so they puts en to sprayin' plants. There's this chemical—nicotine sulphate by name—and his job is to spray they roses and kill the bugs. Old man Gaunt hates they bugs eatin' his roses. Ed gets sick wi' it over and again. Don't turn the old man's head, though, and gone two years, the boy's dead. Course everyone knows it were that spray what done for en—everyone except Squire Gaunt. And en bein' a magistrate, there ain't nothin' to be said.

Zo that leaves Walt—the girls are in zervice and the eldest brother is buried. Avore he went to Gaunts, Ed had been on about a life in the New World. America or Australie. Walt ne'er thought much of that—not at first—beens he had his eye on a draper's girl from Blandford. And she'd zmile sweetly on en too, but he needs make a livin' before he can go axin' for a girl's hand.

Anyhow, he's proud. Doesn't want to sail off somewhere foreign. Zays he'd rather go into zervice hisself. They all has a laugh when he comes up with that one! Hands like a bull's vace, he's got.

Zo 'e gets a meal o' his pride. He were a-facin' workhouse when his Aunt Lizzie recommends en to Mrs Tilly's Service Agency and they finds en the work. They had a need for vootmen. Well, there ain't no vootmen about Wimborne. Up Kingston maybe or Canford, but none spare, you see. So Walt's hired. Turns up at the Harrises' place, up St John's.

And the story goes that the Harrises' housekeeper spots en right off. Walt an' another farm lad who ain't never even been in a house like that avore; they looks as likely as two hogs in livery. Housekeeper puts em to practisin' in the kitchen under the direction of the maid. How to hold the plate, which zide to zerve from—all that. Puts the fear of God in em too. They put a finger wrong, she zays, and she'll bat em about the ears til they's hearin' bells day and night. And only the devil'd tell what'll happen if they drops zomewhat. They ends up so a-feared of droppage they're too fearful to pick a thing up.

The evenin' comes and the guests is zettled and Walt is all dressed up in a collar and gloves and he's a-zerving zoup fro' this girt bowl when he breaks into a sudden vlush. Red as a beetroot. The housekeeper's watchin' and right off she guesses why. There's several young ladies at table all dressed up and vine, but one o' em's been Walt's fancy. He's zervin' her zoup now, but he's zerved her somewhat else avore.

It's vunny enough for to hear told, but ain't no joke for Walt. Housekeeper's watchin' his eyes and each of they young women, 'cause she's a-countin' on just one look for her to know whom.

Reaches downstairs like lightning. As they pass, all eyes turn to Walt and the housekeeper. Walt starts sweatin'. Who could it be?

Well, he ne'er did give her away. Whoe'er it was, the housekeeper ne'er knew, else the whole town should a' heard, but that were the end of Walt's life in zervice. One day.

Av'er that he just 'bout scrapes through the end o' the zummer. Works the quarry, does the last 'arvest up Cranborne.

Then comes they Christian volk sellin' the idea of a free passage to Australie. They come up village halls givin' talks about it and no doubt they meant well. No doubt they did. And not havin' gone theyselves, no doubt they knew no different.

It weren't a happy thing for Walt, though. Didn't e'en want to go, but what else could he do? It were that or the workhouse; couldn't sit around makin' buttons. Zo he took a ship that year—in October 1841.

That were that. Almost. His volks—Art and Jane—ne'er heard from en again 'til the day they died. And it were a long while—long av'er that—the story comes back.

Walt took work in they gold mines in Victoria. You'd think he'd got it made, wouldn't you? Gold mines? But he took a lung complaint fro' the dust. Who knows if he got hisself any gold. Didn't help en. He died fro' it. Unmarried. 1854.

THE PEACOCK SHAWL

~

Wimborne Minster, Dorset, Spring 1849

I thought only of India, dead choirboys, and of lovers separated by oceans and injustice. After two days locked in the music room, all others barred, it was hard to believe I had nothing at all to show for it. And this after weeks of the same; it seemed I could neither write words nor compose music.

So one morning, I thought I might fix on the key. I chose E-flat major because it can sound so wistful, and by defining a specific aspect of composition I hoped to constrain my imagination and thereby force some product from it. Yet after the morning's effort, the key was still all I had.

'Quite maddening,' I told Harriet over lunch. She smiled and patted my hand.

'Dear Evelyn,' she said. She is the wise old owl, who knows how all ills shall be resolved. She suggested I should take myself away from the piano and let my mind settle.

She knew nothing of the reasons for my troubled

thoughts, but I followed her advice and walked around to Purkis's shop on the Square. It seemed a pleasant enough diversion, although not in the least settling because there were still notes in my head and I kept worrying away at them like a mad old maid picking and resewing the same stitches.

On arrival at Purkis's, I asked whether he might have any new songs 'from London' and to my delight he had three by Eliza Cook. I bought these immediately (for four shillings each) and then turned for home.

So it happened that as I was leaving, with the bell of his shop door still ringing, I began to hear my tune. Not as if I was creating it; rather, as if I was remembering a composition I had learned long ago, even though it showed itself to be entirely new.

The whole first section played out exactly as I had hoped it might, curled around the E, forever venturing away to explore musical curlicues and arabesques, and never quite settling, like an eternal nomad. This came entirely without effort on my part, it simply flowed into my thoughts ready formed, and it was exhilarating—a bracing wind on a clear day—to have the music display itself to me; it was such a divine melody, as balanced, flowing and poised as any Italian sculpture.

I had heard it all the way through before I was halfway home and so I set about trying to repeat it in my head, but I realised immediately that if anything resembling another song should enter my thoughts, it would displace my inspired composition. It was in great danger. I scuttled back down West Street directly, keeping my face lowered for the precise purpose of avoiding an encounter with any other person. And that was when Harriet's niece saw me.

I knew it was Anne by her hems; she was standing on the corner of Church Street, and she offered me a greeting, but I closed my eyes and carried on by. Yet I think that did for it. I could sense it was lost, even though I continued in hope.

Since no one was home, I told Mary I was not to be disturbed and went directly to the piano and I even managed to catch the first few bars. But what came after would not reveal itself to me a second time. Not in the same way at all. Worse still, once I had corrected what I thought were my notation errors in the opening, I could not reproduce the same freshness and life when I replayed it. More revisions only took me further from the original, scrawling over the inky notes, so that eventually even that small section was gone.

It was, indeed, incontrovertibly lost. It had drained through my hands in the time it had taken me to walk home (a period that would barely register on a presentable pocket watch) and no matter how I tried to recreate it, what came out of the piano was unutterably dull in comparison.

I cannot think I ever experienced a failure more distressing. It was made worse because, even as I was suffering it, I was aware the impression on my emotions was quite out of proportion to the weight of the event. It might have been ridden out with perfect equanimity by someone more hardened to such sensations, but it is a weakness in me to feel with such alacrity. I stood among the blotted shreds of wasted music sheets, weeping. And whenever a teardrop hit the paper, it sounded like the death of another crotchet.

That was how Harriet found me: standing still, considering whether the slenderest bones in my fingers might actually snap if it proved impossible for me to relax my fists. She placed her hand on my shoulder and waited for me to speak.

Harriet is my Grace Darling, forever rowing out to retrieve me from whichever storm-tossed rock I have wrecked myself on.

'It was beautiful,' I told her. We stood quietly for a moment, then I explained the only other thing I knew about the song I had lost. 'E-flat major.'

~

Anne Ellis, the orphaned daughter of the late Barnard and Florence Frampton, and niece of my companion, Harriet Frampton, called on us late in the afternoon of the day after I lost my song. Her visit threw me into a distressed state of alarm, but to explain quite how or why would make no sense without first explaining the moment's ancestry.

I could describe many threads: how my husband came to die of pneumonia; how Harriet came to inherit her home on West Street; or how it was we moved here together from Westminster. But the only really important story is that of my acquaintance with Jane Pugh, because if I had not known her, Lady Falmouth would have shown no interest in me and I would have no story to tell at all.

So it starts with my headaches. Afflictions I suffered daily from the time we moved into West Street. And one day I was trying to work (I write songs, as may have become apparent) but the pain was simply too much. In tears, I asked Mrs Rolls—Harriet's housekeeper—where I might find a remedy more effective than the chemist's powders. She shrugged and muttered, 'Well, there's always Jane Pugh.'

Seeking help by any hand, I determined 'Jane Pugh' must be my deliverance and insisted Mrs Rolls take me to her. She led me to a tiny cottage at the end of a run-down-looking row on King Street and the woman who came to answer the door peered up at me like a curiosity. When Mrs Rolls explained the reason for our call, the woman smiled very kindly. 'Best come inside, then,' she said, and she beckoned us into her cottage. This was Jane Pugh.

Jane and her husband shared two rooms with two other families. The space we entered was dim and cramped and the air carried tobacco smoke and the scent of lambswool. There was little furniture and too many people for the space, but a stool was quickly found for me. In the dark corners men joked, I believe at my expense, but Jane spoke to them very firmly and a quiet reverence took the air. Then she sorted through several wicker baskets before producing a small pot of dried shavings. This, she said, was willow bark and she swung a kettle over the fire to make a drink from it.

While the water heated, Jane asked me questions about my aches—when they came upon me and what made them better or worse—although I found her hard to under-stand at first, she spoke with such an accent. She called me 'madam', which was abbreviated to 'ma'am' and pronounced like 'mum'. Her S was drawn out to be a Z, so that seven became zeven, and her F a V, so that four became voor. She also employed words I'd never encountered. I turned to Mrs Rolls for clarification and answered cautiously.

When the drink was ready, she held up a ladle. I hesi-tated, not knowing what willow bark might do to me, but Jane was smiling with the kindest, gentlest glint in her big, soft eyes, so I thought I might trust such a face, and anyway being in such pain I likely would have swallowed toad's feet had they come promising relief.

It was the bitterest tonic I'd ever tasted, and seeing my reaction, Jane sipped some herself. Her expression showed her satisfied.

'Ah well, not honey, is it? But stronger is better and this will give you easement,' she said.

So I took all her medicine, wincing with each mouthful and thinking how much trouble I should bring upon Mrs Rolls if it proved to be poison. When it was done, Jane washed the ladle and bowl in a small bare sink at the side of the room and then put some of the dry willow shavings in a jam jar for me. I thanked her most profusely, but for all my entreaties, she would not take a coin for it. Not a farthing.

It was not until the next day I realised I had returned home entirely free from my ache. Jane's cure had worked and I, returning to normal, had barely noticed. I could have sung for joy and I went back the very next afternoon to offer my thanks. She was charmingly reserved, arguing that her help had amounted to nothing more than boiling a little water. I allowed her no such modesty, embarrassing her with compliments until she offered me tea in order—I believe—to change the subject. She was such a beautiful, soft-spoken woman, with that wonderful twinkle in her eye and a very thick head of sandy-grey hair pulled back into a graceful bun, I couldn't help falling a little in love with her.

To Harriet's despair, Jane and I became firm friends. I would visit her when the fancy took me, and Harriet would scowl on my return. On one such occasion she asked, 'Do you care nothing for our standing in this town, Evelyn, that you consort with farmhands?'

I said, 'Little enough,' partly because I felt that way, but mostly to provoke her. She reacted coolly with a slow shake of the head.

'And if scandal falls upon us and we have no friends for defence? Will you go and live with Jane Pugh?'

I asked whether I might have to. Since Harriet owned her own home, I couldn't see how scandal could hurt us, but she was immovable. I took to composing in the mornings and visiting Jane in the late afternoon when the men were all absent from the cottage and Harriet would not trouble me.

Jane would open the door saying always the same thing.

'Aah, av'ernoon, ma'am, you're just in time for a little tea.'

Then, she'd make the tea and we would talk while she sat, rocking gently at her spinning wheel. She talked of her sons and her daughters—she'd two of each living, one of each that had died infants—and she explained her points of pride: the stature of her boys working the farms and quarries, the daintiness of her girls, both in service already. I learned how her husband Arthur—Art she called him— worked the farms with the other men, how they sometimes had to move as far abroad as Weymouth for a wage. And she talked to me of the remedies and how she came to know of them. She showed me how she stripped the bark from willow shoots and how she dried it, then we put some in a pot to brew right then and there.

'Just mind they don't burn thee for a witch,' she said, and she chuckled with a mischievous little laugh.

She told me how camomile solved stomach cramps, and ivy wood cured whooping cough, nettles helped with consumption and moss could aid your eyes. And there were more, many more. Some were less cures and more charms

to ward off ill fortune, but for Jane there seemed little difference. As she talked, she was very engaging, asking me
whether I was lucky or suffered from cramps, before explaining how it might be helped with clovers or cowslip—which
she called 'crewel'.

Her life was very hard; that I came to recognise after
very little time. I took her small sewing projects during
the winter months in order to feed her some money, but
she accepted only the fairest rate for her work. Mrs Rolls
explained it best.

'She values her pride above her purse, Miss Evelyn,' she
said, and I believe she was quite right.

Yet at the same time, she would offer others her remedies
without a thought. There was always a farmhand's wife or
daughter coming to see her. Then, when they gathered, they
would be two or three in the room and their accents would
thicken so I lost all understanding—and I'd know I was the
adventurer. She was consulted most frequently by young
wives seeking fertility, but her gravest concern was always
sickly children.

So it was no surprise to learn how she came by her
knowledge. She told me one afternoon how her mother—
her 'ma', she called her—had nursed her younger brother.
'I were a healthy child, ma'am, I were, but Thomas, he were
a tewly babe. Did bleare like a lamb vrom the day he were
born. None of us thought he'd make a hard boy. But Ma
did set about en with the good of the forest, zee. And I'd to
help her. He caught fever, she bathed en in moss. When he
was a-hurting she gave en willow. He was colic, she gave en
madders.'

It seemed Thomas was afflicted by every ailment that

preys on young children. It was a piteous tale that made me ache for an unpredictable ending.

'Did your mother never take him to a doctor?' I asked.

'Doctor? Oh no, never did hold by em, ma'am. Which is just as well, zee?'

'Why's that?'

Her mocking eye twinkled. 'We'd never a farthing to pay em, had we?' She laughed heartily, with her head back and her hands on her hips.

Later she told me, 'Zometimes we were short of food, but never lacked for money. My ma would vind what we needed in the woods, zee? Never needed pay no one.'

Evidently her mother would take her into the woods to find the right herbs or roots and taught that the strongest remedies came from peculiar locations—the very heart of the forest or the spur of land between two joining rivers.

'There's the best pickings,' she said.

'Why is that?' I asked. And she looked at me with that twinkle in her eye. 'Beens the magic's stronger there!' she said. And then she laughed again at her own melodrama.

Then I asked after the fate of Thomas, and Jane's tone changed suddenly and she sighed, a deep, longing sigh that was drawn from many years of hardship.

'Same as my own two,' she said, then gave me a look I can recall to this day; such dark, deep emotion. With quite surprising bitterness, she told me, 'Don't ever suffer birds in your home, ma'am. Not never.'

'No birds?' I said.

'Keep em vrom your home. Not picture nor pet. In no form at all. For crows have a special care. Don't zo much as suffer em to perch 'pon your roof.'

Then she stopped her spinning wheel, picked up her broom and commenced to sweep the floor with vigour.

~

Some little time after this, I recall, I found myself waiting by the railings that surround the Minster. Through the bars, in among the grass-kept gravestones, I spied a couple of crows striding around with such pride and defiance that I understood with a sudden, visceral certainty the truth in Jane's warning. They were awful creatures: morbid, knowing, watchful and cold. And from that day, each encounter with birds of any kind confirmed the perception, from gangs of seditious starlings to cackling magpies and beady-eyed robins. I could not understand why we had ever considered them endearing.

At home, there were bird motifs on our bathroom lampshades. Fortunately, I was able to replace them without Harriet noticing. I gave away the tea set that was painted with the forms of wildfowl and Mrs Rolls was soon instructing the maid and the cook to bar all fowl from our kitchen.

Harriet knew nothing until the morning she was working through the week's housekeeping. 'We've not had chicken for ages. Mrs Rolls, is the occasional bird beyond our purse?'

Mrs Rolls, of course, looked to me. 'Harriet,' I said, 'you know I shall not suffer birds in the house.'

Harriet blinked, frowned and, after a small shake of the head, returned to her budgets.

~

It was Harriet's constant concern to maintain our standing and good name in the local society. The house on West
Street and the wealth she had accumulated from her railway stocks were not enough for her; she felt we needed the
further security of supportive peers. I cared little for the
opinions of strangers, but for Harriet, our good name was
surety against the risk of scandal, so she was forever chasing
the approbation of anyone with status. It was thus Harriet's
adventures—not mine—that led us to Lady Falmouth.

In our Mayfair days, my singing voice had been
quite admired—I was several times at the same piano as
Mrs Norton and even once sang a duet with Charlotte
Sainton-Dolby. And since moving to Dorset, many of my
songs had been published by Boosey and Company. I had
made a little money from my compositions and word of my
celebrated status spread across the chalky downs. We were
treated to ever more frequent invitations from such exciting metropolitan centres as Sturminster Marshall and even
Blandford Forum. Harriet was always excited by these occasions, whereas I tried to refuse any invitation employing the
word 'soirée' that did not come directly from Paris. It was
pleasing being asked to sing but disappointing how few
recognised the weakness of my voice. Nonetheless, even I
felt a tremor of excitement when an invitation arrived from
Kingston House.

To sing before members of the Bankes family felt
like a very special occasion. I sang passably well, and my
audience was either too well mannered or ill-informed to
expect more. Still, I found myself nervous in such a large
house, and when Harriet tarried over the change of music,
I filled the void. I had already made the announcement,

'Our next song is by Mr Wright. It is called "The Merry Shepherd",' so when Harriet fumbled the pages, I added an aside, 'Not that there are many happy farmhands these days.'

I thought at the time I should not have made such a joke; that an address should be tailored for an audience. My humourless quip was coldly ignored, and Harriet glanced at me with such sharpness I needed a step back. Then she found her page, we set our time and the recital continued. Yet later, after all the music was done, Lady Falmouth herself touched me lightly by the elbow and led me to the window away from the others. 'Do you know much of the plight of our farm workers?' she asked, her voice very low so that it might not be overheard.

I answered from my knowledge of Jane and her family that times were very hard for farmhands. She then asked after further details and listened very attentively to my account. It had never occurred to me that I might ever speak on behalf of Jane and her peers, but this was the situation in which I found myself. Frances (Lady Falmouth) was interested to discover everything I knew, which suddenly seemed to be very little.

'Do they work on the estate, do you know?' she asked. I shook my head confessing that I did not. She looked at me with an expression I thought overly stern. I'd gained the impression the Kingston farms used tied labour.

'Are your workers not employed by the estate?'

'We still use seasonal labour and itinerants are the most imperilled in all the countryside,' she said, then she paused. Her demeanour had a sort of weariness. 'It is a constant concern to me. My brother maintains that the estate must turn a profit, but with prices as they are... well... it is hard on the labourers.'

Then she glanced towards the remainder of our company—who looked uneasy at my monopoly of our hostess—and muttered almost to herself, 'So very few people show any concern.'

Had I the purest soul, I might have explained that she overestimated me; that I had sought Jane out for a headache cure and stayed friendly out of mischief to vex my companion, but of course I said no such thing. We became —instantly—a conspiracy of *the Concerned*. Then, without warning, Frances smiled warmly and changed the subject entirely.

'It is a surprise we have not met before. Your mother is Mrs Rose of Hitchin, isn't she? Yes. So, your husband must have been Mr Edmund Price. The late earl knew him—from Winchester, I believe.'

I was taken aback; references to my mother were rarely welcome and I hadn't spared my poor, awful, deceased husband a thought in months. I covered my shock with an unconscionable lie.

'Why yes, of course, my lady. Edmund so admired the late earl. He took great pride in the acquaintance.'

'You must call me Frances,' said Lady Falmouth.

In truth, my late husband told me nothing about his work and less of his associations, but Lady Falmouth accepted the compliment with grace, and in the conversation that followed, made clear overtures that we were to become friends. Without allowing an outward hint to escape, my heart trilled; for all Harriet's efforts, I had bagged the prize catch.

'I've been invited to tea next Wednesday,' I told her in the carriage on the way home. The road jostled us, and Harriet regarded me coolly, knowing that I should be insufferable after such a triumph.

'So few others take an interest in the welfare of our farm workers,' I explained.

~

It was a torture to Harriet that my association with Lady Falmouth blossomed from the roots of such an unconventional shared interest. After each visit she would ask what subjects we had discussed and I would answer—quite truthfully—'grain prices and the famine in Ireland' or 'the situation in Scotland'. Harriet would sigh deeply—troubled, but resigned.

But the world did not stay so idyllic. After several visits, I began to gain the impression that Lady Falmouth expected something of me. I could not identify a cause for this belief, though I became increasingly convinced with each invitation to tea that I should have been offering something more. Mistakenly, I discussed it with Harriet.

'I wonder if it is something to do with her brother William?' I said.

'You'll not mention him?' she asked.

I held my tongue for a moment, then as I leaned forward, my forefinger leading my explanation, she rolled her eyes, emphasising the gesture by rolling her whole head away from me. I thought her objection ill-conceived.

'But, Harriet, consider the situation: her brother is disgraced and has fled the country for fear he'll be hanged. No one else will mention him. Do you not think a sister's love would remain undiminished by these circumstances? She must think of him, at least?'

Harriet warned me twice over that I would greatly endanger my valuable friendship by the slightest mention of Lady Falmouth's errant brother. So that set the seal. I was right, of course: her brother proved the key.

A few days later, Frances and I were walking under the cedars to the rear of Kingston House. We crunched needles beneath our shoes and swept leaves with our skirt hems. Garden peacocks called every so often, giving off their ghostly screech.

Frances seemed relaxed and open. A pause in the conversation gave me space, so I chose my moment.

'You might pardon me for the intrusion, but do you often hear word from your brother, William?'

Frances did not scowl, nor even frown. She only sighed a little plaintively and looked out across the lawns.

'Poor William,' she said. 'His concern is still for the house and grounds, though there is no telling when he'll see the results of his efforts.'

'It must be very hard for him,' I said, but there was clearly a bottom to Lady Falmouth's well of sympathy.

'Oh, it is. Very hard. But hardship of his own making, mind. His actions were reckless beyond countenance and it has made... well, he seems to have made our family a harbour for such troubles. Now I have a niece...'

'Your niece?' I asked. Frances studied me momentarily and I believe she was deciding whether or not to trust me further with the story. For good or ill she continued.

'Emily is a... a most romantically minded child. It seems she long ago fell in love with the son of a neighbouring family. The Guthries. The youngest son ran away to India many years ago and it appears Emily has spent all these years heartbroken.'

She emphasised 'heartbroken' as if it was a preposterous notion.

'Oh dear. She loves him still?' I said.

Frances looked discomfited by the idea.

'She loves but a notion.'

She sighed and raised her gaze to the distance. 'Still. Nothing moves her from it, certainly not good sense. Just recently a perfectly eligible gentleman—I shall leave him nameless—asked my brother, George, for her hand. A kindly young man, good family, well enough known to her, yet she refused him flat and without the least kindness. Really. A little more wit on her part and it might have made a cartoon in *Punch*. She tells us only that she waits for the return of "her Oswald".'

'How unfortunate. Might he ever come home?' I asked.

I should have held my tongue. She looked at me with a very purposeful expression, as if to say 'well, now, here is your task'. I felt I had wandered into the simplest trap.

'Mr Guthrie does not dare return, because he fears he will be prosecuted for the murder of the old choirmaster, Matthew Ellis.'

I indicated that I was unfamiliar with the story and Frances explained, 'By coincidence, the choirmaster disappeared the night Guthrie left for India and popular opinion has associated the two events and blackened his name. If Ellis's true fate was revealed, if he were found alive, for example, Mr Guthrie's return could be arranged and Emily might have her groom. Assuming he'd take her.'

'No one knows the fate of this choirmaster?'

'Disappeared without a word. Nor was he missed.'

'And we know for sure that Mr Guthrie didn't…?'

'Oswald Guthrie?' Frances said, resuming her distant stare. 'No, he's not a murderer.'

One of those peacocks called. It alarmed me, sounding so uncannily like a child calling 'he-lp!'.

Frances ignored it, turned back towards the house drawing a sudden breath, and asked me, 'How is your mother?' The question took me by surprise, and I struggled to recall any comment from her recent correspondence that could have provided a palatable answer. Angry? Bitter? Caustic? Judgemental? Delusional? Contented?

'Contented. She finds her current circumstances most convivial.'

'Excellent. Come on inside. I believe there is a lemon cake waiting for us.'

Harriet thinks I read too much into minor events. She does not see the veiled criticisms in my mother's letters, so I should not have expected her to agree with me about Frances when I told her how the afternoon ended.

'She showed me to the door and waited while the butler fetched my wrap. And she asked me, "You shall come again, shan't you, Evelyn?" She's never said that before.'

'That still doesn't mean she wants something from you,' Harriet said.

I frowned. 'But it feels so terribly much like she does,' I said.

~

I didn't make the association immediately, which I suppose is a little dimwitted of me. I asked Jane about the story. She looked very grim then told me the darkest parts of the tale: the choirboy in the river, the sudden rumours about the choirmaster and then the disappearances. It all seemed to have happened a long time ago. I was walking home when I realised the connection in the name. Ellis.

Of course, I couldn't hold my tongue. We were at dinner that evening.

'What do you suppose happened to that choirmaster?' I asked.

Harriet said nothing, only shrugged and shook her head.

'He would have been... what? Anne's cousin by marriage?' I asked.

That earned me a sharp look. 'He was Charles's half-brother.'

'Half-brother? So her brother-in-law.'

'I suppose so, yes.'

I waited for a moment, but since Harriet showed no inclination to explain, I pressed further.

'Do you suppose he is still alive somewhere? Or was he murdered? The choirboy's father, perhaps?'

'What, old Cuff? I shouldn't have thought so. It's more than likely he simply ran away. His name was ruined, his reputation... A sordid story.'

'I thought it rather thrilling.'

'Because you treat life like a French novel. This is no fiction, Evelyn. Whatever the choirmaster's fate, nothing good would come from its discovery.'

'Well, not quite nothing. Emily's beau might return from India and they could be reunited.'

'Which, from all you have related, would result only in her disillusionment. Please promise me you will leave this matter be.'

'But how could I? Frances has asked…'

'Frances has asked you nothing. She has asked no favour of you. You cannot even know that your interference would be welcome.'

'No, but…'

'But nothing. This concerns the welfare and the well-being of my niece and her husband. I do not wish to advance our standing at the expense of her good name.'

'Well, why should it be at the expense of her name…?' I asked, stopping myself at a most unwelcome thought. Harriet read my mind very accurately.

'Oh, for heaven's sake, deliver me from your dramas! Neither Anne nor her husband had anything to do with the disappearance of Matthew Ellis.'

'So why not…?'

'Because of the association! You cannot conceive how that man was loathed. It benefits no one to be reminded of his cruelties. It was years ago.'

'You knew all about it?'

'By no means. I knew very little. I was still living in Canford; Anne was with her guardians. It all happened before I even came to London.'

'Yet Anne married his brother.'

'Charles, yes. A very decent and respectable man. You've met him. He was *half*-brother to Matthew and both he and Anne are very dear to me. So, please, Evelyn, promise me you will leave this matter be.'

I stared blankly at her, so she continued to plead with

me. And she did not let up until eventually I relented and promised.

I should be clear about that, as clear as Marley's demise: I made her a promise. However, it never would have been possible for me to abide by it. From the moment I offered Harriet my word, I was divided, and that fissure could not have endured indefinitely.

On the one hand I made a promise to Harriet; on the other I felt an obligation to Lady Falmouth. It was not of my making, and yet somehow I had brought together the conflicting circumstances. As time went on, the division became harder to tolerate. Invitations would arrive from Kingston House and remind me of my inaction since the last visit. Frances and I would talk of local or national affairs, or music or acquaintances, and I would think myself a constant disappointment to her. She always seemed to be waiting for something more.

One can only live so long with a sequence held in the minor key, extending and extending until it trembles with the need for a resolution that seems unachievable, forever curling around itself, searching for the return to the major, longing for the return home.

I did not break my oath with a single fracture. It started with gentle enquiries that could be passed off as innocent. I sipped camomile tea with Jane in her thinly furnished cottage and she told me further details of the story and pointed me in the direction of others. The cordwainer had fragments. He bent my new ankle boots to his last, relating dark resentments against the pusillanimous vicar and the corrupted schoolteacher. The hairdresser said the choirmaster's brother was thick in the affair, then swore the undertaker knew the whole story. The undertaker—surprised at my enquiries—revealed nothing. The old coach driver's wife said I should mind my own business even while she told me tales of smuggling contraband. Mrs Rolls, after warning that Harriet would disapprove, claimed to have known the unfortunate choirboy—a cherubic lad with an angelic voice called Henry. And our maid, Mary, knew the choirmaster's half-sister, a woman who insisted that depictions of her brother were mistaken, and that he was instead an admirably pious individual. With all such fragments the picture grew ever fuller, if never much clearer.

Morning frosts became morning dew. Snowdrops filled the forest floor, then crocuses and daffodils appeared. Jane and I picked bluebells from the riverbanks, but my mind was never at peace. When I returned to the music room and tried to work, I thought only of India, dead choirboys, and of lovers separated by oceans and injustice, and I could neither write words nor compose music. And then one day, in an attempt to break my paralysis, I fixed my mind on E-flat major, and a song came to me; beautiful and lively, but before I had a chance to write it down, I lost it.

~

Those, then, were my circumstances when Anne Ellis came to call. As I have already related, Anne is the niece of my companion, Harriet Frampton, wife to the half-brother of Matthew Ellis, the missing choirmaster. She called on us late in the afternoon on the day after I lost my song.

It was a dull, cool spring day and Anne was wrapped up well against the cold outside. Her visit was not unexpected—she had sent a note ahead—so Mrs Rolls had lit the fire in the parlour and cook had made us a fruitcake.

Anne was (and still is) undoubtedly a charming creature. Dark-eyed and long-necked and she had taken particular care that day to dress for our appreciation in her elegant finest. As I came into the parlour, she was still removing her bonnet so was in the middle of the room in a splendid, full-skirted burgundy dress on which I complimented her.

'Why thank you, Evelyn,' she said. 'I have been waiting to wear it for weeks. How are you? I saw you yesterday in the Square. I wasn't sure you noticed me, you looked... I was concerned.'

I was about to explain that she'd think me ridiculous if I told her the reason why, when we were interrupted by Harriet joining us. Her broad smile showed how pleased she was to see her niece. They kissed and held hands for a moment and then we all took our seats as Mary brought in the tea.

As we sat, Anne opened up her shawl, laying it more fully over her shoulders. She did not open it out for display with any ostentation or self-consciousness; she adjusted it as one might do a collar, or a lace sleeve, so that it lay on her shoulder gracefully.

Harriet knew immediately, although she talked over her reaction. 'How is everyone, Anne? How is Charles?' she said, but we had both already seen the long, opulent form of the peacock embroidered on the shawl, trailing its long feathers down almost to the carpet.

Charles, we were told, was quite well, just returned from a trip to meet his suppliers in Bordeaux. Anne had failed in her efforts to refrain from worrying about the sea passage.

I heard her, but her words had no meaning because I was watching the shawl. It would not have been possible to bring a larger representation of a bird into the house unless it had been a full-sized oil painting, angled in through the door. I was entranced by it. Appalled. Astonished.

It was not unlike hearing my song present itself to me. There was no need for me to consider how to interpret this signal. It was plain. It laid itself out to me quite as obviously as the embroidery itself. I watched it moving as Anne shifted in her seat in conversation, the bird's magnificent tail shimmering with the waving of the material. I recalled the peacock's call in the garden of Kingston House. The cry for 'he-lp!'. All those *eyes*.

After Anne left, Harriet took me to task for my reaction. She was deeply upset and ended her tirade in tears, while her words drew me to the dawning realisation that I had sat motionless throughout Anne's short visit, staring fixedly at her shawl.

At first I said nothing in my defence. Only after Harriet had withdrawn to her room and I had reached my final conclusion was I able to respond. The first ten minutes of my pleas to be forgiven were conducted through the closed bedroom door. When, finally, she admitted me, wet-cheeked and red-eyed, I lied bare-facedly, telling her that I had become transfixed by some music that had come to mind, that it was nothing to do with Anne or the peacock shawl. I repeated the fabrication until at last she chose to believe it, then I promised to make amends, took my own bonnet and shawl and went to see Anne on West Borough.

Her housekeeper showed me into a small parlour at the front of the house. It looked recently decorated and was

tasteful, although the wallpaper was a blue pattern fes-
tooned with depictions of songbirds. I struggled to tear my
eyes from them, while Anne took some time to join me. The
powder on her cheeks disguised the trace of tears, but she
could not remove the redness from her eyes.

I threw myself at her mercy and blamed my impul-
sive, uncontrollable creative mind, apologising profusely
for my behaviour. And while the details of my explanation
were falsified, the apology was not. I held no ill will against
either her or her husband. Indeed, the precise opposite.
On Harriet's account, I planned to promote their fortunes.
Anne was generously forgiving and bade me not to dwell
on it for a moment longer. I lied in consenting to that wish
because I knew Harriet would have me dwell on it for some
considerable time yet.

~

The next time I saw Frances, Lady Falmouth, she appeared
tired, though pleased to see me. I was shown into the drawing room and found her at her writing desk, a tall painting
of her mother looming over us.

She smiled. 'Evelyn, so nice of you to join me.'

I sat in a small two-seat chair to her side and we talked
a little in our habitual fashion until at last I found my
courage.

'Lady Falmouth, you remember you told me the sad
story of your niece's affection for the young gentleman banished to India?'

She lifted her chin, showing evident interest. 'Ah yes,'
she said.

'I think I have stumbled upon a possible solution,' I said.

She did not react strongly. A slight smile. 'Pray, do go on.'

I swallowed back my nerves, conscious that I was taking a step that might never be retraced. 'Your Mr Guthrie...'

'He is not mine.'

'In as much as he is a piece in a puzzle. Is his continued absence not a convenience?'

'A convenience? For whom?'

'So long as he stays in India, the assumption remains that he is the culprit, and nothing is done.'

'So we need to find the culprit?' Frances asked.

'I believe not. I believe we need do very little,' I said. Frances leaned her head sideways in a show of curiosity.

'The choirmaster had a brother...'

'The wine merchant, Charles Ellis.'

I should have guessed that she would already be acquainted with the surrounding details. Perhaps she already knew as much as I. 'He is married to the niece of my dear companion, Miss Frampton, so I wish him only good fortune.'

'I understand. He is well thought of. A respectable merchant.'

'Respectable. Yes, in his own person certainly, but he is not so proud that he isolates himself from more question-able characters. And it is rumoured among such characters that he is skilled at bringing certain valuable goods into the country... as if by magic.'

Frances studied me for a moment while she became cer-tain of my meaning, then sighed, as if disappointed. 'And unnoticed by the collector of excise duties, no doubt,' she said. 'Something of a tradition in this county.'

I studied my fingers for a moment. 'I understand that it

is even something of a local industry. Goods are moved from cottage to cottage as far north as Salisbury.'

'It was far worse during the war. But no doubt it continues.'

'Inevitably, then, over lands that are part of either your estate or the Guthries'?' Frances said nothing in response to this. She watched me. 'Aided by locals who pay you rent?' She frowned. 'Between your two families, you control the coastline between Christchurch and Weymouth. So, if your tenants were induced to refuse him assistance, his business would be sorely damaged, would it not?'

Still Frances did not answer. I was beginning to fear my suggestions would be scorned, but I continued with a forced air of confidence. 'So now suppose he found himself in such a corner and was offered an incentive to resolve Mr Guthrie's predicament? Even if he did not himself know the circumstances of the choirmaster's disappearance, is it not likely that he is familiar with those who do? Why not make Mr Guthrie's return an obligation on someone better qualified to resolve it?'

Frances said nothing for a moment. She watched me for several seconds, then her gaze grew more inward until at last her thinking was done and she raised her head once more.

'What... what form of incentive do you think such a man would find tempting?'

At this I smiled, because the answer was so very simple.

'He already has the faculty to acquire money. But he cannot easily buy respectability or standing. If you can grant that, I believe he will find the proposition compelling.'

Frances stroked her cheek, nodding gently. 'And how do you think he might resolve the situation?'

'Ah well, of that I have no notion. But to catch a thief...'

'You set a thief. Yes indeed, that's very clever. I shall have a devil of a job explaining it to Squire Guthrie.'

And that was when I chose to hold my peace. Frances very quickly changed the subject and did not return to it until I was leaving. She gripped my arm as I walked to the door.

'Thank you, Evelyn. You've been very helpful. I hope we shall do Mr Ellis a good service.'

She smiled. And all the way home, I wondered if I had done the right thing.

I learned nothing of the consequences of my actions until years later. Frances did not mention it again. She continued to invite me for tea, treating me more kindly as time went on, and to my great satisfaction, our association endures, but precisely how events unfolded I doubt I shall ever know. Nonetheless, it is abundantly clear that if these events had never taken place, I would not have come to compose my most celebrated song.

We were in the parlour; I was sewing a silk strap back on to my purse while Harriet worked at her embroidery. I was humming contentedly because that great schism in my soul had been closed. I was no longer divided. And quite suddenly I recalled the songs by Eliza Cook that I had bought from Purkis but never played. I went directly to the music room and was leaning over the piano stool ready to open it and take them out when I started to imagine how they might sound.

Except the song in my mind continued playing. Not Eliza Cook's, because I had never heard her songs. This was coming from nowhere. Instead of lifting the stool I sat on it and captured those first few bars, and as each was caught, the music in my mind spooled on. My excitement grew, because this was now familiar to me: the experience of having a song play itself, invent itself. My only restriction was being able to write fast enough, because the notes came in a flood, inexorably flowing on from one another; obvious, inevitable, logical. And when I had it on paper, I set it out again more neatly and, almost in a state of exultation, started to play.

When Harriet came to the door, I was again in tears, although tears of delight were quite a different experience. 'That's beautiful,' she said, 'what is it called?'

And the name came to me instantly.

'"We Always Come Home",' I said.

THE SMUGGLER'S TRICK

Poole, Dorset,
October 1850

Is it a trick? Or is it more of a wonder? A wonder of modern science. Last evening as the sun was descending towards the Americas, the *Sherborne Abbey* was sighted making steady progress up the English Channel battling a troublesome north-westerly.

Upon this intelligence reaching the offices of the Lloyd's agent in Plymouth—which it did as the last fishing boat was docking in the dying light—it was submitted to the post office and transmitted by electric telegram, taking but one sixteenth of a second to arrive at the leaden halls of London. There it was received gratefully by the ship's owners and noted diligently by her insurers.

That was yesterday. This morning at precisely 8.07 a.m. the news was further relayed to Mr Charles Ellis Esq., wine merchant and ship's agent, and a little later it was delivered entirely separately to Mr Horace Domoney, customs officer for Poole and the surrounding area.

Anyone with any interest in her has therefore been expecting the *Sherborne Abbey* to dock at six this evening since before the ship's crew even sighted St Anselm's point.

Collective hubris perhaps, but matters have progressed as projected. No more than five minutes ago, on the additional intelligence that the lofty masts of the *Abbey* were entering the harbour, both Charles and Domoney emerged from their respective offices and made their ways to the quayside to stand waiting, holding their hats to guard against the thieving gusts of wind.

Twenty years ago, any old salt would have known the affair to have been a folly. Bringing a two-master into the harbour with a stiff northerly blowing and the sun going down risked overpowering the kedging crews and foundering the whole collection on the muddy shores of one of the harbour islands. Branksea, most likely—Purbeck if the gods were truly against them. But times change. They need kedge no more. Instead, a tug went out to meet the *Sherborne Abbey* powered by a modern coal-fired steam engine. Thus endowed with a surplus of might, it has blithely hauled her through the narrow channels, shrugging off the unhelpful winds, if it noticed them at all.

So now we reach this extraordinary conclusion. Not forty-eight hours since first being sighted, more than six months since her departure, the *Sherborne Abbey* is drawing her voyage to a close. The tug is thrashing her blades in the water, belching steam and smoke into the air, while the much larger barque graciously allows herself to be warped across the final few yards to the dock. As the wind rattles her sheets and the distant sunset shines through her shrouds, lines are thrown from the *Abbey*'s side and the sailors are shouted off to their final tasks. She is home.

'Shall you unload her by night, Mr Ellis?' asks the customs man.

Mr Ellis raises an eyebrow and looks down on his companion.

'Oh, I wish I could, Mr Do-Money. Save myself a third of a day.'

'And why should—' Domoney begins, before interrupting himself with a little grimace. 'My name is Domoney, Mr Ellis. Not Do-Money, nor Doh-Money. Domoney. As well you know.'

Then he sighs away his remaining frustration and returns to his theme. 'I do not see why you should not dock the goods by night, Mr Ellis. It is done in plenty of other ports.'

'Is it indeed? You surprise me. But the reason is plain enough and the dockers are as much at fault as the deckhands. Godless pagans, the lot of them. There are bogglers in the mist, Mr Do-Money, devils in the darkness, unworkable witching hours, fairies, fiends and imps for every last saint's day.'

'Indeed... I... yes—it's Domoney, Mr Ellis, not Do-Money—do you mean to say they will not work for fear of demons?'

'A mutinous superstition, but that's sailors for you.'

Domoney looks at the two fellows securing a spring rope as thick as your arm to the quayside bollard. He brushes his moustache with the back of his finger and contemplates the sailors as though their endeavours might reveal their beliefs.

'Perhaps we should be grateful to the saints for protecting us, Mr Ellis. I mean, who's to say the sailors are wrong?'

The eyebrow is raised again. 'When it costs me a third of a day in wages, then I shall say so, for one and all.'

At this, Mr Domoney cocks his head as though he is reluctant to disagree but forced into it by his conscience. 'Man does not live by bread alone, Mr Ellis,' he says, as if that should be explanation enough.

Charles mutters, 'Marmalade,' but does not repeat himself when Domoney asks what was said. Anyway, he is momentarily distracted by a sudden and mischievous gust of wind that attempts to blow his cap into the harbour and he must secure it before he can return to his commentary.

'Mr Ellis, we must all fear for our mortal souls, must we not? And I do believe the devil would take them as soon as look at us, and it is assuredly the case that he has his demons who are ever ready to snatch our spirits down to hell. Do you not agree, Mr Ellis?'

Charles is now paying full attention to the customs man. He ignores the deckhands securing a gangplank to the ship's bulwarks and the mates shouting from the decks to the rigging. 'Please continue,' he says.

'We should be praying most earnestly to those saints, Mr Ellis, truly we should. They stand between us and the demons that would claim our souls for the devil.'

'Good Lord, do you think so?'

'Why, I am quite convinced of it, sir.'

'Fascinating. Do you know there is a man in my employ who says he's seen the ghost of Bramblebush Corner? Some old merchant's donkey killed by smugglers. He swears it is there to be seen—roaming the dunes of South Haven by night. What do you say to that?'

After a moment's consideration Domoney answers, 'I'd

say he is an honest man, sir—in that at least. And Bramble-bush Corner is a site to be avoided, if you value your immortal soul.'

'Really? Is that so? Well, no doubt you are quite right, Mr Do-Money.'

'It's… it's Domoney, Mr Ellis. Domoney. Now then, I have a question for you, which is this: would you welcome a guard for your cargo? My customs men stand ready.'

Charles says nothing. He is watching the crew and his head has not turned. He hasn't even raised an eyebrow. Meaning enough. Domoney persists.

'Keep a watch? Make sure nothing untoward occurs…?'

'A kind offer, Mr Do-Money—'

'Domoney.'

'Of course. The ship's crew will post a watch, naturally, so it is quite unnecessary. Unless you… expect some misdeeds.'

'Timber was it? Your cargo?'

At this, Charles turns himself fully towards the customs man. 'Newfoundland timber, for the most part. It will go by rail to London. A good many crates of fine wine from Bordeaux, wool fleeces from the Basque country and some Chantilly lace, if my agent has done his work. All on the manifest, and all licensed, Mr Do-Money, plain as your hand.'

The customs man shuffles his feet momentarily, hands hiding deeper in his coat pockets—perhaps to cover their plainness.

'You are… I mean to say… there are many honest men of commerce, Mr Ellis, who think well of those in their employ, being generously minded, if you will… whereas I am engaged by the government to be singular in my lack of trust.'

'Singular is it? So I understand you mean to question those in my employ. Is that it? And how might I explain the presence of your men, Mr Do-Money, should the chairman of the Town Corporation happen past my ship at night? He'll think me a common criminal.'

'They shall be most discreetly positioned, Mr Ellis, and gone by daybreak, I assure you.'

Charles draws a deep breath before releasing a heartfelt sigh. 'Well, I cannot stand in your way. The quay is free for your men to wander. Post your picket, if you must. They'll have a quiet night, mind.'

With this he turns his attention to the ship's captain, who has descended the gangplank with an armful of papers. They clap each other on the back and turn to walk away from the customs man.

Domoney, who might consider himself the more senior target for paperwork, is left on the quayside. He looks up at the ship's crew, who are gathered in a rowdy bunch on the deck, watches them for a moment, then turns on his heel and walks back to the little customs post.

The door is old and it creaks as he enters, and his deputies look to him with faces half lit by table lamps. Perhaps it is the light, or maybe it is provoked by the change in atmosphere, but Horace Domoney's demeanour is quite different as he addresses his men. His face more furrowed, his scowl more severe, and the light in his eyes shines now with an almost savage intensity.

'The *Sherborne Abbey*! She's our quarry. Watch it the night through. Watch it like cats with a cornered mouse!' he growls. 'He means to make a fool of me, I can smell it!'

And as two of his deputies bundle past him to do his bidding, he stops a third with a hand against his buttons.

'Get your civvies on,' he tells his man. 'Get to the Nelson. If they don't go there, try the Portsmouth Hoy. They'll be in one of the two. They're just getting their pay now and by the end of the night one of them will have lost the lot. You find that one and tell him he can have it all back if he comes to me and explains how they'll be unloading that ship. But you make sure you wait, now. You wait 'til he's gambled it all away, see?'

His man accepts his task and slips out through the door. Domoney stays—stands by the customs-house window, and peers out at the ships at the quayside. The masts are thin silhouettes now, with the day's light almost gone.

'Do-Money? I'll give you Do-Money...' he grumbles.

~

Charles Ellis would have chuckled to hear it—not that he does, of course. He's in the office on the very top floor of his warehouse, at home among the papers, ledgers, books and files that he uses to keep track of his commercial interests. And with him is John Street, his employee and old friend.

'Oh, Charlie...' says John, shaking his head.

Charles, chewing his lip, misses a beat before looking up.

'You disapprove, John?'

John snorts. 'Disapprove? Just wants to keep our veet on the ground, zee.'

'And why should you not have your feet on the ground?'

'Can't reach—if your neck's hangin' vrom the gallis...'

'Oh, he shan't catch us, John. Too flat-footed himself, that one.'

'Hm, not zo much a vool as he makes out. He's snuffled your truffles already.'

'Really?'

'Should ha' stuck with the Swanage route. Least we could hear they customs men a-coming.'

Charles sucks his teeth, drumming his fingers on the desktop. 'Yes, but we can't. If I'm banned from both Guthrie's and Bankes's land, we can't move an inch down there.'

'Wha's he want, anyhow?'

'Guthrie? He wants his brother back from India. He has it in his head that I can arrange it.'

John frowns—his face darkens like a sudden autumn storm.

'S'that summit about your brother?'

Charles looks up. Rubs his chin. Looks back at his own fingers as they drum on the desk.

'If they had just stayed put instead of running off like that. No surprise they should draw suspicion. Squire Guthrie seems to think I can put the record straight somehow.'

'Well p'rhaps you could?'

'Really? How might I? The fact of the matter is, John, we have no more of a clue who killed Matthew than any-one else—and we were there. I didn't see anyone, did you?'

John shakes his head vigorously.

'So I don't see how I may be of assistance to Guthrie. You know he offered to pay me? Said he'd have Bankes make me Alderman of Wimborne. When I said there's nothing I could do, he grew most agitated. He's told every villager and crofter south of Sturminster to watch out for us. We are practically wanted men.'

John Street is staring hard at his employer, chewing his lip. Charles suddenly sits up in his chair.

'So! Nothing for it. We'll get this shipment past Do-Money and then that's it. We'll just pay the duty.'

'You might just pay the duty on this 'un…'

Charles appears to give it a moment's thought, but no more.

'I can't. It's not on the manifest.'

John grunts, and Charles closes the books on his desk. He is done for the day, and they shall return to their rooms in the New Antelope Hotel for the evening. They're descending the stairs when John makes his final observation.

'… z'not like you never changed a manifest afore…' he grumbles.

Charles scowls after him, having not properly heard his words.

'We shall have the better of Do-Money, John. Don't you fear it.'

'Humph,' is John's answer. And it is not a happy humph, because John does fear it. He fears it deeply, as well he might. He fears it through the rabbit stew he shares with Charles in the Antelope's dining room, and he fears it in his bed that night, eyes heavy, listening to the sailors singing in the High Street.

When, at last, his fear has become so tiresome that he resolves to do something about it, the hour has passed three in the morning and he has barely slept.

Everything is quiet in Poole town's streets. As John's boots hit the cobblestones the sounds echo from the warehouse walls, and down by the dock the night air is pungent with salt. The harbour glitters, lit by a gibbous moon and a million stars.

John does not tread lightly and he finds his path in the middle of the road. He is not a man for cribbing.

Along by the *Sherborne Abbey*, the quay is furnished with rows of great metal bollards, bent forwards like frozen waves with lines trailing across to the ship's sides. In the middle of all those lines there is a small glow of light and a figure hunched up, sitting upon one of the bollards. He turns as soon as John's footsteps reach him, so John greets him quickly to reassure him.

'Evenin', John says, and the figure raises a hand.

'Evening, John. How you keeping?' is the answer.

John frowns, then, as he comes close, he recognises Mark Woolcott—a Wimborne man.

'Ullo, Mark. Never knew you was with Domoney. What you up to here then?'

'Cor, I'm bored out of my mind, John. Should ha' stayed in Davie's shop. Cold, tired and hungry too.'

'Watchin' our ship?'

'And iz not much entertainment.'

John reaches into the inside pocket of his coat and is pleased to discover the cold metal of Charles Ellis's hip flask. It brings back the sudden and fleeting memory of a night trek up Durly Chine.

He pops it open and taps Mark's shoulder with it. 'Here, this'll warm y'up.'

'Oh Lor', John. You'll get us shot!' says the customs man, but all the same he accepts the flask and takes a good sip from it.

'Zeems fair,' John answers. 'Zeein' how you're a-gettin' us hanged.'

Mark looks up with a pained expression as he hands the flask back.

'Won't come to that though, will it, John?'

'Won't it? Your man Domoney ain't much of a one for a joke.'

A grunt is the response; a reluctance to argue the incontestable.

'What's his game then, Mark?' John asks.

Mark looks up with heavy-lidded eyes and quietly chuckles.

'Funny really. He sends Tom out to follow the sailors, thinking they'll soon lose all their wages playing Crown and Anchor then he can sweet-talk em. Except they was better at dice than I dare say they are at sailin'. T'was the dockers they fleeced.'

'Is that right?'

'One o' your men.'

Street's look turns cold and direct. 'Who's that then?'

'Old Bob Hanley. Got hisself in a right pickle. Lost his shirt. So Domoney gives en half-a-week's wages, and he spills the beans. Word is you plans to haul your load up from tunnels under the quay. So Domoney says he'll have the other half his wages if he can find the tunnel. Hanley said it should be easy.'

'He said that?'

'He did.'

'I'll wring his bloody neck...' John says, and he starts rubbing his aching knuckles.

'Now, John... if I don't get shot, and you don't get hung, then you can leave his neck alone, eh?'

Another humph from John. He takes a swig from the flask then hands it to Mark Woolcott once more, and they both stare into the darkness while John's knuckles ache.

'Well... I fear he'll not get his full wage...' John says. And after a few more minutes, he closes the flask and bids the customs man good morning. Then he makes his way back to the Antelope. Feet clumping on the cobblestones and John muttering to himself;

'Hmm... he's snuffled your truffles all right.'

~

So it is that the next day starts with each man boasting how he has the advantage of the other.

Charles treats himself and his companion to breakfast in the Antelope—a noisy affair as the coach passengers for Blandford and Dorchester ready their luggage by the archway—and Charles grins at John's news from the night before.

'Oh that's capital!' he says. 'Oh yes, quite capital!'

And though John frowns at him, Charles does not explain his plans, only instructs John to fetch himself over to Conway's to order a delivery.

Meanwhile, in the customs office, Domoney is actually rubbing his hands with glee as he anticipates his day ahead.

'Today's the day!' he tells them. 'Today's the day!'

And he sets about checking the tides, explaining to his men that they must know their timing. 'We can catch it right and walk in on him and find his contraband stacked under his floors. Oh my, to see his face. This is something to anticipate. This shall be rich!'

Not that all their company seems keen to join in their

respective celebrations. Mark Woolcott is hovering at the back of the customs office, avoiding his master's presence so far as he is able.

There is equivalent discomfort over in Charles's warehouse, where a certain Bob Hanley appears alarmed as he is taken into the confidence of his employer. Charles wants to show him a concealed door and invites him down into a secret coal bunker.

'Clean it up for me would you, Bob? Clear out the clutter for a consignment I've ordered.'

He is not a naturally treacherous man, Bob's not, and it does not sit well with him, so he makes every effort to confess his predicament, but Charles will not afford him a chance to fully explain himself.

'Mr Ellis…!'

'Bob, you're not to mention this place. If anyone asks, you are to say it is for coal and nothing else. And when you're done, bring me up the key, won't you? And be sure to lock the door!'

Having said this, Charles turns and makes back towards the steps.

'Mr Ellis, I must have a word!' Hanley insists, but it is all for naught. Charles waves a hand dismissively.

'Later!' he says and before Bob can intervene, his employer is gone. And there's poor Bob, left alone in the bunker. He peers at the floor for a moment, looks up the rusty coal chute to the roadside doors and can do nothing but shrug.

Having reaped this intelligence, it is no great challenge for Bob Hanley to slip away from the warehouse to bring it to its sponsor. The morning is lit by a dull, cloudy sky, so the narrow lanes, like gorges with warehouses for walls, are all of a greyness. With the collar of his pea coat turned up high and the peak of his cap pulled down low he could be any of a hundred dockers whose habit is to walk in the shadows. It might seem that the centuries' habits have made such men permanently shy of the forces of prevention, were it not for the fact that Hanley's circuitous route takes him to the creaking door of the customs house itself.

'Fetch me Domoney!' he insists, once inside. He looks back through the door before closing it and once Domoney shows his face, tells his tale with all haste.

The rumour is true, he reports. Charles has a basement with a trapdoor. He has seen it—cleaned it, even. Ready for 'a delivery', he was told.

Does Hanley talk about coal as he was instructed? He does not; doesn't even mention it. And upon his swift and well-paid departure, Domoney's glee shines brighter than ever.

He turns to his printed tables and demands of no one in particular, 'How are the tides?' then traces his finger along columns and rows until he reaches his answer. 'Just a little longer,' he says. 'Just a little longer.'

～

Just (to be precise) until twenty-three minutes before ten o'clock in the morning on 17 October 1850—that's when the tide has reached its lowest ebb. Boats are thick in the harbour. To look from the Poole side across to Hamworthy is to look through a scribbled pattern of masts, lines and web-like shrouds. At the heart of it, the unloading of the

Sherborne Abbey is in full swing as huge clutches of New-foundland timber are craned out the ship's hold and lowered onto waiting carts. John has not been idle. He has talked through the manifest with the ship's first mate and relayed the order of unloading to the waiting carriers; he's dismissed the crane handler's complaints, chivvied the recalcitrant cart drivers and waved greetings to the whistling dockers. And now, with a gap in the demands on him, he has come to stand beside his master.

'What they want all that lumber for then?' he asks, looking up at the craning load.

'Railways,' Charles answers. 'They are building railways at a pace and they need timber.' He nods up at a sailor who has climbed the rigging to ward the crane rope against tangling. 'I tell you, John, those men are gods to me. You wouldn't get me up that height for all the tea in China.'

John squints up at the masts.

'Not zo bad…' he mutters.

'Really? I tell you, I've seen them up there at sea, in the cold and the rain. Don't know how they endure it.'

'Beens you was born to a warm hearth, Charlie.'

'It's because I have good sense, John. Would you want to be climbing up there on a winter's evening?'

'They'd not have I. Too much zoil a-twixt me toes.'

'Oh, but you put too low a store by yourself, John. Far too low.'

John peers up to the heights of the ships' masts, drawing a deep breath. Charles is watching his expression, looking from the scene back to the observer.

'What do you think Bill would make of it?'

'Ah, well, he's a type, is Bill. Might call en "tinely"; knows where he wants a-be and that's a-home. Whereas I always envied Cornelius a little. If I'd a chance to zee the world... ride atop o' one of they girt bits of tackle...'

'You surprise me, John. And they'd take you more readily than you imagine, but don't set off just yet—look, here's our customs man.'

And they turn as Horace Domoney steps over the crane tracks, striding across to them. He opens his mouth as he approaches but isn't given a chance to speak.

'Your attentions are most flattering, Mr Do-Money!' Charles calls out.

'It is Domoney, Mr Ellis, Domoney!'

Charles looks up at the timber load, hands behind his back, rising on his toes, clenching his jaw. Domoney blinks at him.

'How so do my...'

'You told me your men would be gone by dawn. Yet I still see them. I count seventeen seagoing vessels in this harbour, Mr Do-Money—seventeen. There are another twelve coastal vessels and seven newly arrived, not including the *Abbey*, yet you parade your men around my ship like she were flying a Jolly Roger. I will have you tell me the meaning of it.'

Domoney stammers for a second, glancing back over his shoulder at the three uniformed customs men. It is long enough pause for Charles to resume his reproach.

'Your attention is an affront, Mr Do-Money. A slap in the face, d'you see? You charge an insult against my enterprise!'

At this, the customs man, reddening in the cheeks, attempts a protestation.

'Now—'

'What possible justification can you have for this?'

'I have information!' Domoney announces bluntly.

Charles focuses his full, angry glare on Domoney.

'You have *information*?'

'That's correct, Mr Ellis,' Domoney continues, sounding almost apologetic for his outburst. 'The old smugglers, you know, they used tunnels. They say this dockside is near hollow with the passages beneath it.'

'So they say—storm drains, as I understood it.'

'Storm drains some of them. Widened a bit others.'

'And this is your information?'

'No, Mr Ellis. My information is more specific than that—so it is. I have it from them that knows, you see, that a merchant such as yourself has been opening those tunnels up. But you'll understand, Mr Ellis, that in order to use them, you'd be needing a warehouse nearby, with a basement that has access to one of those tunnels—see? So not every merchant that imports his goods through Poole is a candidate, as it were. And then there's the timing, because it's no use unloading on a high tide, the entrance being likely underwater or out of reach. So you've to time your arrival.'

'Is that right?'

'It is, Mr Ellis, it is. So there's some simple reckoning to be done. There are those docked on the Hamworthy side, which may be ignored from the start, given that the dockside is solid by there. There are those that arrived on the high tide last night but have no connection with the port, *Foreign Dawn* for example, and then there are those who might be unloaded to a warehouse nearby, docked in the right position, that arrived on the high tide, in time for the morning low. Of which, Mr Ellis, there is only one.'

Domoney jabs his thumb backwards at the *Sherborne Abbey* to which—in order that he might address Charles directly—he has turned his back.

'So that's your business, is it?' Charles says. He raises his chin a little as he says it—an expression that leans towards defiance. But he is betrayed, it would seem, not by the expression on his own face, but by that of John Street. It is John's eyes that widen a little too much, his brow that furrows, his mouth that tightens. And the change is not missed by Domoney. He glances from merchant to employee and back again, before a little smile creeps out from under his moustache.

'Do you have a basement to your warehouse, Mr Ellis?'

Despite John's terror-struck appearance, Charles seems unruffled. 'I'm not sure I care for your insinuations, Mr Do-Money. We have a coal bunker. Not sure it has pretensions to the level of a "basement".'

Domoney looks up at him with rosy-cheeked delight, waving over his officers. 'Never mind pretensions, Ellis. Time we inspected it!'

'Out of the question!' Charles says, nodding at the *Sherborne Abbey*. 'We're docking a whole shipload.'

'Oh, but I shall brook no delay, Mr Ellis,' Domoney declares, almost laughing. 'You may attend or not as you like!'

Charles looks to John, but John expresses only alarm. Charles, seeming defeated, turns on his heel with an irritated harrumphing noise. 'Oh, very well. If only to end your delusion. I have told you many times, Do-Money, I have nothing to do with contraband.'

'Of course you have, Mr Ellis. Of course.'

So they leave the quay—Charles, Domoney and the little band of followers—and march into the narrow confines of Castle Street. Domoney is smiling gleefully as he scuttles alongside Charles, but his happiness turns to sudden alarm when a warehouse gate opens and lets out a dray horse drawing a canvas-covered cart.

'Wait! Stop that cart, men!' Domoney calls. But before the customs men have reacted, Charles has shouted them down.

'No, Domoney! No, no, no! That's not my warehouse. That's next door. We're here. This is my place!'

Charles is standing next to a small wooden door and the cart is drawing down the street with a second emerging from the gate. Domoney looks to his deputies.

'It's true, Mr Domoney, sir,' says Mark, 'this is Mr Ellis's place. Not that next one.'

Charles has held his own door open and is gesturing for Domoney to enter. Next door, the second cart draws away and the gate is closed by unseen hands, while Domoney, looking on with a bitter suspicion, hesitates. Finally he turns and takes Charles's invitation.

'At least you have my name for once,' he grumbles, stepping through the doorway.

Once inside the building Domoney barely hesitates. Without waiting for the merest hint of an invitation, he leads past the foreman's clerking desk, around an oak-beam pillar, beneath the wooden staircase to the far corner of the ground floor, where he waits for Charles to join him.

As Charles comes alongside, Domoney even has the effrontery to haul empty wine racks aside and reveal the hidden door.

'Your basement?'

'The coal cellar…'

'What shall I find in it, Mr Ellis?' Domoney demands.

'I can't be sure. It was certainly empty this very morning, but there may have been a delivery since. Who can tell?'

Domoney laughs. 'A delivery. Oh, I am sure there has been!'

Charles's face straightens, whether as a result of being challenged or from having someone laugh at him directly would be hard to tell.

'Come on, open it up…' Domoney says. But Charles offers only a bitter little smile.

'I have not the key, I'm afraid, Mr Do-Money.'

He holds his hands out wide to display his innocence and the men around him look quickly from Charles to Domoney. What shall he do next? But Domoney's good humour is unmoved. He reaches into the pocket of his jacket.

'Of course you haven't,' he replies, holding up a long metal key. 'That's because I have it!'

John and Charles look at each other in alarm while Domoney turns towards the door. He unlocks it and beckons his men behind him. 'Come on!'

Domoney squeezes through the low entrance, followed by two more of his customs men, with Mark bringing up the rear. This last one of them shrugs at John as he passes, signalling his regret that matters are so far out of his hands. But he gets no further than the other side of the entrance.

There are muffled calls from within the basement, which John and Charles cannot decipher, then Mark backs out— an awkward manoeuvre given the restrictions imposed by the size of the doorway. The other customs men have had a chance to turn around and they re-emerge in order. Domoney is the last to clamber from the steps.

'Ellis! Ellis!' he is calling before he is even clear of the hole.

'Mr Do-Money?' Charles responds, an angel of innocence, going by his tone.

'It's full of coal!' Domoney shouts. He holds up one of his blackened hands by way of evidence.

Eyebrows are raised. Charles turns to his companion.

'Mr Street, did you allow someone to put coal in my coal bunker?'

'I did so, zir. 'Pon your instruction.'

'Most careless of you.'

'Very funny, Ellis. Where is the brandy? The furs and the cigars that were unloaded this morning?'

Charles shakes his head, evidencing bewilderment, but Domoney is insistent. He points back down the passage. 'They were unloaded this morning. Passed up through the hole, into that basement!'

Charles has his hands in his pockets and can but shrug. 'Well if that is truly the case, Mr Do-Money, they must be—I assume—*under* the coal.'

Domoney's good humour has at this point entirely evaporated and he comes threateningly close to Charles—the impact of which is diminished almost to nothing by his comparative shortage of stature.

'Oh, you think you are so clever, Ellis. But I shall have the last laugh yet.'

And without turning from Charles, he calls on his deputies.

'Fetch me coal sacks. And shovels. We shall clear the coal. For I have no doubt what lies beneath it.'

Charles sighs very heavily.

'Coal dust, Mr Do-Money. That's all you'll find beneath the coal. But you shall do as you please. Send for me when you wish to offer your apologies.'

'Bah! And it's *Domoney*!'

So, while the customs man organises his team, Charles returns to his office and the morning is passed to the sound of scraping, clanking, grunting and complaining. And when the sound of shovelling slows, he comes down again to inspect the growing number of coal sacks on his floor.

'He's got someone on the ship,' John says quietly, standing by his side.

'Hm. Maybe he has. Or it may be he's bluffing. But you be ready with the horn, John, in case he gets too adventurous.'

Upon this word, John leaves the scene, retreating up the stairs, taking two at a time, and Charles finds himself a storeman's stool and waits for the last of the coal sacks to be brought up.

'I trust you'll be putting my coal back in its bunker when you have finished playing with it,' he tells Domoney when the soot-besmirched customs man finally emerges.

'Where is it, Ellis?'

'Why, in those sacks where you put it.'

'Not the coal. Your contraband!'

'Oh dear, do you not believe the evidence of your own eyes? I have no dealings with contraband.'

'You brought up barrels of brandy, furs and cigars! Through a tunnel from the quay.'

'Pure fancy, Mr Do-Money.'

'Domoney! And it is not a fancy. We have the tunnel. Come, see if you can explain this!'

And so saying, Domoney summons Charles down into the coal bunker. The air has settled a little once they reach the blackened floor, but dust still lingers. The three other customs men lean on their shovels, grubby-faced and forlorn.

'Explain that!' Domoney demands, pointing at a trap-door.

Charles looks at it blankly. Domoney is left pointing.

'What explanation does a drain cover need, Mr Do-Money?'

'Your men passed contraband through it! Where did it go?'

'My men? Heavens, no. My men have it that the tunnels are haunted. A sailor off the *Sydney*, so they say. Crawling the tunnels until the end of eternity.'

Does Domoney's expression shift? Not so that it might be noticed. Indeed, the very way he stays motionless for a moment—the way his face does not change—might be seen as expression enough.

'If you wish to inspect the drains, Mr Do-Money, you are more than welcome,' Charles says, then he steps forward, catches the hatch by the ring, and hauls it open. Immediately the salty air of the sea invades the room. And something else comes with it. A sort of momentary chill. And a quiet, distant murmuring. Is that a voice?

Faces turn towards the hole, slowly—cautiously—as if the ominous noise comes from something no one wishes to disturb. And then the faces turn back as each man looks to the others. Charles frowns. Domoney scowls.

'What devilry is this?' asks the customs man.

'Oh... I'm sure it is just the wind in the drains,' Charles says.

'There is no wind,' mutters one of the men.

So the little congregation stares at the hole in the floor, listening to the low moaning until at last Domoney says a short prayer and snatches up an oil lamp. For all the glowing light, his face is still bloodless.

'Have I to go myself, then?' he demands of his men. They move nothing but their eyeballs.

'I shall accompany you,' Charles says. 'Not that I think we need fear the sailor of the *Sydney*, but... should you need assistance...'

Domoney does not seem to think kindly of Charles's offer. His face as dark as doom, he points at the opening and says, 'You'll be first, then.'

Charles controls his affronted twitch and steps forward as if it is an honour. 'Most kind,' he says, removing his hat.

As soon as they are in the drains, Charles's stature becomes a liability. His knees are by his elbows and his hair brushes the bricks of the tunnel roof.

'You see, Mr Do-Money,' he explains, shuffling along a little distance, 'there is not room for both men and barrels in these drains. The plot you suspect is too impractical to have been real.'

'Ellis, will you stop...!' Domoney replies, interrupting himself with his exertions, '... will you stop calling me Do-Money! My name is Domoney, like Dominic, as you know perfectly well!'

The water at the base of the drain is splashing onto Charles's trousers and it distracts him from an immediate reply.

'Wait! Where does this go?' Domoney demands.

'Well, how the deuce should I know?' Charles says. 'Do you think—'

A low sound, a deep, moaning voice, interrupts him, and the pair of them hold fast. The sound continues to echo down the tunnel.

'The wind, I'd say…' Charles whispers.

'It comes from this direction,' Domoney growls. 'Come!'

Charles catches his arm. 'Do you think it wise? What might we encounter?'

But Domoney lifts the lantern so that both their faces are given ghoulish shadows.

'I'll tell you what we shall encounter, Ellis. One of your men, trying to frighten me with childish noises!'

'Ah. Do you think? They wouldn't do that, surely?'

Domoney has already turned away and is splashing down the tunnel with surprising dexterity.

'Not unless you told them off to it! Knowing my views on saints and demons. Here… look… another door!'

There is a creaking noise and then a slapping of metal and wood upon stone and Domoney disappears upwards and out of the tunnels.

Charles can't see Domoney ahead of him, but he doesn't need to. He knows perfectly well that Domoney will emerge into a basement remarkably similar to Charles's coal bunker, save for the absence of coal. So it proves. He pulls himself into the room and finds Domoney standing, staring at a part of the wall, his head cocked to one side. Charles looks at the wall, wondering what is remarkable about it, only to realise that Domoney is not looking, but is listening. From the floor above there is the sound of a broom and a workman's whistle. It is the tune of 'I Loved a Shepherd Girl'.

Quite abruptly, Domoney turns and sets off up the stairs. Charles follows, and once they have reached the ground floor and more natural light, they find themselves in the company of John Street in an entirely empty warehouse.

'Street! What are you doing?' the customs man shouts.

'Why I's a-sweeping the floor, Mr Do-Money. Domoney, beg pardon.'

Charles takes time to familiarise himself again with having space for his full length. He brushes himself off and recovers his breath, but Domoney doesn't pause. He strides to the warehouse doors, slams the locking bar open and hauls the door open. Charles follows at his own pace and enjoys the change in the air as they transit from the wooden, echoing halls of the warehouse into the open-skied, tall-walled confines of Castle Street. They both look at the next-door entrance—Charles's own.

'Is everything to your satisfaction, Mr Do-Money?' Charles asks.

Domoney turns to him with red eyes of ire.

'This is… this is… next door! Those carts were yours! I'll see you hang, Ellis. I shall see you hang!'

And with these unkindly words, Domoney marches away, silhouetted by the bright light from the harbour, shoulders hunched, fist crushing his hat.

Charles half turns to John. 'John, would you please tell the customs men that once they have replaced my coal in its bunker Mr Domoney awaits them at the customs house.'

'Right-o!' says John. And as he passes, Charles claps him on the back.

'Well done.'

~

Domoney is not at all calmed by his return to the customs house and his mood does not improve when his soot-covered men join him. While he sits at his desk and grimly stabs his pen at a small collection of papers, his men look to each other, none daring to be the first to speak, and go meekly about unnecessary tasks.

They all jump when Domoney's anger erupts with a sudden thump of the desk.

'He knew!' he shouts, his fist still pressed against the paperwork. When he stands, the violence of his sudden movement propels his chair backwards into the wall. 'Because someone told him!' he declares.

The customs men look shocked at their master, the whites of their eyes being more prominent for the soot on their faces. All but one. One face does not look at Domoney—one face stays lowered towards the floor. Domoney clocks it then turns away. The men wait his next direction with anxious patience.

'Get out! Leave me alone! Go and clear the soot from your faces,' Domoney growls.

They file past him—lonely boots clomping over the floorboards—and Domoney waits until the last of them reaches the doorway before stopping him.

'Woolcott. A moment of your time.'

The man stops.

'Do you know the punishment for customs men in the pay of smugglers?'

'No, Mr Domoney.'

'You do not? They would find themselves in clink, Mr Woolcott, branded the same as the paymaster.'

Mark's face goes pale so quickly that even in his anger, Domoney is concerned for him.

'Sit you down, man, before you pass away.'

And so they sit beside Domoney's clerking desk.

'I... took no money off en, sir,' Mark says quickly, 'only John Street's a friend. Known en since we was children. He's a good man and I shouldn't wish to zee en hanged.'

'Of course not. Of course not, Mark, none of us should want to see another man killed. But there also needs to be justice. And good society needs protection from the criminal classes, does it not?'

'I s'pose it does.'

Domoney leans back in his chair and studies his officer, although Mark still keeps his eyes lowered.

'And do you think these men criminals? What do you know of them? Tell me.'

'Good men, sir.'

'Is that all? You've not heard rumours? Gossip about their business? Rumours from their past?'

Mark looks alarmed at this. 'Their past?' he says.

He knows the tugging feel of a near-caught fish does Domoney. He'll not snatch too soon, nor waste his bait. He places his hand flat on the desk beside him. A meaningless gesture, but they both watch as his fingers spread wide, like a squid on a deck, then close into a fist.

'What about their past?' he repeats.

'Why... nothin'...'

'Nothing except?'

'Well...'

'Hmm?'

'Well, it were only that business of Lily Wilkinson's grave.'

'Ah yes. Poor old Lily. I know all about her grave,' Domoney lies, never having heard the name before. 'Tell me how *you* were involved in that affair.'

A sudden fright on Mark's face. 'Oh no, Mr Domoney, I weren't involved. I only heard about it from my brother, see…'

~

So it was a trick, after all. Not quite the clean outcome Charles had planned. Still, he thinks himself quite the cleverest smuggler. Until, that is, John Street calls on him two nights later at his home in Wimborne, bearing ill tidings.

They sit by the fire, hunched forward on the edges of their respective armchairs, faces glowing.

'The *grave?*' Charles whispers, lowering his voice so that his wife might not overhear. 'How should he even know about it?'

'His brother were thick with old Wilkinson. Far'z I can tell they just figured it out theyselves. He's proper cut up at having to tell Domoney. Don't mean no harm to no one, don't Mark.'

Charles sighs heavily and after a moment's staring at the flames sits upright.

'Well, don't let it trouble you, John. We did nothing wrong. None of us,' and he grips John by the shoulder as he offers reassurance. 'We are honest men, John.'

'Oh ar. Right honest smugglers, us.'

They stare at each other for a moment longer, then John shakes his head. He has decided. A drastic action, but it is a decision.

'No. There's nothin' for it. I'll away to zea, Charlie. I'll be gone and have done wi' it.'

'Oh, John, really? For a rumour? That's a hard life. And a hard decision…'

'As soon as Mark tells me I thought I should be away. Could you get I on one o' they ships, Charlie?'

'Well, I could, but…'

'Well then, would you have it done, Charlie? As a favour?'

Charles sighs very heavily. 'John, are you sure this is what you want?'

It is indeed what John wants and nothing Charles can do will persuade him otherwise.

So it happens that three nights later they are standing on the dunes of North Point, by the entrance to the harbour. A longboat is approaching from a ship standing off Sandbanks and the whole scene is lit by a moon hanging low over the Purbeck Hills.

'When shall you come back, John?' Charles asks.

'Honest truth Charlie, I don't mean to. I'd rather ride out the zeven zeas than vace the hang-gallis.'

'You did nothing, John.'

At which point John turns to his old friend and grips him by the arm.

'Charlie, you do I a favour? You keep in mind that they magistrates don't care f' right nor wrong. Zeen that enough. They care for themselves and their bank books. If it favours em to hang 'e, they'll hang 'e. If not then they shan't. Wrong or none don't make much difference. You remember that, Charles.'

'Very well. In return, John, you must promise me this: if

you ever change your mind and decide to return, you send me word first, will you? I'll make sure the landing is safe. But you must promise me.'

And with these agreements made, the men shake hands and John walks down the beach to the waiting boat.

~

So Charles's trick was not the only show in the circus. Nor was it the last trick. That never seems to come. Several nights later, Charles's face is lit again by a desk lamp, wick turned up high. It's a face that sees more light from oil than it ever does from the sun.

He is chewing his lips. Looking from one handwritten letter to another. It might be the lamplight, or perhaps he is unwell—indigestion perhaps, or perhaps it is the task he has set himself that pains him, the blank paper in front of him.

Perhaps that—because before he draws the blank page close, before dipping his pen in readiness, he draws a deep and very heavy sigh.

NELSON'S FLEET

~

Wimborne Minster, Dorset,
August 1852

Young John Warland found HMS *Victory* behind the white-washed greenhouses, where the nettles grew long over broken glass and flagstones. He'd never been there before, his mother having always called him back, shouting, 'There's glass, John!' from the kitchen door. But this morning he had been left with his sisters.

Eliza was studying and Sarah had already hissed, 'I'm *not* playing Nelson!' before he had even asked her. So, with his missing arm tucked into his shirt and his bad eye patched, he'd wandered around the garden, batting at butterflies with a bamboo stick until he had ventured into forbidden territory—and there she was.

His excitement was unquenchable. He trampled the nettles aside and dragged her out, turning her right way up. Water had gathered in the base and the soil darkened where it spilled, while spiders the size of your hand scuttled for cover. He dragged her along the path in front of the nursery shed, metal singing raucously as it scraped over stone, and brought her to a halt on the lawn. She was easy enough to move, even with just one arm, and he could easily take her down to the meadow and launch her from there—if he was allowed.

Seeking Sarah in the house, he found her unmoved, legs swinging pointlessly under the table while she continued staring at those impenetrable stories. There was no clear way of asking her without confronting the fact she'd already refused him once.

'What is it, John?' she said.

'I found the *Victory*!' he told her. 'We could sail her... if you like.'

She turned back to her stories, sighing theatrically. 'What are you talking about?'

'*Victory*. Behind the greenhouses. We could actually sail her! You may be Hardy. If you care to. You shan't have to kiss me or anything.'

Sarah lifted her head. He tried to think of something else he could offer. She'd be his flag captain, so it would have been good to give her some flags. But then she squashed her face up like a bitter old spinster. 'Do you mean that old tin bath?' She made it sound dirty when it should have been exciting.

'We could take her across to the meadow!' he explained, but it did no good.

'John—John, take your hand out of your shirt, you have two perfectly healthy arms—I already told you I am not playing your ridiculous Nelson games.'

He stayed still. Her tone was far too harsh. Upsetting. And he reviewed what might be considered ridiculous about his games but there really was nothing whatsoever. On his last birthday he talked of ships with Uncle Charles—who had sailed all the way to France and back—and *he* didn't think John was ridiculous—so Sarah was wrong. Although it didn't do to say so, when people were wrong.

'Well… can we play over on the meadow? You can just as well read your story paper there.'

'I can just as well read my story paper here, John,' Sarah answered. There was a taunt in her tone and had their mother been in the room she would undoubtedly have issued a reprimand on the basis of it. He withdrew, wounded.

As he climbed the stairs, running his hand over the smooth-curving wood of the banisters, John muttered to himself about his sister. She did not understand leadership. Nelson, as an example, was known for the compassion he showed his crews and they loved him in return and fought all the more fiercely for it.

The upstairs corridor was a hall of closed doors and Eliza would be behind the furthest. He rested his chin on the door handle first, listening. It was the wrong shape for a chin-rest. He turned it and allowed the door to draw itself open.

'D'you not know how to knock?' Eliza asked, clucking out the rhythm in her words.

'I… didn't want to disturb you,' John reasoned. His eldest sister was sitting at her writing desk with a large book before her. She had her hair in a bun like an adult.

'Well? Now that you haven't disturbed me, John, what is it you want?'

Her eyes were red like she'd been crying and the sight almost made him jump. He sifted his recent memory for explanations but found nothing.

'John? For pity's sake! What do you want?'

'I want Sarah to come with me over to the meadow,' he heard himself say.

Quite why Eliza then chose to shout at him, John couldn't discern. In his estimation, she had precious little justification. She called him 'an annoying worm', complained that their mother should have contented herself with two daughters and stormed past him to the banisters. From there she screamed down to her sister with a volume and pitch so extreme it made him wince. Sarah—with unbelievable composure—appeared, stood at the bottom of the stairs, and bluntly refused Eliza's order to take him to the meadow.

While Eliza and Sarah launched into an argument of increasing violence, John tiptoed down the stairs, past them, and out of their company. He sniffed, wiped his nose on the back of his hand and slipped unseen into his father's study. It was distressing to be thought a worm—most distressing. He should never have been so rude to someone else, but crudeness was a characteristic of his sisters. That they still expected to marry was a cause of wonderment to him. He could see they were insufferably foolish, and he was but six.

He climbed onto his father's desk chair, swung it round and wondered what Eliza had meant about her mother contenting herself with daughters. The study was a blur, flying past when the meaning revealed itself. Eliza, his own sister, had wished him gone and never to have been born. The swirl of colours settled back into the room, but it was blotted by snotty, salty, tear-wet, clench-fisted anguish. When his tears cleared enough, he wiped his hands on his shorts, sniffed angrily, and opened his father's polished walnut-wood desk.

The box that held his father's hunting pistol had a felt base. It slid out silently. He'd thought of doing this so many times.

~

The Good Lord plagued Egypt with frogs and locusts as a punishment, but why would He visit John and Sarah upon Eliza Warland? She is sure she has done nothing to warrant it, yet pretending her younger sister is a spiritual ordeal that she somehow has to overcome with patience and virtue is the entire fabric-thin barrier that prevents Eliza from reaching out and actually throttling the girl.

'Mother left you in charge, not me,' Sarah is insisting, which is true enough in its finery, but Sarah is unwilling to accept the broader consequences of her claim.

'So, you should do as I say and take John to the meadow!' Eliza says.

'No, because that would make *me* in charge!'

'But you never do anything! And since Mother's immaculate logic does not permit me to join Bible classes, I have to stay here and study, so I must be left *alone!*'

Sarah answers that this is none of her concern, which is infuriating not only because it is true, but also because it emphasises how utterly intractable she intends to be. Eliza screams her frustration.

~

Selina Warland will step from the offices of her lawyers onto West Street with too much on her mind. She'll sigh —thinking back over the intricate conversations recently concluded—and she'll shake her head a little as she recalls her earlier argument with Eliza, her eldest. From West

Street's shade she'll cross a sunlit square towards the Wilts and Dorset Bank muttering silently. Having queued in the echoing cool of the bank, she will chat briefly with the cashier, complete her withdrawal and then re-emerge into the sunlight.

In the summer sun of the Square, Selina will find herself further irritated. She'll be annoyed by the flies that follow the horses everywhere and she'll be troubled by heat and the loose hem on her skirt that keeps catching on her heels. Her thoughts will continue to produce soured memories of the ill-tempered reproaches she directed at Eliza, accompanied by Eliza's hurtful responses. She'll cross the street to the butcher's shop, recalling her own motherless childhood, wondering how an example might have helped—had her mother lived to offer one. With just the three children she shall have few chances to correct any mistakes—but will survive the risks inherent in further issue.

She shall wait to be served, reciting thoughtful and considerate arguments that she might have used with Eliza, and shall emerge with the weekly bill settled but her spirit still in turmoil.

~

It was not a childish matter to charge a pistol. You had to open the powder glove carefully and let in just the right amount, adding a little extra to the pan. You weren't supposed to spill any on the desk, but John wiped that away so it wouldn't matter. Then you had to get the shot in. His father could do it with just two fingers, but the point was to drop the lead ball into the barrel and follow it with the plunger. With the shot pushed hard into the gunpowder, it might stick for a while, but, his father had explained—before his mother had claimed John was too young—you had to keep the gun upright to prevent the ball just rolling out.

He replaced the case, wiped more powder off the desktop, closed the desk lid and sat cross-legged on the floor with the pistol in his lap. The cat curled her tail around his legs. Clearly, he was not too young. He had expected someone to come into the room and scold him but no one did.

Since neither of his two unmarriable sisters would take their part, he would need other actors. He stroked the cat's neck and asked, 'Atticus, how would you like to be Hardy? He was in charge of the flags.'

Atticus purred at the suggestion.

Sarah came calling along the downstairs corridor. 'John! Where are you? I have to take you to the meadow. Eliza says so.'

He hid the pistol under his tunic and called back, 'Can we take the cat and the hen?'

When Sarah appeared in the doorway she no longer needed to shout. 'Why d'you want the cat and the hen? And what are you doing in Father's study?'

'Atticus will be Hardy and Henny will stand for Collingwood, since neither you nor Eliza want to play.'

'Oh, John, for heaven's sake, come on!'

So he gathered his navy under Sarah's supervision and ferried them all across the road to the long-grassed meadow. HMS *Victory*, the old tin bath, floated imperiously by the river's edge and he found a bucket for Atticus and a saucepan for Henny to sail in. Conveniently, Sarah was not dedicated to her task. He coaxed her back to the house for a glass of milk and she stayed there with her story papers, presenting him his chance to set sail.

It should have been a grand affair, the send-off of the fleet, but his senior officers proved reluctant to take their commands. The hen flapped and the cat scratched and just getting them into the bath was wriggling with problems. He held them both tight, pushed off from the bank and once they were out in the stream transferred them to their respective ships.

'Atticus! That wasn't nice,' he said, rubbing his stinging wrists while the cat glared at him from her bucket. Henny flapped in her saucepan for a few moments, looking around at the water, but then she seemed to accept the inevitable and quietened down.

'Now, don't you alarm yourselves; there's nothing to fear from the water,' John said, checking the string that held the fleet together, 'Nothing to fear,' although the current had taken them—not quickly, but very firmly—carrying them to the middle of the stream and alongside the meadow. Soon the Solent would flow into the English Channel and they would be on course for the Atlantic! They would ride the weir like leaves!

'Nelson chased Villeneuve all the way to the Caribbean! The cowardly Villeneuve wouldn't fight!' John told Atticus.

His battleship interrupted him by wobbling again and he wondered how he might reach the riverbank if he wanted to.

~

Eliza looks up from her Bible. It is as though she heard a noise, but if she did, it is not immediately repeated. In the downstairs hall the clock ticks melodiously, and from the open window comes only birdsong. She bows her head to the Book of John once more, twirling a strand of hair from behind her ear.

Of course, it is simply impossible to concentrate with so many thoughts chasing around one's mind and in any case one cannot learn by reading alone—she ought to be *taught*, like her friends. But for all that, when she looks up again, it is because of a clear noise. This time she is quite convinced that she has heard something from within the house.

She jumps up, muttering, '… never any peace!' and with the book under her arm, descends the stairs in a flurry of classically trained steps.

Her sister Sarah is in the drawing room, feet swinging under the chair, bread and jam and a glass of milk laid out beside her story paper. Eliza leans against the doorframe.

'Where's John?'

She is expecting to hear that he's stealing food from the larder, but her sister is wide-eyed and wants for an answer.

'Oh, Sarah! You said you would look after him. I'm not paying you pear drops for this. Is he still in the meadow?'

'I *am* looking after him!' the younger girl says, jumping down from her seat, 'I think… he's in the meadow across the way. I only came back for a minute.'

'Forgot about him completely, more like. How could you leave him there?' Eliza stands aside and lets Sarah pass, out of the room.

'He's fine,' Sarah insists.

~

The walk home from the town centre will take Selina Warland twelve minutes and she will arrive a little before midday. Her momentary satisfaction will be destroyed upon finding the picket gate swinging on its hinges and it will frustrate her to think how many times she has told her children to be sure it is kept closed. Then she will happen upon puddles and wet footprints drying on the tiled path and her face will tighten.

To step over the water, she will lift her skirts an inch or so because she will have dressed that morning thinking of dusty streets and accounts to be settled, not puddles to be avoided. So doing, she'll dismiss the footprints with a variety of scenarios, all of which keep her three children safe—some river fowl that needed rescuing; a spilt bucket or an innocent game. She'll imagine John chasing his laughing sisters around the house in a good-humoured water fight and she will sternly and adeptly avoid the thought of anything more unfortunate.

She'll doubt herself, though, seeing green river weed on the steps by the door. She'll offer herself a heavy reproach for leaving Eliza in charge when she is still just a child herself, and to settle the matter—to seal the pact with fate and to completely banish the possibility of any misadventure—she will commit to never again leaving the girls in charge of their younger brother. And then she will enter the house.

~

Collingwood and Hardy allowed their squadrons to get out of formation in the bend before the weeping willows. Admiral Nelson, his one good eye still capable of spotting the slightest irregularity in his fleet, sent the necessary signals, but his captains disobeyed him. He was heard to sigh with exasperation.

'Villeneuve will blast us to smithereens if we aren't lively!'

He tried to reach over the side of his tin bath to manoeuvre Henny's saucepan back behind him, but the slightest act of imbalance made the edge of his tub dip towards the water's surface. All he could do was stare with naval disapproval as eddies in the river's bend sent Henny floating ahead with Atticus meowing angrily alongside.

And then, just when the fleet was at its most vulnerable, a call came from the crow's nest. The enemy was sighted!

There was nothing for it—he risked a capsize, but all the same, he leaned out far enough to wet his hand in the river's cold water and push for faster progress. It was his sister's voice. He could hear her shouting at him.

'Go away!' he commanded.

~

Sarah comes running back from the meadow, just like the prodigal sister Eliza knows she is.

'He's gone!'

A moment's fear and then Eliza is running through the front door and across the road. Down by the river's edge, the long grass of the meadow is trodden flat and strewn with abandoned playthings and seemingly random domestic items. There are saucepans, a picnic blanket, books, buckets, a model sailing ship, sheets, even a chicken basket.

'What were you doing?' she demands. 'That's the cat pannier! Where's Atticus?'

Sarah opens her face into innocent protestation. 'He was playing with her… her and the hen.'

'The hen? Oh my word! Whatever will Mother say? So you've lost John, the cat and the hen?'

'I haven't lost them!' Sarah shouts back. '*You* were in charge. Besides, John went off, not me!'

'Well, you can explain that to Mother. Where did they go?'

Sarah looks towards the river and Eliza follows her gaze.

'Oh no! He's not in the river?'

'There was a bathtub… an old tin thing he dragged across from the nursery sheds. He had it down by the water and was seeing if it would float.'

'And you let him?'

'No! He came back to the house. I told you!'

Sarah is beginning to get tearful and Eliza suspects that only a small amount of harshness will tip her over the edge. A feline, malicious curiosity gets the better of her.

'*Really*, Sarah… this is all your fault!'

With surprising predictability, Sarah breaks into tears. 'It is not! It's *your* fault and I hate you!'

Eliza shrugs it off. 'Come on. We'd better hope he isn't drowned already!'

She sets off marching through the grass, craning her neck over the reeds. As she rounds a clump of bulrushes, she gains a broad view of the river and her heart almost freezes.

John's head is visible above the edge of a tin bath that is wobbling in the water as he dips his hand over the side. Every time he moves, the tub seems to lurch into capsize, only to pull back at the last second. The cat looks—quite rightly—terrified. The hen will surely drown.

Sarah joins her, sniffing. 'What is he doing?'

'He's Nelson, of course. He's always on about Nelson, never stops about Nelson. Come on—we'll call him in.'

She runs along the bank, skirting the clumps of nettles until she reaches the path. 'John! Come here!'

He looks up, but his face is thunder. She's never seen him looking so cross. 'Go away!' he calls back. Eliza stands like her mother would: feet apart, hands on hips.

'John, you come over here this instant!'

Instead of answering he ducks into the tin bath and, after a little pause, re-emerges pointing something that he holds with both hands.

'What's he got?' Sarah asks.

~

Selina will be confounded by pools of water on the black-and-white tiles in the downstairs hall. She'll hesitate between panic and rage as she tracks the footprints up the stairs carpet, unable to draw any conclusions. She is susceptible to fears when already prey to guilt—she knows this of herself—so she'll provide her own reassurance.

She'll call out—of course she will—she'll use that summoning-questioning tone that is native to every English mother: 'Eliza? Sarah? John?' and when she hears a response, she'll close her eyes to keep a lid on the relief. Then she will realise that she has heard only two voices. And she will recognise something in their tone.

~

Lord Nelson had already suffered wounds that would have been fatal for many. He had lost both an eye and an arm, and there are those who claim he had premonitions of his demise at Trafalgar. Whether or not that is true, he was careless of the danger, standing clear on the poop deck as the *Victory* sailed into the melee. There they were, two ships of the line under full sail, drawing alongside the port beam. Nelson signalled his commanders.

'Line astern!'

The enemy hailed him, commanding him to heave-to. He shouted back his defiance and they hailed more forcefully. He adjusted his admiral's hat and barely whispered his command, 'Roll out the cannon!'

His father's pistol was still dry under the blanket and John was quite certain of himself. He was no worm, and Eliza might want him dead, but he would shoot her down instead and that would be the end of her. Then he would sail over the weir where his mother had said he could never go and she would see that he could, even if she said not.

It took both hands to pull back the firing pin. He had to grip the barrel with one hand, then lean right over it, using all his weight pushing down to get it to lock into place.

~

John might be pointing a pistol at her, but Eliza doesn't believe him for an instant. Her father does not keep the weapon charged and John most certainly hasn't the wit or strength to load it.

She stops on the river path and stamps her foot. 'I should be at Bible classes! Why on earth would Mother not let me go?' Then she raises her voice to shout out to the bathtub. 'John! Put that down! You'll hurt someone.'

Her brother calls something back, but it is incomprehensible. Suddenly Sarah is at her side, clutching at her arm and pointing down the river. Just before the weir at the sawmill, the River Allen passes under a clump of trees. There are thick, low-hanging branches that reach out over the water. The girls rush onwards, trailing hairbands and petticoats, and hop through the undergrowth by the riverbank. They've done it before, but never with such haste or with so few words: Sarah forms a hoop with her hands and Eliza uses it as a step. They jump up, then swing from branch to branch out over the water and are in place before John's flotilla reaches them.

'Why would he take Atticus? Or the hen, for that matter?' Sarah complains.

'I have no idea; Mother is going to be so angry with him. You grab the handles and hold him still. I'll pick him up.'

Eliza readies herself, but events do not bend to her will so easily. The branch is higher above the river than she had judged, so it is too far down to reach the bathtub. Sarah misses and John floats beneath them. Eliza quickly lifts herself over the tree trunk and lunges at him from the other side, but as she reaches out, she is confronted by that ridiculous gun. He aims it right at her and his face is a red ball of effort as he wrings both index fingers around the trigger.

He turns away, eyes clamped closed—as though he truly believes the gun will go off. Her heart leaps as she realises the danger is real.

With the loud explosion comes a light spray of wood bark that hits her neck, stinging her skin.

'You devil!' Eliza screams. 'You outrageous, murderous, unpardonable *demon!*'

She reaches out, flailing with vengeful arms, but John is paddling. Her chest is heaving and her nostrils flaring with anger and burnt with the stench of gunpowder. She stands on the branch looking down at the slow-moving river for an opportunity for revenge, but her gaze settles on the thin grey-green line by the mill. She can already hear the roaring of the weir—she can smell the damp air kicked up from its violence.

'Off!' she says to Sarah. Her sister jumps at the serious-ness of the command and they rush along the trunk of the tree. 'We have to reach him before the sawmill. He'll drown.'

Sarah runs alongside her with just the same urgency, but looks up with fear. 'He shot you!' she says.

'He missed,' Eliza explains. 'I'm going to murder him!'

As they race along the path, she is trying to imagine how she might reach her brother before the sawmill. If he could be washed close to the bank, or if the river might be shallow, she will find a way, but when she reaches the wood yard, her hopes are confounded. John and the cat seem impossibly far out. She could swim to him, but there is no chance of reach-ing him in time. The river is carrying him towards the edge with muscular intent—silvery and serpentine.

Where the water tips over the edge of the slope it smoothens out before rushing down to a constant roaring wave, where it turns into frothing turmoil. They call out, 'John!' tracking him from the timber yard, but there is noth-ing to be done now, and it is doubtful they can be heard. Two mill-workers in dungarees look up with concern, but it is too late.

Eliza has time to scream, 'Oh my heavens!' and Sarah, 'Oh no!' then John seems to notice them. He lifts his hand, thumbs his nose, and waggles his fingers.

'Oh, John!' Eliza mutters, sad—disappointed. She knows she could tell herself he deserves it; after all, he just tried to shoot her, but that's not the way she feels. Her last, desperate hope, as the bathtub reaches the fall, is that it might catch against the edge of the slope, but the water is too deep and her brother too light.

He salutes, sitting upright, then the tub slips over the edge and plunges down with awful speed.

～

She shall find her daughters sitting on the bed in their brother's room, soaked to the skin with water pooling at their feet, no sign of her son, and for all the years she lives, Selina will never again see such a look on their faces nor feel such fear for them. Their illnesses will alarm her, their marriages will excite her and she'll share their pain in childbirth, but not even in her graceful, thankful, dying days shall she revisit such a feeling of fear.

Eliza will speak first, her hair bedraggled and glistening wet. 'It was John…' she'll say and Selina won't know whether to command her to explain the outcome or hold her tongue that time might be stilled and she might never know.

'He took Father's gun.'

Her daughters will remain wide-eyed and helpless as she looks between them trying to understand the connection between the way their clothes are stuck to their skin and Richard's old hunting pistol.

'He fired it at us,' Sarah will tell her, her tone one of wounded complaint, as though the intent could be more hurtful than the bullet.

'Where is he?' Selina will ask, trying to keep an appearance of bravery. She'll find her mouth so dry the words will stick like paste. She will be refusing to consider the prospect of telling Richard the unfortunate fate of his only son.

Then the girls will turn to the bed they are sitting on and their mother will notice the motionless lump lying there, head covered by the blankets—inert. After all three rounds of chickenpox and measles, each bringing countless nights of life-threatening fevers, this is her most hated fear—that she might one morning encounter a child motionless in their bed.

She will pull the blanket back with her own hand, revealing the unmoving head, the thick hair still black with water, the ashen face. She will look down like she is gazing upon an impossible apparition.

Her youngest daughter will break the news. 'He's not dead!' she'll complain, as if her mother is overreacting.

Selina shall look back at her son's face, seeing his eyes for the first time, and Eliza will nudge him hard with her elbow. John, staring blankly at first, will scowl at the blow.

'Yes, I am!' he'll insist.

To the astonishment of her offspring, Selina Warland will respond to this claim by quietly sitting on the edge of the bed, reaching out to her children as if to gather them to her, and then bursting into tears. Her sobbing distress will persist for so long that all three of them—Eliza, Sarah and John—will combine in comforting her. But when the anguish of relief passes it will be followed by a rush of sublime anger!

In the years to come, when the tale is recounted, it will be remarked upon as much for the prodigious ferocity of Selina's temper as for the drama of events or the humour of John's self-certainty. Selina will never quite find herself able to laugh about the affair.

~

Admiral Lord Horatio Nelson was killed at the battle of Trafalgar on 21 October 1805. His statue was erected as the centrepiece of Trafalgar Square, London, and he became one of the greatest heroes of British naval history.

~

Atticus the cat swims to shore, creeps away and never returns.

~

The hen will surely drown.

THE WORLD'S END

~

Wimborne Minster, Dorset,
August 1859

The mid-morning sun had beaten the world into hiding; the fields stood motionless in the ripening heat and only the crickets raised a sound, filling the air with their cree-crick-cree-crick, making it seem all the hotter.

Bill and the chestnut mare were in the shade of the stable. He had a hand palm-flat on her shoulder as he brushed her quarters with a reassuring rhythm, the hiss of the brush marking long, drawn-out beats. Drops of sweat fell from his brow, splashing darker colours onto the cobbles, and when he drew breath, the scents of horse and straw stung his nostrils.

The mare flicked her tail in agitation. He kept to his rhythm. Then her near hind leg came up and smacked back down on the cobblestones. He hardly blinked.

'All right. I know.'

She was having none of it. She stamped a second time, the clatter echoing sharply from the farmyard walls. It seemed to cast her anger like a shadow on the hot stillness around them.

Bill stood back and straightened, and looked her in the eye.

'C'mon, Penny. It's naught. He'll be gone tomorrow.'

He moved closer to her and stroked her neck, while she bobbed her head a little. 'It's all right,' he told her. 'All right now.' Soon she was calmed, while the crickets still called.

He ran a hand over her muzzle, picked up the leather harness that needed waxing and ambled to the stable door. His eyes were way off on the clouds as he mumbled his agreement with the mare.

'You're right, though. Shouldn't be a-feared to zee us own brother.'

He reached over the door for the bolt, slapped it open and stepped out into the sun. And there he stopped.

There was a figure at the far end of the track, just coming though the gate.

He shaded his eyes and watched the man walking towards him.

'Here he is, then.'

As his brother approached, Bill had time to appreciate the changes that time had brought. It was a surprise to see such an old man. Cornelius's face was tired and lined and his eyes were squinting and small. He had nothing of Bill's weight or strength—his arms were thin and wiry.

Without removing his hat, Bill nodded a greeting.

'Corny.'

His brother stopped, a big grin showing his amusement

at Bill's reception. He shook his head, as if he thought Bill a hopeless child.

'You knew I was coming, then.'

Bill ran his finger over the worn strip of leather.

'I hears you're out by Stur.'

'Rooms at the World's End Inn.'

'Oh ar? They's having a good old get-together, is they?'

The smile faded from Cornelius's face.

'They've not seen each other for a long time. They're brothers, Bill.'

But Bill just hardened his jaw.

'Dare zay,' he conceded, relinquishing nothing.

A bead of sweat formed on Cornelius's brow, broke from the pore and trickled down his cheek. His tongue lapped it from the corner of his mouth and his eyes tightened.

'I was asked to bring word that your master, Squire Guthrie, requires his horse and trap.'

Bill twitched his head up, managing to show his faint disapproval with just the weight in his eyelids.

'Zay which? Bay? Chestn't?'

'Black stallion.'

Bill snorted. 'What's that, then? Women out there?'

'My master was entertaining Miss Emily Bankes, who has lately been joined by her sister.'

'"Lately been joined"? Sort o' talk's that?'

Cornelius didn't answer; he was sticking instead to the stiff formality of his task. Resigned, Bill turned towards the carriage house.

'Ha! "Lately been joined!" Come on. Th' can help me hook them up.'

Cornelius followed him and took direction from his

grunts and the jerk of his chin. They put a saddle in the trap for Bill's return, harnessed the chestnut mare and tied the stallion behind.

All the while they worked at it, Bill was watching his brother with sizing eyes, noticing the scar on his neck and the forefinger missing from his right hand. He couldn't deny his brother's honest efforts, but when he had to lift the canvas cover back on its shelf, Cornelius hadn't the strength alone and Bill all but took it from his hands. He sneered as he did it, feeling that alone stood witness for a range of failings, but Cornelius wouldn't meet his gaze.

And while Bill made fast the traces, his brother held the mare's bridle and talked to her like they were old friends. It was a relief when the trap was ready and they could climb aboard.

'Walk on then, Penny,' Bill directed, and the chestnut mare tugged them forwards before settling into an energy-preserving amble. Bill let her walk slowly. It was hot. The horses had to be spared for their masters and delivered untaxed.

Cornelius was smiling at the chestnut mare, while peering out from under his hat as if he had nothing to answer. Bill could think of plenty of accusations. He glanced sideways at his passenger as each new one occurred to him. They had descended St Margaret's Hill before either spoke again.

At the corner by the gateway to the hospital, there was an old man with a handcart and two dogs by his side. Bill drew Penny to a halt.

'Art.'

'Bill.'

'How's Jane?'

'Not zo good, Bill. But she's a tough old bird, she'll come a-right.'

Bill bowed his head with satisfaction and the old man whistled his dog away from the horse.

'Much on?' Bill asked. Art dipped his head back the way he'd come.

'Drayton's herd. Cassn't find else. Gertie'll harvest soon, mind, zo he'll zee us through.'

'Well, you send word if there's ought th' needs, now.'

'That's right kind of you, Bill. God keep 'ee.'

Bill just clicked his tongue to get Penny moving again and they resumed their steady rhythm. Cornelius asked after the conversation.

'Who was ill? His daughter?'

But Bill didn't answer. His sideways glance was full of contempt.

'Much as thee'd care,' he muttered.

Cornelius chewed his lip for a little distance, sweating, as they both did. Then Bill started shaking his head, unable to contain himself further.

'Your ma… Cried for a week, she did. Then another week when she hears you've taken to soldiering.'

Cornelius was hunched over on the driving bench, focusing on his boots.

'You could ha' just told her. You could ha' just a-said goodbye.'

His stare was demanding an answer, but nothing came.

'Couldn't you?'

Cornelius brought his head up and appealed with his hands.

'Bill, we had no time. Major Guthrie was told he could leave and join the army or stay and hang for murder. I had no choice.'

'He weren't told nothing! Who told en that? Pair of you just took off! He were a vool, and you were a vool for a-following. No one would have thought twice if you'd just stayed put.'

Cornelius had no reply and would not meet Bill's eye.

'Anyhow. That's why you left. What o' the next fifteen years when you sent no word, nor wrote nor nothing? Hey? You should ha' zeen your ma, Corny. You broke her heart, you. You, her favourite. Went to her grave weeping over you.'

Cornelius sat quietly penitent as the roadside daisies drifted by.

'Didn't hear nothing 'til old Healey come home one leg short of a cricket. Poor soul. And that were five year. You could have sent word, but no. And I'll tell you why. You've a cow's heart, that why.'

'I had no choice.'

'Cow-heart.'

'If they'd known where we were, they'd have followed. Guthrie made me swear secrecy. I swore, Bill. How could I have broken my word?'

'Bah! Broke your mother's heart instead.'

'I'd no choice.'

Bill had no answer for this. Instead he hunched over the reins and watched the road.

'Zo now you're back? On account o' that trial, no doubt.'

'Major Guthrie's name was cleared.'

Bill spat with contempt at this.

'That were years ago an' all. Pay much for his clean name, did he?'

Cornelius kept his gaze ahead—wouldn't look at Bill.

'He paid no one. He wasn't sure if it was true at first. It takes a long time for news to travel. I know what you think, Bill, but I tell you, Major Guthrie had nothing to do with it.'

'Zo who put up John Street's name then?'

'He confessed.'

'Bah! Confessed! John Street din't do nothing. How could he confess when he weren't there? He never wrote no letter. Never! An' they just tried en when he weren't there either. Shoulda hanged en when he weren't there 'n' all and had done with it.'

Cornelius looked sideways with a sort of hangdog expression. He wasn't arguing.

'I was told he went to sea?'

'Aye. That he did. Always had a hankering for it.'

'So who killed Buggermaster then?'

Bill turned to his brother with a hard, dark expression. Then he shook his head. 'Well, it weren't none of us. And it certainly weren't John Street!'

They drove out through Cowgrove and on towards Barford, nodding at the few other people they passed while the silence between them grew. Eventually Bill was chewing his lips, regretting his outbursts, uncertain how to retract his angry words.

'India was it, then?' he grumbled. Cornelius nodded. 'What's that like then?'

Cornelius lifted his head, chuckling as he looked up the road to review their pace.

'You've not been outside Wimborne, have you, Bill? Not past the World's End, I shouldn't think.'

'Nope. No reason to.'

Cornelius grinned as if there was humour in the World's End.

'If I told you what India was like, you wouldn't believe me.'

And he looked so pleased with himself, Bill wanted to push him off the side of the trap.

'You'd have to see it yourself.'

'Huh.'

'Ain't you ever wanted to? You've never even seen the sea.'

Bill shrugged.

'No reason to,' he repeated.

'But wouldn't you *like* to? Just to see a little more of the world beyond the Stour?'

'An' what's the whys of that then?'

'Why? Why to see things... to grow... for betterment, for self-improvement!'

At this, Bill raised his eyebrows, leaning away.

'Oh ar? Improvement is it?'

'Yes,' Cornelius insisted. 'Improvement.'

'That an improvement?' he checked, nodding at Cornelius's missing finger, 'Or that?' looking at the scar on his neck.

'No...' Cornelius conceded.

'Good. There's no need to lose parts, then? To improve the' self?'

'Lor' me, Bill. That was just the army. No, I'm talking of progress. D'you understand? Like the railways. Tell me you've at least seen the railway?'

'Zeen the station. That's enough. Stinky, noisy place.

Railway? Progress?' Bill shook his head. 'Look, zee thik field there? Week or so, it'll be harvest. Then he'll plough and lay zeed. Then he'll grow again and ripen and harvest again. It don't need progress.'

Cornelius was grinning and trying to interrupt, but Bill would have none of it.

'I seen your progress. Art Pugh and all his gang spent two summers in no work for they steam threshers. They's no food an Jacob's paying less for his harvest but can't sell grain for tuppence, and who the blue blazes do you think's improved by all that?'

Cornelius's mouth was hanging open as he looked around the landscape for his argument.

'That's politics, not progress.'

Bill grunted and left the words to the air. They sat, rumbling down the road without a word, before Cornelius picked up the point.

'That was him we saw earlier was it? Art? Have they all work now?'

'Zome o' em. There's em as burnt the threshing machines, they's in Australie. There's Ted Crick and Jerry wassisname—Thatcher—they's both hanged. Chapman's Common got took over by the Vicar Cookesely and his board. But aye, there's work. Banke's banned they machines. God knows there's enough others that hasn't.'

'Jerry Thatcher, hanged?'

'Ar. Bloody vool.'

'You don't think they should have burned the machines?'

'Don't think they should a' got themselves caught. The rest of it? Don't make sense to me...'

At which point they suddenly lurched forwards because

Penny had stopped still in the road. Bill fumbled, rushing to resume his seat, coughing self-consciously, as though he was embarrassed by the antics of the horse. He cleared his throat before clicking his tongue.

'Get on now, Penny.'

The horse moved off, but Bill was still rolling his shoulders to reposition his shirt. In the corner of his eye he could see Cornelius smiling as he looked from horse to driver. They drove for some time, travelling in slow, steady silence with Cornelius watching his every move, and to bring it to an end Bill pulled up a wrap of buttered bread and two apples from under the seat. They ate as they drove. Eventually Cornelius gestured at the chestnut mare with his half-eaten apple.

'How does she know where to go then?'

'What? Penny? Does as I tells her.'

'But you've not so much as twitched those reins since we left the stables.'

Bill shrugged, not knowing if he had or not.

'Does she know your thoughts?'

Bill turned sharply on his brother, squinting from the sun that was over his head.

'Zee, you make that sound like it's wrong. That's what you do. Somewhat I's never zo much as thought on and you make it out as it's wrong. Sure enough, Penny understands me, much as an old mare might, which is better'n zome folks, but it's just as it is. That's all. Just as it is. There's no need for you to come an start a-making it right or a-making it wrong, no need at all.'

'I've not said a thing about it!'

'No, but there's plenty as is said as needs no words. An' that's the truth.'

Cornelius stared back at him while Bill's gaze jumped from his brother's face to his tunic and back. Then Cornelius's wide-eyed look of wounded innocence melted into earnest concern.

'Bill, I'm sorry. I meant nothing by it, really I didn't. You and I, we just live different lives now, that's all.'

Cornelius licked his lips and searched the floor for something more to say.

'I've seen things, see. I've seen a lot of the world. It's exciting, Bill! That's the matter. I've always been excited by it. And you would be too, if you'd seen what I have.'

'You reckon?'

'Of course! Look, I'll tell you what. What if we go up to the railway tunnel once we're done with the horses? See the train go by at full steam?'

Bill shifted on his seat and rolled his shoulders.

'Can't think why I should need to see that.'

'No, Bill, no need. But it's a thing to see, truly it is.'

Bill looked up at the broad thatch of the World's End Inn curling into view. He started wrapping the remains of their meal.

'If it means zo much to 'ee.'

~

They prepared the horse and carriages for their two masters and Bill was surprised how familiar the major was with Cornelius. Compared to Bill's own master, the major was almost friendly. Once the courtyard had stopped echoing to the clatter of hooves, he remarked on it.

'Part of the family then, eh?'

'He treats me very well,' Cornelius agreed.

They both knew the same could not be said of the Squire, so his change of subject was welcome.

'Come on. I'll get a flask of cider from the landlord; we'll go and see the train pass by.'

And so they did. Cornelius carried the stone flask and they walked until they reached the embankment where they sat to watch the tunnel mouth for the train.

'So what happened with Chapman's Common then?' Cornelius asked.

Bill smacked his lips, savouring the cider.

'That's all beyond me,' he muttered. 'They vixed up zome board, the vicar and that. But virst no one's allowed no trapping or shooting, and then no pasturing. Can't zay as I understands it. Foreshare's gone, zee? Not common land no more like that.'

'And the threshing machines?'

'Ar, well, that's all about of the same time. Sprung up like daisies they did. Suddenly there's a whole crop of men, Crick, Thatcher, Johnson, they've no work in the harvest and Cookesely has taken over the common zo they can't even put a cow out to pasture, much less shoot a rabbit for the pot. No surprise they took to burning the things.'

'And what happened?'

'Word comes out of Lacy. Old man Bankes puts bans on the lot o' em. No machines on his land. Course there's plenty of others that uses em, but there's not many as cares to cross en. Not many at all. Hard times, though. Hard times.'

He took another bolt of cider and handed the bottle to his brother. There was a blackbird on the hedge behind him, standing tall and chirping loudly, and a small flock of starlings were pecking at the grass around them.

'What you do for Guthrie, then? Tickled his teats with somewhat?'

Cornelius peered over the cider bottle and into the past.

'Calcutta. He was set upon in the street. I grabbed the cutlass that was swung at his neck. He kept his head, I lost my finger.'

Bill looked at the stub, trying to imagine.

'That India, was it?'

Cornelius tried to smother his grin.

'Yes, that was in India.'

They looked up at the hill as the birds took flight and the shrill whistle of a train broke out of the tunnel.

Bill found himself tensing, wishing he'd fled with the starlings. It was a ghostly sound to his ears—screaming and unearthly.

'Here it comes,' Cornelius muttered, but nothing could have prepared Bill for what came next. The thing exploded from the mouth of the tunnel. There was first a puff of smoke and then, like a terror-stricken horse bolting from its gate, a huge black cylinder screamed into the cutting, blowing out immense breaths of smoke, one on top of the other, roaring, thundering and burning at once.

Bill jumped two feet back up the slope in the instant it appeared, scrabbling for grip.

'Oh, the devil!' he cried. 'The devil!'

The train's whistle blew again, and Cornelius was looking up the slope at him, at first amazed but then reeling with laughter.

Bill didn't let go of the grass, as though his grip on the ground might save him.

'What?' he demanded. 'What's zo funny?'

He stared after the train and its carriages as they curled beyond a growth of young beech trees, trying to see anything human in it. Cornelius was lying on the grass, tears of laughter glinting on his cheeks.

'I've a cow's heart!' he called. 'Just look at you!'

It took a while for Bill to see the funny side. At the start he was certain his brother had meant to humiliate him, but Cornelius was so full of apologies that Bill softened. He explained over and again how the train had come at such a pace as he had never seen, until he could finally laugh at his own surprise. As they walked back to the inn, they were chuckling together.

But the sun was sinking low and the shadows stretched too long.

'If I'm lucky, Bill, I'll have some time tomorrow. I'll call in and see you if I can. I should like to see where Ma and Pa are resting.'

Bill nodded, keeping his eyes on his brother's golden-lit face. He told him of the churchyard and the flower-covered corner. They shook hands before they parted.

By night-fall Bill and the chestnut mare were back in the cool of the stables. There was barely enough light in there to pick out the walls, but he knew the place for everything and had time enough to feel his way. The horse was steaming, for the night's air had turned cool, and the vapour caught what little light the moon was yielding. Penny raised her near hind leg and stamped on the floor.

'It's all right, now,' Bill muttered, 'it's all right.'

And when everything was hung in its place, he shuffled

to the stable door. His hand reached for the bolt, he slapped it open and stepped into the night.

His eyes focused on the stars as he mumbled his agreement with the mare.

'You're right, though. Progress? I hope they knows what they's about.'

SHAKESPEARE'S THIEF

~

Wimborne Minster, Dorset,
June 1860

Thomas Dewbury was comfortably invested in one of the first-class carriages, where he was trying to ensure his lines were not influenced by the rhythm of the train on the tracks. As he spoke, his fingers played along the quilted material of the handholds.

> 'And, most dear actors, eat no onions
> or garlick, for we are to utter sweet breath; and I
> do not doubt but to hear them say, it is a sweet
> comedy. No more words: away! Go, away!'

Jasper looked up from the *Illustrated News*. '"*Nor* garlick,"' he said.

'What did I say?' Thomas asked. Jasper and Cecilia both answered him.

'"Or garlick."'

He flicked the strap away. 'For heaven's sake!'

Since Jasper meekly lowered his eyes to his paper, Thomas chanced a peek at Cecilia. Her face was pristine and her hair sublime, but her newspaper blocked his view of her décolletage. He turned back to the flickering countryside.

"'And, most dear actors, eat no onions nor garlick...'"

A small herd of heifers was running from the train, alarmed, as a cloud of steam and dark smoke loomed over the meadow.

'Oh, tosh! A plague on Bottom!' said Thomas.

Neither Jasper nor Cecilia looked up from their reading.

'I say it would be a damned sight easier to settle on my lines if Willy would settle on my part!'

He was aiming the comment at Cecilia, who had Wilson Barrett's ear, but Jasper answered first. 'Hasn't he told you? I thought you had Oberon?'

'He has still to decide,' Cecilia said, her lips and neck remaining deliciously poised. 'If he makes his connections from Dublin in time then Maclane shall be my Oberon, and Thomas here...'

'I shall have the undoubted privilege of playing your Bottom,' Thomas concluded.

Cecilia's lips twitched a little, though her gaze stayed level. Jasper, on the other hand, rolled both his eyes and his head. 'Oh, for pity's sake, you two! It's like a music hall.'

Cecilia finally smirked. 'Quite right; Thomas, bring your attention a little... *higher* if you would.'

He stifled a laugh, wholeheartedly ignoring the angry stare from Jasper and indulging himself, instead, in the mischievous gaze of one of the country's leading actresses. Sadly, she broke away to lean her head towards their prompt. 'Are you acquainted with Mr Maclane, Jasper?'

'Michael Maclane? Yes, I am. And if my word has weight, you'll trust him with nothing.'

'Oh really?'

'Maclane... is a thief!'

Jasper made his declaration with such force that Thomas and Cecilia raised their eyebrows in unison. Their expressions stayed open, inviting more details, but Jasper reclaimed privacy behind his battered paper.

'You've worked with him before?' Thomas asked.

Jasper flicked the paper straight. 'Princess's in fifty-eight. He's not to be trusted.'

They looked at each other. 'So says our prompt!' Cecilia said. Thomas nodded, fighting to stop his gaze slipping down from her face. She saved him by precisely positioning her paper once more. He turned back to the window as hedge followed field followed hedge and Bottom's dull lines echoed in his thoughts: *I will roar that will make the Duke say 'Let him roar again...'*

'Oh look, here's hope for you, Thomas,' Cecilia said. 'It says the majority of his race bring their fate upon themselves. They are all feckless, apparently.'

'Feckless, are they?' he answered as a clump of trees blurred past, catching her reflection in their darkness.

'In the majority.'

'Well, there's nothing to say, my dearest Cissy, that Maclane's not of the minority—then he'd be the opposite of feckless. And what's that? Fecked?'

At this, Jasper cast down his newspaper with final severity and did his best to storm out of the carriage without treading on Cecilia's skirts.

'Oh dear,' Cecilia muttered once he'd gone.

'Well, what *is* the opposite of feckless?'

Cecilia peered at him straight-lipped.

'You're too hard on him, you know.'

The train rocked them to one side and back.

'I don't solicit his attention, Cissy...'

~

The Station Hotel in Wimborne Minster was far better than might have been expected. The carpets were new, ran the lengths of lamp-lit hallways and were as brightly coloured as any in London; the saloon shone with brass fittings and a mirror behind the bar was as broad and proud as one in a Piccadilly food hall.

'I don't know what you were anticipating,' Jasper grumbled, swirling the brandy in his glass. 'We weren't going to stay in cowsheds.'

'I'd no idea a provincial hotel could be so well appointed. We could be in the West End.'

Thomas turned on his stool, admiring the surroundings. 'Except for the view of course. Did Cecilia say she was coming down?'

'Everyone's coming down; we're all dining in the same place,' Jasper answered, knocking his glass on the bar a little too forcefully. 'Why are you so anxious for Cecilia?'

'I'm hoping to find out which room she has,' Thomas said. He couldn't stop himself from grinning, even though he knew Jasper would be annoyed, but Jasper was dismissive.

'Room fifteen. She's sharing with Lilly Farren.'

'Sharing? Lord. Who booked...? Oh, no, of course: you did. I say, do you get along with Lilly? You couldn't entertain her for an hour or so this evening, could you?'

He glanced at the stairway and then back at Jasper. Several other members of the company were descending, and the saloon was filling up. Jasper was scowling.

'So that you can bed her milky-breasted roommate? God's teeth, I hope Maclane shows.'

'You think he'd take her from me?'

'Perhaps. But that's not my aim. "An ass's nole I'd fix upon your head."'

'Ah. Very amusing.'

Thomas turned to the stairs again but this time only because everyone in the room was looking that way. Wilson Barrett was descending with an actress each side of him, and Cecilia and Lilly following behind. Lilly caught his eye, but Cecilia was talking over Barrett's shoulder.

'"By the pricking of my thumbs..."' Jasper muttered.

Their manager stopped on the stairs, stretched his arms wide, grinned, and with a booming voice offered them a welcome that laid claim to the whole county.

'It is such a *proud* thing to see this company gathered. And we have such an honoured part to play! Tomorrow we shall start the preparation for our presentation; we'll build our stage and set our scenes! We'll have a couple of days to make ready and on this Sunday, Miss Emily Bankes will marry Major Guthrie and, following the ceremony, we shall perform William Shakespeare's *A Midsummer Night's Dream* in the grounds of Kingston House!'

They were, he told them, the finest Shakespearean actors on the stage (Jasper quietly observed that all others were out of season) and they were all to dine that evening at the Laing's Hotel in the town square—by implication at Barrett's own expense, although according to Jasper,

Guthrie had suggested the venue and offered to foot the bill.

Barrett finished his address by holding up a hand to acknowledge the subsequent applause. At last he completed his descent of the stairs and the room broke into bustling, chattering energy as everyone headed outside for the carriages. Thomas, observing the melee of embarkation, decided to walk and was surprised by Jasper's decision to join him.

The evening proved warm and the scents of flowers and grasses graced the air. Thomas was also charmed by the ease of the town with its tidy shops, neat bridges and a river so thin it was barely more than a stream. Near the centre they admired the church—the Minster of the town's name—and Jasper related how the Norman tower housed a venerable chained library. Thomas could not but wonder how he came by such information.

'Do you happen to know when the last train arrives?'

'The last train? Around midnight I believe. He could still turn up tomorrow, you know.'

When they reached the town's central square they encountered Lilly outside Laing's Hotel, pacing the pavement, trying to keep her skirts above the road's soil. She noticed them as they crossed the square.

'What-ho, Lilly, you look like you've lost someone.'

'Hello, Thomas. Out for a smoke; I'm a slave to Sweet Threes. Hoping I might find somewhere secluded. Never mind. I should warn you: Maclane's here. Inside already.'

'Well, how did he do that? We've just walked from the station; he didn't pass us!'

'Arrived much earlier. Got it wrong about the hotels, been here since lunchtime.'

She had a sorrowful, sympathetic expression that he immediately wanted to escape, so he pushed the door open to the saloon and stepped into an atmosphere thick with tobacco smoke, beer fumes and chatter.

Maclane was immediately recognisable. A tall man who could have been the dashing gentleman lover of a light comedy. Cecilia was in the small group of people around him.

Thomas's eye fell greedily on the smooth skin of Cecilia's chest, but then he realised how straight she stood; how her bosom was prominently displayed. His attention jumped to her face.

He could not have been more alarmed. Her cheeks were lightly flushed, her gaze fixed upon Maclane, and she was open-mouthed, like an innocent child, utterly enraptured.

'Oh, by all the saints!'

Barrett saw them over the crowd and called out.

'Jasper! Thomas! Come! There's someone to meet!'

He introduced them with lively enthusiasm. It might have been a little easier if he had not seemed to find the whole encounter amusing.

'You're taking Thomas's part, Michael, so you'd as well be nice to him.'

Michael Maclane was very civil, calling for drinks for Thomas and Jasper while making certain they were accommodated before pursuing his own line of conversation.

'Now I'm to offer my Oberon, Willy, which is a wise choice, and you've told me we are to perform... this Sunday, is it? Which gives us time enough to rehearse, eh?'

Their manager looked at the floor with a slow nodding of his head, but without yet choosing to answer. Michael

Maclane was more than capable of addressing his own questions.

'We all know our lines, and Jasper, I am sure, will marshal armies to build a stage that rivals creation. But all the way from Dublin, Willy, I've been asking myself the most important question of theatre, of poetry and of drama.'

On cue, Wilson raised his head and asked, 'Which is?'

Maclane lowered his tone to a threatening grumble. 'When do we get paid?'

The company roared with laughter as Barrett smiled and gripped his actor by the arm.

'Miss Emily Bankes, you know, has made two very wise judgements. Very wise. Her first is to admire the theatre. And she is an avid admirer. Avid. It is at her request that we have transported an entire London theatre to the provinces. And her second act of great wisdom concerns Major Guthrie. It is said he returned from India with the wealth of a maharaja, and Miss Emily Bankes, through her great and deep wisdom, has chosen to marry him!'

The company laughed again and Barrett spoke over the hubbub to assure Maclane and everyone else that their post-nuptial payment would be prompt.

Drinks arrived on a tray. Cecilia passed a pint glass to Maclane and, as he took it, his thanks were offered through a lingering glance—but without words. Thomas groaned.

~

Kingston House—or Kingston Lacy as some of the locals called it—was an admirable building: tall, broad-windowed, and made up to look like something Italian or Venetian. When Thomas followed Jasper to the south-facing grounds he came upon a lawn that was alive with work. There was a space where carpenters had set up and were busy adjusting set, scenery and stage, and an array of tents that housed make-up, costumes and props. Men and women marched purposefully in every direction and small groups of actors stood in clumps reciting their lines. Then there was the stage itself—an enormous construction with a tented awning stretched over it. And these were not the only preparations; clearly there was a feast for guests on the other side of the lawn, where a large field kitchen belched steam into sky.

Thomas wandered through the melee until he found his fellow actors but before he could start working they were all called to Barrett's side. Miss Bankes wanted to meet them. As they waited for the presentation, Thomas found himself beside Cecilia, who was momentarily separated from Maclane.

'Have you still got your purse?' he muttered.

She looked puzzled.

'Oh, I'd forgotten. Do you think I should worry?'

'They say the devil has a certain charm…' Thomas suggested.

He didn't say much more because Emily Bankes was particularly keen to meet the actresses whose faces she had seen on posters and cards. But he consoled himself with the hope he'd sown a seed of doubt.

That evening the company dined as each saw fit. Cecilia was nowhere to be seen. It was bad seeing her with Maclane, but it was worse if they disappeared.

'Oh, let her be,' Jasper advised. Thomas had no choice but to comply.

He found Lilly in the hotel bar and she told him, 'You have admirers who might be more constant, you know.'

'Jasper, you mean?'

'He's one.'

She didn't identify any others and Thomas had no desire to press her. To himself, at least, he could bluntly admit that no one had breasts like Cecilia's—and Maclane was clearly stealing them away from him.

He thought there was something in Cecilia's sadness on the afternoon of the final rehearsal and was cheered by the thought she might have found fault with her Irish beau. It proved to be hope without fulfilment.

~

Act 2, Scene 1. Thomas crept in from behind the stage and leaned his head against one of the tent poles, part holding, part hanging from the canvas drapery. The faces of the audience were lit cool white by the moon and orange by the kerosene lamps, while their eyes and mouths were little dark Os with wonder. They were transfixed; watching while midges and moths whirled unnoticed past their faces, more utterly transported to Athens than any of the professionals on stage.

The major was with his new bride in front of the whole wedding party—echoes of Theseus and Hippolyta. Their watching eyes danced left and right as the fairies joined the stage. Thomas stood aside as two taffeta-clad girls clumped up the steps beside him, trying to be as light as spirits.

When they'd passed, he looked up and saw only Cecilia and Maclane on stage. And they saw only each other. Her voice was like a bird's trilling.

'What, jealous Oberon?—Fairies skip hence.
I have forsworn his bed and company.'

There was a light in her eyes that wasn't reflected from the lamps, nor did it come from Titania. As Maclane moved, Cecilia courted the stage around him and he puffed his chest and kept his shoulders towards her. 'Tarry, rash wanton. Am I not thy lord?'

'Then I must be thy lady,' answered Titania, and she paused. It was only the slightest pause—a beat left in the summer night's air—probably not enough to have troubled Jasper, but Thomas caught it. 'But I know when thou hast stolen away from fairyland...'

Her field had been ploughed, as Shakespeare would have had it. It was in the pause, and in their argument too—the way they danced without touching, held each other's gaze, the way she lifted her chin as a challenge to Oberon and his head rose to meet her gesture. They reeked of each other. It was infuriating to imagine when they had found the time, or the privacy, but there wasn't any doubting it.

'Didst not thou lead him through the glimmering night
From Perigouna whom he ravished;
And make him with fair Aegles break his faith,
With Ariadne and Antiopa?'

Thomas drew himself behind the curtain and retreated to the backstage tent. He could still hear Cecilia and Maclane's melodic voices above the hushed urgency of the stage-hands and the timid accompaniment of the orchestra. Lilly stopped by his side and touched his arm.

'You all right, Tom? Look a little pale.'

'Feeling sick. Have you seen those two?'

'Oh... yes. Not discreet, are they? Never mind, eh? Listen, you'd best be ready. You're on soon!'

Thomas sighed and nodded. He made himself ready. He got to the stage side for the cues and stepped through it all. He peered out from inside the ass-head mask and looked in vain for the sincerity Cecilia had shown Maclane.

'And thy fair virtue's force perforce doth move me
On the first view to say, to swear, I love thee.'

But she didn't mean a beat of it. Her focus fell on his mask and her voice was thick with actor's guile. Thomas played it out and watched with wonder when at the end the audience stood, shouted and whistled at the final curtain. They'd had displayed to them true emotion and then three couples acting out thin lies and they were too provincial to demand more than the fakery.

He found a bottle of champagne the moment the post-performance celebrations began. With help from the bottle, he tried to pull himself into better cheer for Wilson's sake, if nothing else. The major entered the tent with his fussy little wife and Wilson started introducing everyone. Thomas stayed out of it until the greeting was inevitable.

'Major Guthrie, this is Thomas Dewbury, who played Bottom.'

'Ah! Capital!'

'Thomas: Major and Mrs Oswald Guthrie.'

'This is the chap with the ass on his head, my dear!'

They both chuckled and nodded and Wilson ushered

them on around the tent followed by the coterie of leading players, still in their fictitious pairs—except for Maclane and Cissy, who were truly lost in each other. Thomas studied the champagne bottle for want of anything else to do. The label named an importer in Wimborne Minster.

Lilly leaned close to Thomas's ear to avoid being overheard.

'If Barrett becomes any more obsequious, I'll have to assume that Guthrie actually shits money!'

She also wanted to know if Thomas knew of somewhere she might smoke a cigarette without scandalising the whole county.

Thomas found her a quiet storage tent, brought a brace of glasses and a half-full bottle and shared a couple of Sweet Threes with her. When the bottle ran out, he found another, and they carried on talking and talking. Lilly could chatter and giggle about anything and Thomas was happy to stay with her. Eventually someone started trying to take the tent down and they came out to find the party over and the stage struck. A prelude to dawn was showing through the treetops. A fine dew was settling on everything.

Jasper called out to them wearing his stage-management frown.

'Where have you two been? I've been searching all over. Lilly, darling, the wagonette is leaving from the front of the house right now. Thomas, you and I are in the little carriage. There's a man waiting for us.' He turned and looked at the half-packed tents and piled-up equipment. 'Everything else will be dealt with in the morning. Come.'

Thomas walked with him as Lilly hurried over the lawn, then he was surprised to see a gathering still occupying the terrace. He picked out Cecilia's silhouette with the shawled figure of Mrs Guthrie. Jasper coughed apologetically before he explained.

'The leading actors—Titania, Oberon, Helena, Lysander, Hermia and Demetrius—have been invited to stay in the house for breakfast.'

Their shoes crunched as stones squirmed on the gravel down the side of the house. On the drive a single small-hooded carriage waited and a stocky man in a broad-brimmed hat soothed the horse.

'We're the last for the Station Hotel,' Jasper announced.

'At th' zervice, zir. If thee'd care to take th' zeats.'

Jasper looked at Thomas, chewing at his lip.

'We're, um... the last for the Station Hotel?'

'Th' zeats, sir. If 'e please,' the man repeated, gesturing to the carriage.

'Seats! Yes, of course.'

Thomas climbed up first, wishing above all else that he was back in London. Jasper followed, closing the carriage's tiny door before the driver hunched himself on the bench before them where he sat, muttering at his horse and smelling of hay. They set off at a funereal pace.

'Anything amiss?' Jasper asked. Thomas brushed some tobacco ash from his cloak and wondered how he could possibly answer.

'No, I should gauge it all perfectly... fine. Nothing amiss. Everything is... as might be expected.'

The carriage rumbled down the long drive, the seats rocking gently. 'Jasper, am I cruel? To you, I mean. Lilly thinks I am utterly heartless. Even Cecilia mentioned something.'

Jasper's chin went up in the air, his lips twitching, and at the same time his cheeks coloured quite distinctly. 'I have never asked you for anything, have I?'

'No. Not at all,' Thomas answered, 'and I've always assumed... I mean... you have other opportunities?'

Jasper looked away and Thomas followed his gaze up to the fading stars before the answer came. 'They're not so common as you might think. And more dangerous than you can possibly imagine. What is more, they do not always come from sources that are entirely desirable.'

He had a way, Jasper, of waving his whole body when he was summoning up the most precisely appropriate words; it was as if he was forging them from the very air.

'Major Guthrie, for example, was married this afternoon...' he said.

'Good Lord, no!' Thomas replied.

Jasper merely raised his eyebrows.

'But surely—I'd have thought he was singularly attractive?'

The prompt scowled at him, glancing again at their driver. Before answering.

'Are you quite senseless? Consider his situation! "Spotted and inconstant man." The simple folly of it. He's bait for the gallows!'

Thomas considered the point while glancing into the woods following the sound of chattering wildfowl. Jasper most certainly lacked his own taste for chasing from blouse to blouse, so perhaps such constancy mattered.

'She wasn't the youngest blushing bride, was she?'

'I suppose not.'

'He was accused of murder, so Lilly has it. Spent years

in India not knowing his name had been cleared, while she pined away here waiting for him.'

'Hmm. Very romantic,' Jasper muttered as they both looked blankly from the carriage.

'And of course, it was Miss Bankes's uncle who was—somewhat famously—outlawed to Italy on account of some poor guardsman.'

'Pity the guardsman.'

'Well, quite. Not sure how anyone would have thought the major a murderer, though. Doesn't seem the type at all, especially if what you say is true.'

Their driver shifted on his seat, rolling his shoulders, and Jasper gave a stern sideways glance. As a consequence, they completed their journey without further conversation. The carriage took a slow, ambling ride down the hill into town as dawn rose over the valley's meadows—it was quite beautiful.

In a style typical of Jasper, when they reached the hotel, he suggested to the driver that now the man might rest. The old hand muttered something about being already late for 'milkin'' and when he clicked his tongue the bay mare drew the carriage away—without so much as a twitch of the reins.

'One could almost be lulled into admiring the rural idyll,' Thomas suggested as they climbed the carpet-softened stairs.

'You've drunk too much,' Jasper answered.

A little later, lying in his hotel bed, Thomas stared across the room at Jasper's sleeping form and sighed for his own part. Perhaps he really was too cruel. Not that there was anything to be done about it. If Jasper had been stifling sobs as he fell asleep—and he fancied that was what he'd heard—it would have no more consequence than keeping him awake. He couldn't do anything remotely similar. The equivalent would have been to continue to dote around Cecilia even though she was claimed by Maclane. Half devoted, half resentful. It made no sense.

The following day he read. Jasper went back to the house with other crew members for their final get-out, and the rest of the cast either packed or rested, recovering from the night's revels. Cecilia made no appearance and Thomas made no effort to seek her out.

When he came downstairs on the Monday, the front doors were latched open and trunks were piled up, ready for departure. Cecilia strode across to him from the breakfast room. She was dressed for travelling in a velvet jacket with thick skirts and an impractical bonnet, but her eyes looked puffy and sore. When she took his arm, there was real urgency to her grip.

'He's asked me to go to Paris!' she whispered. Thomas drew a blank. It seemed inconceivable she was seeking his advice; his support even. For a moment he thought of Jasper.

'France?'

'Of course, France. Where else?'

'Cissy? Well, don't tell me you're sheltering the thought at all?'

Her mouth was left hanging open for a moment and hope's light fell on Thomas when she frowned and shook her head.

'No... that'd be ridiculous, wouldn't it? I've only just met him.'

'That's a reason; and in its company is the possibility he

might murder you, steal all your belongings and throw your body from the train...'

'Oh, Thomas, he's not like that... Where is Jasper? Oh Lord!'

'You want for Jasper's advice? You are wanting indeed.'

The company of players was gathering in the hotel lobby and on the pavement to its front, and each person that passed Cecilia glanced at her and then looked anywhere but at her a second time. Wilson Barrett's great frame appeared in the mottling windows as he used his booming voice to direct the movement towards the station.

Then Michael Maclane came in from the corridor, approaching Cecilia with a sigh of resignation.

'I must be away, Cissy,' he said, not even looking at Thomas, 'I've a carriage for Poole—then a boat to Wey-mouth and on.'

Thomas could see the smooth sheen to his cheeks where he had just shaved. Cecilia's hands, which had been weigh-ing on Thomas's arm, lifted themselves and were transferred to Maclane without decency's pause.

As the couple walked towards the door, Thomas cursed quietly and picked up his travel bag. Jasper came in from the street.

'She's not going with him?' Jasper said.

'You knew he would ask?'

'I thought it probable.'

Maclane stowed his bag on the carriage, then stood with Cecilia's hands in his. The part of the company that watched them staring into each other's eyes did so with brows raised, while the more conservatively minded carried on with their travelling preparations as though nothing was happening.

'They're going to kiss in the street, I swear it!' Thomas muttered, although he was wrong. Maclane mounted the carriage and Cecilia came striding back towards them, tears draining from her face. With a backwards wave, Maclane dismissed the gathered audience and the carriage moved off. Cecilia stopped beside them.

'I warned you he was a thief,' Jasper grumbled, still fiddling with keys in his pockets. Cissy looked offended.

'He's not like that. He stole nothing from me.'

'Did he not?'

'No, he... Oh!'

That moment, it seemed to Thomas, changed everything. Jasper showed a librarian's knowing turn of the head while Cecilia could not have managed a better expression of astonishment if she'd suddenly discovered herself to be standing naked.

She raised an arm and called out, but the carriage was already beyond earshot, so Cecilia turned to her only plausible hope, Wilson Barrett.

'Willy! Please! Stop them!'

The big man frowned most severely. 'You cast me as Theseus? And you are now whom? Hermia?'

'Oh, never mind, just stop them! I implore you!'

Barrett ground his teeth for a moment, swallowed, then drew breath.

'MACLANE! HALT THERE!'

It was a wonder the horse did not bolt at the sound of it. Barrett could have shifted the leaves off the trees with his voice.

The carriage stopped, the mare stamping her foot in protest, and Maclane and his driver turned in their seats.

Cecilia meanwhile had pulled her bags from the piled-high luggage. She gripped her skirts and ran—without effecting much more speed than if she'd walked—the full distance to the waiting carriage.

As she lifted her bags on the back, Thomas sighed heavily. He watched her climb up to the seat, then turned to the prompt.

'Well done, Jasper.'

~

The fields that followed the hedges that followed fields held no more interest for being seen in reverse order. They were not even recognisable from the train journey outward. Jasper was reading silently, sitting opposite and rocking gently with the motion of the train, but Thomas had read every available book and Lilly was inaccessible in the second-class carriages.

'Paris,' he said. 'Some Finian conspiracy: that's why he's going there.'

'Fenian.'

'Precisely. Poor Cissy—she'll be ruined.'

'You never know, it might be the making of her.'

'I hardly see how. And what about Maclane anyway? Is he like your major? Is he… you know?'

'No,' Jasper answered firmly.

'Well then, Jasper, I don't understand. You called him a thief and you were right, though I'll confess I thought you meant watches and purses…'

Jasper kept his eyes on his book. Thomas leaned a little closer. 'So who could he have stolen off you, I wonder?'

The prompt finally looked up through his darkened brows.

'Michael Maclane had an affair with my mother,' he grumbled.

'Ah.'

Thomas sat back. Jasper had such a wiry frame and weary outlook it was easy to forget how young he was. The countryside flashed past.

'That's a love triangle Shakespeare left untreated,' he said.

Jasper turned a page. 'Hamlet,' he muttered.

THE VOICE O' STRANGERS

❧

Atlantic Ocean,
May 1861

The table by John Street's bunk was built into the fo'c'sle bulkhead, leaving only one end supported by a thick, dented leg. The retaining lip was chipped and rough from the attentions of bored sailors' knives; there was a tally carved along its length—reaching sixty in gates of five—and the outline of a mermaid near the corner.

As the *Pilgrim* pitched in the Atlantic swell, Jansen's tin mug slid the length of the table, chimed against the end, and slid back. The rest of the port watch was asleep, and above the creaking of the timbers and the snoring of the watch, the mug made no sound at all. Still, John pulled himself up and when the mug next skated across to him he caught it. From the bunk above, Jansen grunted gratefully then returned to his slumber, but John still stared into the darkness. Mug or none, how should he sleep now the captain needed killing?

The lad Bute had thought nothing of an invitation to

Bible readings. Why should he? Not fifteen; curly-haired and wide-eyed as a lamb.

'You read, young Bute?' the captain had asked.

'Aye, sir. My mother's cousin taught me.'

'Why then, come for Bible readings in my cabin. Eight bells of the morning watch every Sunday.'

Bute hadn't hesitated to say 'yes, sir' and the captain had hardly mumbled, 'Anyone else care for Bible readings?'

John had jumped with his answer, 'Aye, sir,' making Captain Morden's oversized eyebrows darken his face with a scowl.

'Street, isn't it? Know your hornbook, Street?'

His *hornbook*? The question cast him as a child in the church hall.

'I... I do, sir. And I's a God-fearing man, sir.'

The captain had very-welled and turned his back and Bute had stared like a coney puzzled by a gun.

John turned on his side, still holding the mug while rubbing an old wound on his knuckle. It was so easy to remember the Bible lessons in the choirmaster's rooms; the close heat from the coal fire, the revulsion and the fear. Harder to forget. He could curse away the memories, but they would not budge; not the feel of the choirmaster's sweaty hands, nor the sight of that bald pate plastered with useless dank hair, nor still the terrifying weak-lipped grin or the musky, wet-leather smell. None of it would shift. Never had.

He pushed off the blanket and sat up to clear his head of it. No one should do that to a boy, nor allow it to be done. He'd sooner kill the captain than let Bute suffer the same ordeal, and that was it—his knuckles ached with the need for it—the captain had to die.

After a few minutes trembling with anger, he lay back on his bunk and the *Pilgrim* rocked him gently as it plunged south through the night.

~

On the first Sunday at eight bells he was by the foremast with the knife in his sock. 'Seen a ghost?' asked the second mate. He swallowed and the second mate laughed, 'Not seasick, surely, Street?' John Street shook his head—he never had been seasick. Bute appeared, standing with his feet too close together and smiling uncertainly.

The captain had combed his hair and he grinned when they entered his cabin. He offered them seats and warm drinks and Bute accepted everything. John wanted to tell him. He'll smile, for sure, but then there'll be touches and little secrets. He'll seem kind, and you'll wonder why until at last the price will become clear. Then you'll feel like you've been steeped in vileness.

He took his seat, deciding whether to strike at once or bide his time for the perfect moment. The captain asked John to read and leaned forward, and for a moment it was going to happen—Murderer John—but when the Bible touched his hands, he let the chance slip away. Morden pointed to the passage and John focused on the words. *And it came to pass after these things...*

There had been a time, many years before he took to sailoring, when John had read his Bible every night, when he'd known chapter and verse for every episode. He knew this passage. He read it proudly: "'An' it came to pass av'er these things, that God did tempt Abraham, an' said unto him, Abraham: and he said, 'Behold, here I am'...'"

He glanced up to see the captain smiling broadly, almost laughing, but there seemed no reason. Perhaps he had already decided a way of getting rid of John, or maybe his intention was somehow hidden in the passage: "'An' he said, 'Behold the vire and wood: but where is the lamb for a burnt offering?'"

John looked up, but the captain simply nodded—still with that wretched smile on his face—and asked Bute to take over.

O but Bute had a reading voice that sang.

'Abraham said, "My son, God will provide himself a lamb for a burnt offering." So they went both of them together. And they came to the place that God had told him of and Abraham built an altar there and laid the wood in order and bound Isaac his son and laid him on the altar on the wood.'

The captain glowed with pride like the boy was his own. 'The lad reads well, doesn't he?' he said, and he meant something by it clearly enough. "'... And Abraham stretched forth his hand and took the knife to slay his son.'"

John's leg twitched and the captain seemed to raise his brow. "'... the Angel of the Lord called unto him out of heaven and said, 'Abraham, Abraham': and he said, 'Here am I.''"

Aiming to take the Bible back, John held out his wide-fingered hand. 'If y' please...'

Morden could frown all he wanted; John knew what he was doing. He was very familiar with this passage. "'An' 'e said, 'Lay not thine hand 'pon the lad, neither do thou any thing unto 'im: for now I know that thou vearest God, zee-ing that thou hast not with'eld thy zon, thine only zon vrom me.'"'

But the captain only nodded, took the book back and finished the reading. Then he leaned back in his chair, stoked his pipe and talked at length about the sacrifice of Isaac. Bute picked at threads in his breeches and the *Pilgrim* pitched on through the Atlantic until the forenoon bell. Like one of those time-draining afternoons in the choir-master's study.

When they emerged from the cabin, he was still not a murderer. He strode across the deck, the boy by his side.

'John, have you rounded the Horn before?' Bute asked. The *Pilgrim* was on a port tack, yardarms three points to the wind.

'Rounded th' Horn? Why's that then?'

Bute skipped to keep pace with him. 'I wondered... is it as dangerous as they say?'

John stopped and looked at the lad as though staring could teach him. 'There's plenty more dangerous 'n the zea, boy.' But the lad looked back without an ounce of under-standing.

He ate his meal pondering Bute's likely fate. He would meet his corruption one way or another, that was for sure. If not by Morden then between the thighs of some toothless whore forced on him by a drunken crewman. And who was to say her ministrations would better suit him than the cap-tain's? After all, there'd been plenty of Minster boys who'd made light of their Bible lessons. Perhaps it was only Bute's coming from Sturminster that caused him to care, but still, he put the knife in his sock when the next Sunday came.

They read of Jacob's vision. *And he dreamed. And behold there was a ladder set upon the earth, and the top of it reached to heaven; and behold the angels of God ascending and descending upon it!*

Bute joked that it sounded like sailors climbing the shrouds; something the captain found so funny he ended with tears in his eyes. Bute giggled self-consciously and John observed, allowing himself a smile.

That week they crossed the Equator and watched dolphins play in the bow spray. They read of Joseph's coat and the brothers—Minster choirboys—who sold him into slavery—cruel, educated young men, dark-eyed with betrayal, whose sport was putting bruises on choristers' arms.

The week after that, heading into the South Atlantic, they bent on storm canvas. They'd already repaired the ratlines, varnished acres of wood, replaced stays and greased chains, so now they prepared for the Cape Horn tempests.

The bad weather came on the first dog watch the following Saturday. Seas towered behind the *Pilgrim*'s stern and the captain stayed with the helmsmen night and morning. They worked their turns, subduing the flailing sheets in the rain, ending each watch exhausted and soaked. The captain roared at any helmsman who let the course wander and Bute, who had taken to John's shelter, wondered at his ferocity. In the quiet of the fo'c'sle, John explained why, using his biscuit to demonstrate. 'Zea's always trying to catch 'er, push 'er round. An' if she goes…' His other hand swept over the crust that was now sideways on. 'Bangen girt wave'll broach 'er.'

Bute looked aghast at the biscuit. 'What then?'

John shrugged. 'She vlounders. We drown.' Bute was still

horrified by the biscuit, so John put the whole thing in his mouth. From his bunk above, Jansen laughed at them.

'At last, bumpkin! Someone who can understand dat strange language of yours!' he said.

'Dorzet lad, i'n' he?' John answered, ruffling Bute's hair. 'Best of this storm, though; no more Bible reading. Not 'til we's round the 'orn, shouldn't think.'

But his calculations proved wrong. The captain sent his usual Sunday summons. They had to dodge the breaching waves to get to his cabin, jumping into the lifelines as water swept across the deck. Consolation came from the black stove's warmth.

'I'm not a superstitious man, lads, but a storm is no cause to relinquish our Bible-reading.'

They read from Samuel II. The story of David and Bathsheba. *And David sent messengers, and took her, and she came unto him and he lay with her.*

John blushed at the captain's choice of reading, while the waves hammered at the hull. Everything groaned and creaked to overwhelm their words. *Set Uriah in the forefront of the hottest battle, and retire ye from him that he may be smitten and die.*

The captain's dark eyes were full of intention as Bute raised his sweet voice nearer coarseness to battle the noise. *But the thing that David had done displeased the Lord.* Was John to be pushed to the forefront, lost to the seas? He studied Morden's eyes, but the captain stayed solemn. Fear grew in John's breast like a warning buoy clanging in the fog. He rubbed his aching knuckles.

'Will the storms get any worse, Captain, sir?' Bute asked.

Morden laughed. 'Let's hope not, eh, lad? But you know

what they say? Below forty south, God cannot help you. Below fifty south… *there is no God.*'

He leaned in close as he said this, face like a gally-bagger. The boy stayed wide-eyed. 'Where are we now, Captain?'

'Forty-eight south, my lad, forty-eight south.'

John stepped into the gale, his temple throbbing as he pieced together the captain's intentions. He was sailing them into Godless seas so no one could stand witness when he put John in the forefront, like Uriah. Then Morden would have Bute for himself. He'd said as much.

The *Pilgrim* pitched deep into a trough as he and Bute crossed the deck and John had to pick the lad up and throw him into the shrouds, barely leaving himself time before the seas came over the bulwark. When the decks were clear they jumped down, but the knife caught on John's boot and cut into his leg.

He burst into the fo'c'sle shoving the door out of his way.

'Moses! It's like tending lambs!' he spat. Sitting in the bunk, he pulled the knife out and buried it beneath the blanket. Bute, in a nearby bunk, looked up with frightened eyes and quickly turned away.

The storm went on, day and night. They weathered it well at first, but its ferocity grew. The night when it cracked the hull, John hadn't been asleep two hours before they were called into the howling darkness to deal with a loose topgallant. Seas like monstrous shadows rose and fell all around them while the sail flapped wildly above. They climbed the shrouds and fought for control of the canvas, struggling for grip with fingers numbed by the cold.

The old masts were throwing them up like corn to be

threshed but there came a sudden pitch that signalled a mountainous wave. John wrapped himself round the yard-arm, shouting at Bute to hold fast, and he felt the *Pilgrim* yawn forwards as she fell into the trough that came after.

She must have dropped a full yardarm's length, and smacked the sea with such a force that John's legs slipped from the lines. It was a deliverance that the bow emerged from the water. Three tons of foaming brine, white enough to see, were sweeping the decks before John was upright. Like the others around him, he recovered his grip on the canvas and they looked left and right to catch their rhythm and then, as one, hauled on the canvas and continued to pull it in—someone else, the second mate most likely, would be checking the damage.

It took two hours to get that topgallant sheeted in; desperate work, but without the steerage they'd have been like John's biscuit and they knew it. His arms were weak with strain, but they'd not made the deck before the call came from the mate, 'Man the pumps!'

The *Pilgrim*'s crash from such a height had cracked something. They muttered about the luck it hadn't splintered her and pushed the capstan gratefully, though it was dawn before they were called off. They got to their bunks with limbs like wet leaves as the starboard watch took their turn. They were, as the captain had said, all working together, and Jansen slapped John's back. Young Bute looked hollow-eyed, but he didn't know the danger he had avoided.

'Don't worry, Bute, worst of it's over. We'll be into Stanley now.'

Bute looked back at him with hope all over his dimly lit face, tempered with very little understanding. He didn't know of Port Stanley and probably hadn't realised the hull was cracked. And it was way beyond him to see how he'd been saved by the need for repairs.

All the men were grumbling as they found their bunks. Jansen was the only other one with enough understanding to look satisfied. 'Least ve'll get some sleep. He von't turn for Stanley 'til we're sout' of it.'

John grunted and crawled into his corner. Jansen was probably right.

As if in tribute, he dreamt of Amsterdam, its gabled warehouses and narrow streets. It had stunk of fish that last spring he was there.

The dawn was steely grey and sharp cold. The men were staring for'ard as they climbed the shrouds. They coughed their way into the rigging, relieved to have seen the back of the storm, but those who knew this passage were troubled by the dark shape on the horizon.

It couldn't have been the Falklands with the dawn on the port—they were heading south. And it could only have been South America if you ignored the bearing and the port tack. As John edged out onto the yardarm, he nearly lost his footing for staring, but there was no mistaking it. Jansen was shocked.

'Gotdamn Stateneiland! Vot the man doing?'

'He's a-tryin' a kill us all.'

'Ve'll never make it!' Jansen insisted.

'Never make what?' Bute asked.

'Never make it round de Horn,' Jansen said.

'Hull's leaking. We should be harbouring for repairs,' said John.

'Leaking?'

'Where 'ee think a-pumping's vor? We're a-zinking, lad!'

The crew was alive with gossip and no one could see the captain's reason. The men worked their watch in fear as the weather deteriorated and their pessimism grew. At the start of their next watch, seawater washed through the fo'c'sle door as soon as they opened it and they had to wade onto the deck.

Then the wind shifted against them. It strengthened and started howling like something alive. An hour into the watch the topgallant split, leaving great lengths of canvas snapping in the gale. When they'd dealt with the sail, they manned the pump, leaving barely enough energy to drag themselves back to the fo'c'sle and eat. In the back of his mind John still meant to use the knife, but there was nothing he could do from the rigging.

The storm went on another three days, seemed to abate for a few hours, then started again. They pumped until they were hanging from the handles, mindless with fatigue. They ate biscuit and slept four hours at a time. The first mate had taken to shouting at the captain, but it made no difference. Morden showed no fear—not of the mate, not of the seas, not of God. He smiled.

Day followed night as the *Pilgrim* tried to make its way west. After another three days on the port tack they risked everything in the dangerous manoeuvre of going about and spent three more days on the starboard tack. Then they did it again. Port; starboard; all the time pumping, pumping, while the *Pilgrim* sat ever lower in the water.

John woke suddenly. He'd seen the captain and choirmaster standing in the vestry, the choirmaster saying, 'God will provide himself the lamb for a burnt offering, my son.' Then he said, 'The lamb he'll provide is the *Pilgrim*,' but Morden had started laughing. 'Below fifty south *there is no God!*'

He shook his head and realised the first mate was telling them the main fore-royal, their last topsail, had torn itself to shreds. All hands came on deck, but the wind was monstrous. John had never before had to pull himself along the bulwark to make headway against the wind. They crowded round the mate, shouting.

'We can't go up in this!'

'You'll do as you're damn well told!'

But as they argued, the main royal mast cracked, then bent, then carried away. A tangled mess of ropes and splinters were left flapping in the wind.

'Now you have to get up there. That lot'll bring down the main mast!'

The mate started ordering them aloft to save the rigging from beating itself to pieces and to set some sort of sail to give them steerage. They climbed, knowing a loose grip would see them carried away.

John was soon by the topmast stay, high above the deck and trying to figure out how to clear the mess. The thick collars of his reefing jacket were fluttering like leaves, blocking his view, and the *Pilgrim* was so low in the water she looked four parts sunk. He had the strength still, but his mind was beaten. He stared at the thrashing, tangled ropes without comprehension.

Jansen edged towards him, shouting and pointing to a line. They each took an end and began drawing it back, pulling in a flailing strip of canvas, at the end of which was a broken block. The captain, standing on the quarterdeck, was watching—peering right at them, making John feel like Uriah at the forefront.

He and Jansen both had a strong grip and they tied off the rope, working gradually closer as they brought the canvas strip under control. But the shorter the line, the wilder became the thrashing. When they almost had it, John reached out, leaning over the yardarm. The flapping canvas slapped his hand away. Jansen snatched at the rope, shortening it and clearing John's view of the captain, who was smiling up at him: Uriah. The block flipped again, the rope shortened, and the block crashed into John's temple.

His feet slipped from the lines and he felt Jansen's grip on his jacket. He had a rope under his shin and his bad-knuckled hand had a half-conscious grip on the yardarm.

'COME, BUMPKIN! Raise yourself!'

He shook his head, lifted himself and got his feet on the line. The block obliged by swinging into his catch like the tin cup on the table. Sea spray mixed rain with the blood that poured from his head.

Once the topmast was lashed into place, John set his mind to the next task: murder.

He had to fight his way down the rigging, battling the *Pilgrim*'s attempts to shake him off by letting go of nothing without first gripping something else, then he pulled himself through the waters that washed across the planks to the quarterdeck. *That thing David had done displeased the Lord.* But there was no Lord here.

As he approached, Morden called out to his fellow helmsman and pointed to port. The *Pilgrim* broke the next peak and John saw what he was pointing at: in the distance, a line of darkness above the jagged peaks; a wave larger than anything he'd ever witnessed.

He met the captain by the helm as a huge sea boarded them from the starboard bow. He and Morden lunged for a handhold as the weight of water pulled at their legs, but the helmsman hadn't seen it coming. John watched him being washed to the bulwarks and reached for the wheel in his stead.

Now John was alongside the captain and they fought with all their weight to keep the helm from spinning out of control. Morden was within easy reach, but to leave go of the helm was to leave go of the ship. 'Did you see it?' the captain shouted as, together they edged the wheel round.

'I zeen en!' John answered, and his answer echoed his earlier warning to Bute: 'Bangen girt wave!' The *Pilgrim* was slow; she had precious little steerage and the hull was sitting ever lower in the water, but she responded.

'We're a-zinkin'!'

The ship edged further to port and the captain raised his head to search for the oncoming monster. His face and hair were dripping with water, his eyes had withdrawn behind his brows. With one arm still bracing the wheel, John felt for the knife in his pocket. They crested another swell the size of a church and they had a view once more of the oncoming fate. It was a wave that dwarfed everything around it.

'To port!' roared the captain, leading the wheel. The *Pilgrim* ducked into another trough and the captain turned and called as loud as he could, 'All hands! Make fast!'

For when they rose up, cresting the following wave, the trough appeared like a hole in the sea. They pitched forward, dropped, then the bow plunged underwater, emerging only as the monstrous wave rose above them, darkening their view.

It drew the bow up and then pulled it up further. John first braced himself against the helmsman's stand then gripped the wheel, then leaned against the deck. He cursed himself for having spared the captain when they still could have made Stanley. But though the ship all but stood on her stern, she recovered, coming level at the crest. John and the captain struggled to their feet. They both stared into the terrible trough that followed the wave. The lip had knocked the *Pilgrim* sideways and now she threatened to plunge down side-on. It would surely be her last motion.

The two of them pulled hard to starboard as the ship started to gain pace.

'Hold there!' called the captain as the bow came around, then he heaved it back to port, John following his lead, to straighten her. In such weather the wheel weighed against them and they scarce had the course before the poor *Pilgrim* hit the wave behind. Water smashed through the bowsprit and roared at them. It was a murderer's last chance. The seas beyond looked normal in comparison, as though the monster had flattened everything.

John stepped away from the wheel, forcing the captain to take the full weight of it. He felt for the knife in his pocket and focused on Morden's back and he'd have made himself a murderer if he'd only seen the seas that came over the starboard bulwark. As it was, they caught him from behind and swept him under the captain's legs. For a moment, with his head underwater, John had the captain's weight on him while water dulled everything to a few thumps and creaks, but the knife was never used.

When he got out from under the captain, he felt himself being carried with bashes and scrapes by the current. Nothing fell to his grasp until a mesh caught him. He grabbed at it, found ropes in his hands and pulled himself above the surface as a great mass of water tried to suck him away. With an anchor on the ratlines, he saw a hand emerge. The captain had a grip on nothing; the torrent was washing him towards the open, eternal sea.

John grabbed the hand without thinking. Only when he had it in his grasp did he realise what he'd done and what it meant. The warm, desperate grip of the captain had its own message: against all the fearful rhythm of the saying, God was here. Fifty-six degrees south. God was here because God was in them both.

The current hauled at the captain, loath to give him back, but John now felt as though he had returned to himself and he hauled him in—pulling with all his might until the water drained away.

When it was done, Morden lay on the deck like a landed fish. Slowly he raised himself to his knees and looked at the sails. 'To the helm!' he croaked, and they staggered, dripping, across the deck. When they reached the wheel, they pulled at it together, in the same direction, without a nod.

'Man the pumps, Mr Edwin!' the captain hollered.

'She's still a-zinking, Captain!' John shouted. 'Needs bailing with buckets an' pumps an' everything!'

The captain looked over the bulwarks at the sea level then back at John. There might have been something in his eyes that showed a soul, unlike the choirmaster's. Something.

John's stomach turned with fear for what might have been. Morden turned to shout. 'Mr Edwin! All hands to the pumps! Those who can't pump are to bail. I want for empty bilges, Mr Edwin!'

So they pumped. They bailed and pumped. They worked at it like the wind itself was driving them and after two hours the weather started improving. Soon it seemed likely they were pumping out more than was boarding; it spurred them on.

By the next dawn, the *Pilgrim* was riding higher on the waves. The weather grew kinder still and they were able to make a clear course southwest and get aloft to mend the damage. By that evening the sea behaved as though there had never been a storm. A stiff nor'westerly allowed the mate to tell the port watch off for some rest. Three days later they changed tack. They had rounded Cape Horn.

~

John was asleep when Jansen banged on the fo'c'sle table.

'Vake yourself, bumpkin! Cap'n vants you for a choirboy.'

'Wha'?'

'Says it's Sunday. Time vor Bible-reading.'

John swung his feet from the bunk. The fo'c'sle floor was only damp now, no longer a constant washing puddle around.

When he knocked on the captain's door he was greeted by a smile. Bute broke into a grin when he saw him. He looked from the boy to the captain and back again.

'Good to see you again, Street. Thought we might resume our reading. If you're agreeable?'

He nodded and took his seat. Bute was still looking happy, so he also threw a nod in his direction. It was clear the two of them had been in here alone.

'I was telling our young apprentice how a seaman can sometimes be called upon to haul his captain back from the teeth of a tempest.'

'No more'n his duty, Cap'n,' John answered, rubbing his nose. The captain handed him the leather-bound Bible.

'Perhaps you'd like to choose the passage.'

John coughed, then turned to the book of John and found Chapter 10 because it was the passage he knew best. 'When I were a lad, my brother axed our pa how he should know as the Bible speaks the truth. Now we had sheep in those days. Whole flock o' em. An' we all knew as how they sheep'd come when Pa called—but not no one else. Only en. Zo he read us this: "To 'im the porter openeth; an' the sheep 'ear 'is voice: an' 'e calleth 'is own sheep by name, an' leadeth em out. An' when 'e putteth vorth 'is own sheep, he goeth before them, an' the sheep vollow 'im: vor they know 'is voice. An' a stranger will they not vollow, but'll vlee from 'im: vor they know not the voice o' strangers." An' when I heard that, I knew there were truth in it.'

Captain Morden stared at him with a straight face and dark eyes. 'Amen,' he said.

~

He was in the topsails after the reading. The seas were still restless and burly, but John was at home where the masts threw him up and down as a father would his baby. The lines would catch him the moment the bow cast out a bloom of white spray.

He was about to descend when he turned to look back at the dark sky on the southern horizon—where there was no God but the God you carried with you. His focus shortened and fell upon the hand that gripped the rope—and the old scar curled around on his knuckle in the shape of a scythe; a curve, almost a question mark.

It had been caused when the choirmaster's tooth had lodged in it. He'd been smashing his fist into the man's lifeless face so hard that amidst the flying blood a tooth had come away, embedded in his skin. It was years 'til his hand worked properly again. The best part of his anger had come from entering the church to find the man already dead.

Still. He'd been through all that now and the world was a different place. Bute was safe, the captain hadn't needed killing and John was no murderer. Ten years was enough. There was a friend who once said he'd make sure the return was safe, so he'd go back after this trip. Back to Wimborne; back home.

ART'S LAST LAUGH

~

Wimborne Minster, Dorset, October 1862

T'were a wager, zee. 'Twix George and I. George were the type to take a wager on most anythin' but I wanted to zee Art laugh again. It come about beens they wooden vences out on Netherwood Leaze had rotted away zo I tol' Squire Guthrie how I'd take George an' Art Pugh to help I fix em up.

George and me is a-comin' up on Art's place when I tells en. 'He's had a right rare time over the years,' I zays. 'Lost a child to the pox, another to poison, his two daughters gone into service, never hears vrom his son. And o' course Jane died last winter, and cap it all there's no work. He gets dribs and drabs here an' there, but there bissen no life to be had no more. Ain't heard Art laugh in years.'

George don't answer, zo I zays, 'Reckon not even you could make en laugh.'

'Oh ar?' he zays. Full o' hisself is Georgie. Zo avore we gets to Art's place, we've a tanner on it. Virst to make Art laugh.

Zo we's standin' by the gate an' out comes Art, then George—beggin' your pardon—but George lets rip this baggen girt vart. No doubt it were rude, but George's laugh is a-catchin'—a right hobble—an' it were that loud, zo he an' I are near weepin' wi' laughs.

Art—poor trimmer—he's lookin' at us through those thick old eyebrows of his, a-scowlin' an' zerious an' that old poppy of his is stood azide, en not knowin' whether to bark or 'owl. Art just takes his 'andcart by the 'andles. He zays, 'We a-vence-mendin' or not?'

Us headin' up the road in the thin autumn zun. George and I still a-gigglin'. Art an' his dog, grave as a tomb.

I offers en a chunk o' bread. 'Dewbit?' I zays. I were a-thinkin' how skinny he's lookin' and vrom the way he tears into that loaf, zeems he's not had much to eat lately. Course, I never know'd how bad it were. George offers en another apple, an' aver he's scoffed that too you can zee the change in en. Different vace. I thinks to myself—*Don't mess with an 'ungry old farm hand.*

'You remember the Stickman, Art?' George axes en. Art grumbles back. He remembers. Donald Stickman. Were the pastor who taught us all our hornbook. Zome o' em had Ellis, but he were a different cup o'tea. Zundays in the hall. Spindly little gawk-hammer, Art calls en.

'Gawk-hammer, were he?' George zays, an' he reminds us how funny Stickland looked that time his pony took lame and he zaddled up his nirrup. 'Remember en ridin' round town in that gown-coat of his, veet scruffin' the groun'?'

I laughs at the memory, and George is a-chucklin' to think of it, but Art stays grim. 'Man were a ninny,' he grumbles.

Zo George remembers the time old Healey got stuck up a tree. He thinks it good enough f'r a laugh, but Art counts Healey a vool for gettin' hisself up there. 'Only had one leg. Should ha' stayed stood on it.'

George don't give up, though. He brings back zo many old stories. Zome folks I'd forgotten an' all the daft things they done. But Art—he don' think much of any o' em.

Zo we gets to the leaze an' all the way across we's a-dancin' round avoidin' they cowpats to get to the other side, where we starts work on the vence.

Then me an' Art's layin' the lugs out an' George starts up with tellin' gags. One av'er t'other. The wife who never varts in her husband's lap, all that zort o' stuff. Molly and Jim, this and that. Gag av'er gag. Not a zingle one o' em raises zo much as a smile vrom Art. He just looks at George like he's de-da.

Hours this goes on. We'm vixed about-of ten lugs o' vence an' we're packin' up—still a-dancin' round they cowpats. We's a-pilin' broke lugs back in the cart an' George zays how he could ha' been in the army on account of how strong he is. He lifts one of they lugs wi' one hand—I couldn' a done it—but Art rolls his eyes like George was makin' his brags.

Zo I waves George back a step, axin' if he could lift it over his head—an' he takes two steps back and raises the lug. Can he do another? He steps back again and—sure enough—he trips an' valls backwards. Ends up on his arse in a cowpat.

George gets up a-swearin' and a-cursin' and vor a moment I was a-feared it's all gone riggy. Then the stench reaches us.

'Aw!' cries Art. 'Aw my! You don' half pong!'

That's when Art starts laughin'. George is ruddy in the vace, he's that angry.

'That weren't funny!' he zays, but Art disagrees.

'Oh it were!' he zays. 'It really were!'

An' George is chuckin' they lugs in the barrow, covered wi' muck an' a tanner down an' Art's laugh gets louder an' louder. The more he laughs, the more George looks ruddy, an' the more Art laughs. Carries on all the way home, it does. George cheers up a moment, Art chuckles and George comes over all mad again. Quite the day, it were.

Zad though.

Weren't more 'n a week av'er that, Art took to his sick-bed.

We buried en on a Monday in the rain. Zad day. Zad as 'ey come.

There were only one thing I were glad of. I were stood there watchin' the rain a-patterin' on his canvas and I happened to recall that look on his vace—the light in his eye—when George landed in the muck. It were Art's last laugh, but I were glad of it.

THE ALDERMAN IN THE SNOW

~

Wimborne Minster, Dorset,
December 1862

They came in their millions in the late afternoon.
Snowflakes. A silent nursing party, descending breathlessly
and sinking the town into early night with their white comfort; each one unique, each one a paragon of conformity. This
snowflake fell straight, swerving only in the last moment. It
missed Charles Ellis's hat, whirled past his ear in a curlicue
of motion and lit upon the arm of his overcoat, snagged by
a fibre.

Charles had started coughing almost as soon as he
stepped out into West Borough. He coughed until he was
wheezing and was still catching a breath when his attention
was stolen by the exquisite ice crystal on his sleeve.

It was tiny. Twinkling needles that branched out,
stretching with such delicacy it seemed he had discovered
another world in miniature. He was trying to understand its
whole shape, to understand the pattern in the multiplying
branches when, as though obeying some hidden direction,

every arm of the snowflake folded—and it melted into a tiny droplet.

He'd barely time to register his surprise before his chest went into spasm again, enslaving him with a symphony of coughs. They built from minor spasms, growing their intensity until he could not move for coughing, could not breathe for the effort of breathing. Leaned against the lamppost, unable to think. Five, six minutes. Maybe more.

When at last it eased, he was leaning over, and he stayed still for a moment, breathing tenderly, keeping his eyes closed as he waited for the tension in his chest to subside. When he felt safe, he opened his eyes and began to look around. The evening seemed to have darkened, the snow thickened. And on the ground at his feet, a coloured contrast to the universal white, lay a sinister red spot. A perfect circle embedded in the snow, larger than a fleck and red as a sore. He sneered at it, wiped his mouth and checked the back of his hand.

There was nothing to be done. He picked up his bag, threw it over his shoulder, glanced once more at the regrettable blot and set off through the snow, turning left into the dimness of Smith's Lane.

When the brick back walls ended, he followed the shadows; across Westfields, tracking a guess as to where the path lay, grumbling to himself as he went.

'… never should have written it…' he said, then he looked about to check there was no one but the night to hear his thoughts overspilling. He walked on, holding his tongue for a while, lifting his feet high out of the snow, planting them again with each step. His lips began twitching and, once more, his thoughts broke out.

'… not yet fifty years,' he said, and he stopped, staring at nothing, then just as abruptly, resumed his progress. He pushed through the gap in the hedge by St Margaret's corner, grumbling, '… hanged for a murderer,' turned left near the top of the hill and climbed the steeper path to Stone Farm. 'You owe me…? Tell you what you're owed…'

On through the snow and darkness, he achieved the steady, determined progress of one who is used to making his own way in the world. '… diagnosis… alderman? Ha!'

The coughing overcame him again just as he reached Bill's place. A small dog came out while Charles spluttered, and it stood in front of him, barking itself off the ground. Eventually a shadow emerged from the loft rooms, telling the dog off for quiet.

'Who's that?' came a voice, but Charles could only wave a hand. A few seconds more and Bill was beside him asking, 'Mr Ellis? Charlie?' and Charles found himself being helped up the steps.

The warm air and a glass of small beer served to calm his lungs and he was soon heating himself by the coals while Bill scowled and fussed about him, shuffling around the cramped room to make space.

A shovel-load of coals went on the fire to add heat to an atmosphere that was already close and, while Charles still struggled to find breath enough to talk, Bill took his coat and hung it on the back of his door. 'All huckmuck wi' snow,' he pronounced it, and set about beating it clean. Charles, handkerchief at his mouth, couldn't help but smile.

'Huck…' he wheezed, 'huckmuck?'

Bill smirked self-consciously.

'My old ma used to zay that. "Look-zee em breeches.

All huckmuck!" she'd zay. I were thinking on her when that poppy started up.'

'Don't recall you owning a dog, Bill.'

Bill kept on brushing Charles's overcoat as he explained, 'Art Pugh's. Said I'd look av'er en, zee.'

Charles nodded. Through several iterations of breathless speech, he told Bill how he'd been sorry to hear about Art. He watched his old friend put away the clothes-brush and squeeze into a chair the other side of the fire.

'Zad it was,' Bill said, 'but his heart broke when his wife were took vrom en. Tough old bird, but when Jane was gone, old Art...'

Charles nodded again. They both had their memories of Art even though Bill was a far closer friend and for a few minutes they exchanged old tales: his devotion to Jane and the struggles they had faced, clinging on to farm labouring when there was no work to be had, their sons emigrating.

Charles lifted his chest in deep, cautious breaths while the firelight played with the shadows of Bill's frowning face.

'You go about in the cold with a chest like that—you'll not be long a-following en.'

'You may well be right, Bill,' he said, but it did nothing to ease Bill's irritation.

'What you doin' owlin' about this late, anyhow? Playin' Z'nt Stephen?'

'Exactly that, as it happens,' Charles said, and he reached into his bag to pull out a bottle of brandy. He watched Bill's widening eyes and broke into laughter.

'Every year,' Bill said, 'you bring I one o' they damn bottles, an' it's still a surprise!'

It wasn't a stretch to pass the bottle over, but Bill had

turned to open a small chest from which he retrieved two small glasses and an identical bottle. Charles would not have believed it still contained anything had Bill not poured out two glasses immediately.

'That's the last of it,' Bill said, with a grin on his face. He passed a glass and declared, 'A Merry Christmas to 'ee!'

'And to you!'

The brandy was warm and fine; last November's consignment, brought in by Swanage on Ridout's route. 'How you make a bottle last a whole year, I'll never know, Bill. You know I always said you only had to call on me for another.'

'Aye, that you did.'

Bill had never taken him up on the offer and didn't look like doing so now. 'Zelf-control, zee. 'S a virtue, that.'

'A virtue it is, indeed. But you could be as virtuous on two bottles a year.'

Bill scoffed. 'No. You'll not have I a drunkard.'

'Drunkard? Two bottles a year?'

Bill laughed again, rolling his head around. 'I know 'ee. Two bottles one year, three the next...'

Charles chuckled at the idea. 'Oh really, Bill. As if I would...'

'You've not had the chance! Zelf-control, zee?'

'Good God! All these years did you really think I was trying to corrupt you?'

Bill stared back at him like he regretted having said too much.

'No, Charlie. Course not. Pullin' your leg. It was a kindness, for which I's grateful. You've been good to me.'

'I have been trying to ensure you are well looked after,' Charles insisted.

'Zo you have. You kept me vrom the workhouse.'

'And why would I want you a drunkard anyway?' Charles asked. Bill shuffled in his seat and said nothing. 'Bill?'

There was too long a pause before his next reassurance.

'You've been very kind. Plain to zee.'

Charles took a sip of his brandy and turned to watch the coals burning amber and yellow in the fire.

'I wouldn't…' He turned so Bill could see his face and look him in the eye. 'I know I've seen some dark deeds done, but when we're gone, Bill, all that is left behind is our works, for good or ill. We were always friends. You, me and John: we were catching fish in the Stour before we knew how to count.'

'We was, Charlie, and I know 'ee to be a good man. Times change, though, eh? John's a sailor and you's a gentleman— alderman an' all—'zept I'm still here at Stone Farm. Only thing don't change is my station. Knows me place.'

'Well, there's wisdom in that.'

'Aye. Not much else, though. Not much money in it, tha's for sure!'

He laughed, Bill did. Showing off his blackened teeth and snorting like a hog.

'Well then, here's to your health!' Charles said, raising his glass.

'Ay, an' here's to your money!' Bill said, chuckling. Charles smiled and Bill swiftly straightened his face and corrected himself. 'Your 'ealth I mean, Charlie, your 'ealth. An' thanks f' your kindness all these years.'

'You're welcome. Of course, you know that John Street's back from sea?'

Bill's hand froze in midair and his eyes narrowed as he focused on Charles's revelation.

'Back? Where's he at then? Not round here.'

'Poole Gaol. He was taken when he walked off his ship. Twenty years. Sailed clear around the world—twice—so they say.'

It was clear this was a surprise to Bill. His eyes darted around and he looked like he was chewing his tongue.

'Well, that's a cat in a coop. What's Guthrie zay to that?'

'Guthrie? I have no idea. I'm not even certain he knows. Street's for the gallows, though—if something's not done.'

'John? Hang-gallis?'

Charles felt a little sick following the expression on Bill's face.

'On account o' that damned trial? That blasted letter?'

Charles looked down at the liquid in his glass, and slowly nodded.

'On account of the letter.'

'Well, I zaid it avore and I'll say it again. John Street never wrote that letter. He couldn't ha' done.'

'Why not? He knew his alphabet; could read and write as well as anyone I know.'

'Goat's 'orns, man! I'm not talkin' about his alphabet! If John were confessing somewhat, he'd plant his veet afore 'ee, and tell 'ee straight! That's the manner o' the man. More zo than Guthrie, that's for sure.'

'Oswald Guthrie did not kill Matthew.'

'Zo you zay, but it weren't John Street!' Bill said, his voice sharp and loud and his eyes darkened with anger.

Charles sat back, suddenly aware how forceful they had become, but Bill was still glowering at him.

'Things are all a-mized up. If it weren't for that letter, it'd be Guthrie for the hang-gallis.'

'Yes, but that would be no better. As I said, Guthrie was no more guilty than John, Cornelius or either of us. You know that as well as I.'

Charles chewed his lip a moment, swilling the brandy in his glass.

'Zo what's to be done?' Bill asked.

'What indeed. I've been thinking hard on the question ever since I learned he was taken.' Charles drew his hand along the stubble of his chin, staring hard into the fire.

He sat back, finally ready to tell Bill his thoughts, but a cough overtook him, threw him into convulsions that left him curled in his seat. His spittle had a raw, metallic taste. He swallowed quickly but coughed again. With his fingers at his brow he grumbled curses at the demon in his lungs.

'You a'right?' Bill asked.

Charles waved his hand in lieu of answering, holding his chest. It was hard to complete a sentence.

'The magistrates... will only give up John... if they've someone else to... put in his place.'

'Turk of a business.'

'It is that.'

They stared at each other for a minute. Charles drew hard on his chest, but his throat had a constant, niggling itch.

'So, Bill... here's what I've been thinking... I'm meaning to ask you... what if I tell the magistrates... it was me?'

It was a waste to be too short of breath. He'd thought of so many explanations, so many justifications for Bill. As it was, he was stuck, barely able to wheeze out the meagrest description.

'You what wrote the letter?'

'Never mind the letter... I mean to say... it was me that did the murder!'

Bill chewed the thought for a second.

'They'd hang you in his stead.'

'Maybe not. I could tell them... what Matthew did...'

Bill groaned and rolled his shoulders, apparently unhappy with the suggestion.

'... what he did to those poor children.'

While Bill frowned uncertainly, Charles wheezed for a moment or two then found he had, at last, breath to talk.

'If I told them I discovered his acts, heard from the choirboys how he had mistreated them, how he defiled them. In the church of all places, in the church! I might convince them it was not a hanging matter to kill such a man.'

Leaning towards him, Bill suddenly looked so old. 'Might. And what if tha' cassn't? Then what? And who'll swear by 'ee but me? You tell em how he was fouling with the boys and they'll axe, "Name us one!" zee? And who you going to name? We had all this out years ago. Take en to the magistrates, I said. But we cassn't on account of needing to name em as he was fouling with.'

Charles ran his finger over his lips. It had sounded very simple in his head.

'I'll name all of them,' he answered.

Bill leaned back in his chair. 'Ar. Well that was my thoughts, years ago. You zays that now and they'll hang 'ee twice over!'

Charles couldn't quite fill the second that passed as he recognised the truth in what Bill said, but he followed it immediately with unanswerable confidence.

'I shall be fine. You'll see. But I need your say-so; there's danger for you too.'

'Me?'

'There's a risk, you understand, that everything might come out.'

'Will it?'

'Not from my lips, but I can't speak for John, and who knows how the years have changed him.'

Bill dropped his head, muttering, 'Poor John...' Then he peered into the corner of the room, grumbling how it was a turk of a business, then he glanced back at Charles again, moaning about the hang-gallis. Finally, he looked up and asked, 'Ain't there no other way?'

Charles shrugged. He'd not been able to think of one. 'There might be something a lawyer could do, but I couldn't say whether it should work.'

Bill waved the suggestion aside. 'Won't have no truck with em. Mind, it's your neck you're risking.'

'Could be yours too.'

He shrugged at that suggestion, as if it were the least of their concerns. Then he drew a deep breath and released a long, heavy sigh.

'Well, I surely ain't in your way. Tell em what you have to. Get John safe virst, then we'll see what more needs a-doing.'

Charles nodded gravely. It was started. And having been started, an air of sombreness entered the room, slowing the conversation to a near halt.

It was time for him to leave. He explained that he had to visit his sister before the night was done and emptied the very last drop from his brandy glass.

It wasn't far to the door—Bill's rooms were very modest
—but the stone walls and windows were cold in comparison
to his place by the fire. His coat had barely begun to warm. It
was damp and heavy too, thick with melted snow.

When he stepped outside, the sharp winter air stole his
breath. Bill advised him to watch his step and the dog snuffled by his feet. They said their farewells, then Bill muttered
something else that Charles didn't catch. Charles begged his
pardon and Bill repeated himself.

'Just axing. Weren't you—were it—what done for your
brother?'

Snow was already falling between them.

'No, Bill. You know it wasn't.'

~

Charles Ellis descended St Margaret's Hill slowly and carefully. The evening was darkened by the falling snow; there
were no gas lamps until he reached West Street and those
were not yet lit. With the hill behind him, he shuffled
towards the centre of town, coughing lightly every few steps
and wheezing the rest of the time, noting the scarcity of
other people's tracks. As he crossed the Corn Market, laughter broke from the warm-glowing windows of the Bull, and
the smell of ale and tobacco smoke drifted out from the
George. He didn't stop; on past the Minster, over the Allen
and round onto Poole Road, past the police station and the
nursery to where his sister's house stood, proud as its siblings in a neat little row. Established now; no longer the new
houses with unblemished paint and fresh-laid bricks.

He coughed a little as he stepped through the picket
gate, brushing mounds of snow from its surface. He climbed

the three steps, noticed the lamplight leaking from behind curtains, then tapped on the door.

His sister peered out before opening the door completely.

'I got your note... come in, come in... beginning to wonder if you were still coming. Lord, Charles, you must be frozen!'

Selina was in her housecoat with a slightly ridiculous nightcap protecting her hair. She had never been much interested in fashion, but ever since she'd married, she had developed a passion for the latest labour-saving devices. She kissed him—in the French style, on both cheeks—and helped him peel off his snow-laden coat before ushering him into the front room.

She did not disguise her disdain when she told him he smelled of horses.

'Where've you been, Charles?'

His feet were cold and his hands and nose were like ice. 'Up Stone Farm, went to see old Bill.'

He stood before the coal fire and held his palms out to the heat.

'And you walked all this way? In darkness? In the snow with that cough of yours? Dear me!' Selina said, then she wrinkled her nose. 'Heavens, Charles! Does he actually sleep with the horses?'

Charles squinted at his sister. 'Near enough.'

Selina made a small gesture of disgust and Charles consoled himself that he had bought her that right. His work, his wealth and his business had found the money to pull the whole family out of poverty and buy her into a marriage that she might sneer at those souls they'd left behind.

'What news? Anything from Lord Nelson?' Charles asked. Selina gave him a stern look in response.

'Don't call him that. John's fine. He sent a note on Thursday; his ship is still in Portsmouth and I pray nightly it will never leave. He's far too young. Eliza is enjoying the role of homemaking and Sarah seethes with envy. How are Charles and Lizzie?'

'Oh, they're fine. Of course. You saw them last Sunday. Charles leaves for Bordeaux next week, so he's hiding his excitement.'

The tree in the corner was decorated with Selina's natural flair; symmetrical and neat, yet delicate and original. 'I miss the days when they were young and overexcited at Christmas, don't you?'

'No. Not at all. I was ever fearful they might do themselves some mortal injury. I still worry too much to enjoy their company. What's in the bag? Have you been poaching?'

'No, of course not, I have something for you. Arrived yesterday.'

He bent down and pulled out another bottle; the last of his St Stephen's Day gifts.

'Champagne! How marvellous, Charles. Have we something to celebrate?'

'Well, no—in fact, quite the opposite, but save this for happier times, Selina. It's from a very fine vineyard.'

'Your note seemed a little portentous. Not bad news, I hope? Not at Christmas, Charles.'

His sister smiled sweetly, but with only her mouth, so Charles kept a straight face. Her smile faded.

'Oh. So what is it? Tell me the matter quickly.'

Charles sat in an armchair by the fireplace and Selina sat

opposite him. 'The matter… yes, they say it comes in threes, don't they? Bad tidings.'

'An expression. No basis, I'm sure.'

It was not yet certain. Dr Harrison could have been wrong; the blood might have been caused by something else.

Selina was open-faced with eyebrows raised, but there was a sternness about her eyes; wanting to hear, not wanting to know.

'Is it Richard?'

Charles shook his head and looked away.

'Nothing to do with your husband. I'm sorry. It's hard to know where to start. Our brother: you always thought highly of him and described him with respect.'

Her face flickered, a little twitch at the side of her mouth as though it was trying to say something quite independently of the rest of her.

'I did. God rest his soul, Matthew was a man of noble sentiment and religious nature; a pure and incorruptible soul. I've always said he was an example to us; you know this.'

'Yes. And I always knew that to be untrue.'

She stared at him blankly without, it seemed, a ready retort. Charles continued.

'He didn't even have the appearance of a virtuous man. He was slovenly and unkempt, as everyone who remembers him will recall.'

'He had not an ounce of vanity…'

'He was rude, thoughtless and overbearing.'

'He was forthright. Why are you saying this? Stop it. You're being monstrous.'

Charles sighed a very long sigh. He looked Selina up and down, then he glanced at his fingers as they worried the piping on the armchair.

'Did you ever notice, Selina, how unutterably miserable the choir always seemed at service? Do you remember how severe he was with the boys? Or were you too young?'

He studied her face for a reaction, but Selina stayed reserved.

'Not really.'

The armchair, like most of the furniture in Selina's house, was new when she married; he had helped her and Richard bring it into the house. But it was now beginning to show signs of wear. The piping had been toyed with by younger hands than his own.

'Do you know what they used to call him, those choirboys?'

'Nor do I wish to. Boys, especially young boys, can be...'

'They called him the Buggermaster,' Charles said. He had raised his voice to speak over his sister and she was now glaring at him. He moved forward in his chair. 'Do you remember what happened to Henry Cuff?'

Selina's chin had gone up in defence.

'That was years ago.'

'He drowned himself! To get away from Matthew. To escape the attentions of *our brother*!'

Selina started biting at her bottom lip, her worried fingers fidgeting in her lap. Her reserve seemed to be melting into distress.

'This is not just something I made up. I made enquiries and many of the choirboys said the same. Our brother, Selina, was a depraved defiler of young boys.'

Selina's head dropped. She didn't seem anxious to deny it.

'Why are you telling me this now?' she asked, voice weakened with sadness. 'Why now?'

Charles drew another breath. 'That has to do with John Street...'

'His murderer.'

'John was convicted on the basis of a letter that was received after he had gone to sea; he was tried in his absence.'

'I know, Charles. You will recall my presence at the trial...'

'John did not write that letter.'

'How do you know this?'

'Because I wrote it.'

She stared at him coldly, but he waved away her shock using Bill's gesture. 'It was necessary at the time. The problem is that John has returned. They say he has sailed clear round the world and returned to where he started. He is being held in Poole Gaol and unless something is done to prevent it, he will soon be hanged.'

'I do not mean to be callous, but *should* anything be done? He was tried and convicted. I mean, why now?'

'Why? John Street did not kill Matthew! And the only justification for his conviction was a letter I wrote to shift suspicion from Major Guthrie.'

'Well then, surely Guthrie should...'

'He was equally innocent.'

'Well, so say you! So everyone but Matthew is innocent and all are to be saved. Why now?'

Charles checked himself, stared at her momentarily and then let it fall.

'Because John has returned from sea and because... because I am dying.'

He watched his sister try—and fail—to override this most extreme revelation. She carried on talking for a moment, her eyelids blinking like flapping sails.

'That's no reason to open old wounds... what... what can you...'

She silenced herself eventually, covering her mouth with her handkerchief. Charles explained.

'I saw Doctor Harrison last week. He used his scope on my chest. Consumption. He urged me to ensure my affairs are in order.'

Selina was clearly trying to keep a straight, sober face, but tears broke almost immediately, streamed down her cheeks and dripped onto her lap.

'I don't think I should hear this...'

'He said I should attend to the matter with some urgency.'

'There are treatments...' she suggested. Charles shook his head slowly.

'I haven't the time.'

He watched her collapse. Her head sank and her shoulders started shaking as she gave way to a fit of sobbing.

He wanted to console her. He wanted to move from his armchair, scoop her up in his arms and hold her like a child, but she soon lifted her chin and sniffed back her tears, defying pity.

'So... what now? You're planning something childishly noble on account of that scoundrel, Street. Don't tell me—you're planning to offer yourself up in place of him. God, Charles I shan't hear of it. Think what this will do to Anne! You want young Charlie to be the son of a murderer? For the sake of John Street?'

'He's an innocent man, Sally.'

'So are you!' she countered, turning on him with reddened eyes and burning cheeks. Charles stared at the carpet, with its curlicues and paisley signatures.

'Are you not?'

'Well, I wrote the letter for a start.'

'For a start? Great heavens! What else?'

He glanced up at her pale, open-mouthed face, wondering how he might convince her of the truth. She had fixed her eyes on him, and he found for the first time in many years that he could return her gaze and hold it. Her eyes were wet and shining.

'There is a thought,' Selina said, 'I have always banished from my mind. I have refused many times to even think it. Do not—please—force me to voice it now.'

'I didn't kill him.'

She trembled—her eyes closed and head bowed, as though exorcising a much-resented spirit. When she spoke next, she seemed to be forcing the words out.

'So, what… remains… unspoken?'

Unspoken? So much. All the ineffable moments. His brother's pained expression; the darkening robe and random blots that appeared so abruptly on the flagstones; a confusion of final moments; a ghost in the edge of sleep, taunting him: 'You owe me…'; the pooling; the swift transformation of someone who was to someone who was not.

'Charles, I shall ask you once again…'

'I believe he killed himself, Selina.'

She left her mouth hanging open.

'I came upon him in the library with a knife in his ribs, staggering towards me. There was no one else there.'

'You were with him when he died?'

'He bled all over me.'

'Did he say anything?'

'He told me to look after you.'

Charles maintained a blank face to support the lie, watching Selina's reaction.

'And what had Bill to do with it?'

Charles's immediate, panicked sensation displayed the perils of deceit.

'Why... what makes you think Bill was involved?'

'Oh really! You've just come from him. I do not think you so casual that you would do social rounds before bringing me this news.'

'Bill always suspected me. He was the gravedigger and I used his handcart to ship the body to the graveyard. I wanted him to know the truth.'

'Handcart? But... you buried him? Having found him with a knife in his chest, you proceeded to bury him yourself? Why didn't you tell anyone?'

He looked for a moment at Selina's slippered feet, remembering John Street's arrival on his shoulder—his sudden violent outburst, beating a man who was already dead.

'I–'

'You're hiding something from me.'

Charles stared at her. Why bury the body if not to save John from being accused? He had always planned to claim that he feared a misunderstanding—that it would be assumed he was the murderer. To hear it now, it seemed like a child's lie. Selina didn't seem to care.

'How much did you tell Bill?'

Charles had to think. How much did Bill really know?

'I told him I plan to confess, and that I am innocent. He has always known the crimes of our brother.'

Selina bowed her head and addressed him with her eyes lowered.

'I must ask you, if you have ever held me in any esteem and wish me any goodwill at all, please change your mind on this course of action.'

'You still defend him?'

She pulled her head up quickly, fierce in her look, tears glistening in the room's lights.

'Had I found him with a knife in his chest, Charlie, I should have twisted it—and not just to ensure he was gone. I regret that I never had the chance. No one... no one hated him more than I. I was not defending him—never him— all these years: I was defending myself. You always missed that. I defend my own reputation and that of my children. Always.'

~

Few noticed the evening turn to solid night. The snow certainly did not pause to mark the change. It kept on fall- ing—resolute, dutiful—settling comfortably on the roofs of Poole Road, on the police station and the malthouse and on the glass slopes of the nursery. It nestled into the missing- tile gaps above the close-pressed gables of East Brook, and it smoothed and soothed the long view down East Street, where flakes balanced on the hands of the corner clock like ministering angels.

Snow formed wide columns—wide, white columns—to crown the gravestones around the Minster, tributes to the long-forgotten kings in their eternal sleep. And snow trailed invisibly behind the shuffling form of Wimborne's lamp-lighter, smoothing over his tracks, filling in his footprints. It formed small settlements on the top of Charles Ellis's hat as he trudged home through the cold; made thin layers on his shoulders and formed gossamer sheets of white across his back. But for all its blanketing softness, for all its quiet and its dark white calmness, for all that it clung to him, it could bring no comfort to the Alderman of Wimborne.

He stopped at the spot where he had started. The snow had covered his tracks and covered the red blot over. He was not fooled.

He tried not to make a noise. He cleared his boots of snow before opening the front door, then he shook his coat off and went into the drawing room at the front of the house, lighting the lamp by the window with matches from the table drawer. He sat and tried to relax his breathing gradually without causing irritation, but the warm air tickled his lungs again. He tried to hold it, to simply refuse to cough, but it burst through and flecks of blood-tainted spittle flew onto the rug. And then he was bent double, wracked with coughs that would not release their hold on him.

As he was coughing, he sensed Anne sit beside him, felt the hand she placed on his back and knew, as he struggled to breathe, that his labours had woken her.

It came close, then. For a moment he had not enough breath to cough and he had to stretch his back up straight, desperately wheezing half-breaths of air into his lungs, fearing that this might be the end, when he had not yet done all he needed to do. But it eased. It left him, eventually, bent over his knees, gently hauling his aching chest open and closed, temples throbbing, exhausted. He hardly had a need to utter the words.

Anne drew her hand across his back and left it on his shoulder. He studied the lace embroidery on her dressing gown for a moment—a miraculous achievement of artistry in miniature, tiny white threads curled around each other, and he was he was trying to understand its whole shape, to understand the pattern in the multiplying branches when a tear filled his eye. He blinked it away.

'I'm dying, Anne,' he said. She gripped his shoulder, then took his hand. His was still red-cold from the outdoors winter; hers was bed-warm. After a long, silent pause, she lifted her chin. Her voice quivered, but did not break.

'I know,' she said. The surprise nearly provoked his coughing again. How had she known? Suspected maybe, but *known*?

'Doctor Harrison?'

'Mrs Rawlins. She offered me her sympathies, bless her. But your cough, Charles...'

He swallowed back his reaction and ignored the churning fear in his stomach.

Anne was a wonder. The tiny muscles around her eyes flickered and he knew she was choosing her reactions very deliberately. He could only lament the occasions he would miss; the times still to come when she would employ her genius of understanding.

'What can I do?' she asked.

He had to fight to control his own distress because if Anne could keep her composure, it would have been a betrayal for him to lose his.

He squeezed her hand. Swallowed. What could she do?

Look after the children—after Charles and Elizabeth. Live her own life once he was gone, without sadness or remorse. Thoughts tumbled but none of them expressed what he meant, so instead he shook his head.

'I don't know,' he said. It came out as a wheezing whisper. 'But there's something else.'

'John Street,' she said. Though how she knew this also, he couldn't fathom.

'I can't let him die, Anne.'

She shook her head. 'Of course not.' And with quiet desperation turned her head away to wipe her eyes and nose.

'I mean to take John's place, if I last long enough. You understand that?'

He saw the colour drain from her face. She bit her lip and nodded. She had known it already—that was clear—but there was something in hearing it, just as there was something in saying it.

'I've made arrangements with Rawlins. The house, the business. All in your name now. Charlie and Lizzie, both...'

Tears descended breathlessly, sliding down Anne's cheeks, even as she sat with her head up straight. And as she controlled her own emotions, her grip tightened when his words would no longer stand on their own.

'If they come with confiscation orders, Rawlins will protect you. I cannot... I cannot justify myself. In court, I mean.'

She pulled a handkerchief from her dressing-gown pocket and carefully wiped her face and nose. 'You'll not explain?' she asked.

'Selina fears for her reputation. He...'

Now he had to clench his teeth. Recalling John's fury all those years ago, seeing him again pounding his fist into

Matthew's dead face as blood coloured the flagstones. To distract himself, he fixed his gaze on the Delft-blue pattern of birds and trees on the wallpaper. It was designed to confuse where one sheet stopped and the next began.

'What do you know of Richard?' he asked. Anne shook her head. She didn't understand his change of subject, so he explained.

'Selina said... she thought, if...' he said, giving a deep sigh that turned into a long wheeze so he had to control the muscles in his chest. 'Selina fears Richard's reaction if he learns what Matthew did.'

'To her?'

'To her.'

Anne stared at him for a moment then turned away and settled her distant gaze on the space by the door. 'He raped her?'

Charles swallowed back his bile and nodded. He didn't know what to do with the thoughts; the memories of his little sister covered in flour angrily bustling around the kitchen, baking for her two elder brothers. He had always assumed her anger was a sign of her effort and her shortage of time. He had thought light of it, and even made light of it on occasion. Irreversible mistakes.

'Poor child,' Anne muttered.

'She's convinced if Richard finds out, she'll end up on the street.'

Anne turned away, sighing. 'He is from that mould of men,' she said. 'Would it were him in your stead.'

It was the last time he would ever hear her say something unkind. Beyond his windows and walls the snow still fell, its comfort far too cold.

THE WOODPECKER
AND THE MISTLETOE

Lyme Regis, Dorset,
June 1863

The floor of his room in the guest house had a pronounced slope towards the door. It seemed as if it was silently ushering him out, emphasising the impermanence of his stay.

The Reverend Giles Cookesely did not wish to meditate on the impermanence of his stay.

He would also have preferred to remain standing while donning his breeches, but his legs were old and the sloping floor confounded his sense of balance, so he sat on the bed to dress.

He wondered whether it wouldn't be better if all old houses were pulled down and replaced with modern ones. Give them gas lamps and water pipes and let their floors be flat. The new replaces the old. It falls in layers. Time builds its record as one thing falls on top of another. That was how he understood the matter—although his estimations would soon be redundant, for today he anticipated being introduced to time's precise workings.

Once dressed, he stood, pulled his spectacles from his jacket pocket and checked his face in the small mirror that was hanging awkwardly from the uneven plaster wall. His collar was straight, his beard was neither unkempt nor vainly trimmed. But it was there in his eyes. He could see it, so he wondered if it was evident to other people.

It was three days since he had been required, once again, to console Anne Ellis. And what a consolation. It was now four months since she had lost her husband, Charles, an entirely innocent man, a decent, noble, incomprehensibly brave individual, hanged for a murder he did not commit. Still she grieved. And what consolation might have been provided to the poor man's wife? Whatever measure of comfort was available to her, not much of it would reach her via an ailing priest whose faith was little more than a bitter memory.

He had tried his best. He had offered his sincerest assurances that Charles Ellis would find a place in the everlasting heaven, but Anne, dear woman, hadn't seemed too concerned about the eternal; she'd been distraught about her loss. It had made his own hypocrisy ache like a rotten tooth.

He turned to the small number of possessions spread around the room and focused on the two books by the bed. Their position together was entirely coincidental, but there it was. The King James Bible and *On the Origin of Species* beside each other.

It was many years now since he had used the Bible as an augury—it had so cruelly misled him—and yet the impulse remained. He had not yet thought to use the Darwin in a similar fashion, but there could be no reason to think one superstition superior to another. Predators of frailty.

He sat on the bed and—just for amusement—picked up the Darwin, rather than the Good Book, wondering how it might compare.

It was Morton who had taught him the habit. Uncle Morton, sitting on his bed, taking up most of its space and challenging young Giles to ask a question that the Bible might answer. And Giles would ask, and Morton would choose a page at random and the answer would be so direct it would seem a miracle.

He often wondered whether the priesthood would have called if that fat old uncle had not sought to perform bed-time miracles? And he must surely have lied. Giles tried it himself, night after night, but had never once stumbled upon a passage with anything like the relevance Morton produced. He had thought himself unworthy. Unworthy! He'd just not been cheating, that was all. It was all lies and vanity. Everything, except what Charles Ellis did, and it was infuriating that he should be an exception.

He flicked through the pages of *Origins*, sighing. He let the pages stop, and flattened the book, trying—as he always had—to avoid pre-selecting. He placed his finger on a passage. He hadn't a question, but only the memory of Ellis's sacrifice in mind.

How have all those exquisite adaptations of one part of the organisation to another part, and to the conditions of life, and of one distinct organic being to another being, been perfected? We see these beautiful co-adaptations most plainly in the woodpecker and mistletoe; and only a little less plainly in the humblest parasite which clings to the hairs of a quadruped or feathers of a bird; in the structure of the beetle which dives through the water; in the plumed seed which is wafted by the gentlest breeze; in short, we see beautiful adaptations everywhere and in every part of the organic world.

It was not an ugly passage—not as ugly as he remembered. The first time he read Darwin, his text had seemed perfunctory and soulless. 'In the structure of the beetle which dives through the water; in the plumed seed which is wafted by the gentlest breeze.' It wasn't poetry, but then there were passages of the Good Book that were uninspiring. 'And the beetle after his kind and the grasshopper after his kind.'

He closed it carefully, but without reverence because it was, after all, just a book. Just like the Bible. What good was self-sacrifice, he wondered? The way of the Lord, the way of Ellis, but the antithesis, surely, of natural selection. He packed the books into his valise and stuffed a woollen hat and a spare pair of gloves into his knapsack. That was it. He closed the bags and retreated from the room, closing the door on the sloping floor.

Mrs Gover was waiting for him at the bottom of the stairs. She was a Talker: started with a greeting and continued by explaining the progress of her morning. He had long been used to Talkers—most frequently they would collar him at the church door and jabber away without pause until he was able to make his escape. In his earliest days he used to listen patiently, but he had learned. Now he interrupted very bluntly.

'... as my 'usband used to zay...'

'My breakfast, if you would, please, Mrs Gover. Two eggs and a slice of ham.'

Not that such simple bluntness made a jot of difference with someone as artless as his hostess; she simply acknowledged the request and continued.

'He'd zay, "You can't have a hackle 'til the crop's a-gotten in," he would.'

No doubt there was some conversational purpose to this non sequitur, but Giles didn't care for it.

'And I'm sure he was quite right, Mrs Gover. Meanwhile, I am in the habit of taking my breakfast in quiet contemplation.'

She looked at him a little oddly but took off to the kitchen quietly enough, leaving Giles alone in her dining room.

It was a sparse little room with one long table and whitewashed walls punctured by two mean windows that provided light but nothing in the way of a view. Giles retrieved the Darwin from his bag and read until his food arrived and then carried on reading while he ate.

When he had nearly finished, his hostess came back, placed a paper-wrapped parcel on his table and very pointedly backed away without saying anything. His food package for the day ahead. He took a minute more before untying the string and checking the contents. He smelled it immediately and could feel the irritation tightening his chest.

'Mrs Gover!'

She appeared meekly by his side and started talking immediately. Of course she did; she was precisely the type that was forever talking and never listening.

'Mrs Gover, had you thought to *listen*, yesterday when I asked you for lunch in a package, you would have heard me say—quite *distinctly*—that I dislike mustard. Whereas this package has mustard all over it!'

'Oh,' was all she could say, although her chubby little cheeks turned red almost instantly.

Giles clenched his teeth and, for just a moment, closed his eyes to hold back the temptation to strike her.

'Please take it away and bring me the lunch I asked for— *without mustard*!'

Mrs Gover picked up the package with a ridiculous expression on her face showing offended false contrition and Giles wanted to explode.

'And please do not cause me to be late in meeting my nephew!'

She stopped and stared at him blankly.

'Hurry!' he urged, waving her towards the kitchen, 'Quick, quick, quick!'

He regretted his outburst. Once he was walking by the shore, listening to the waves cackling over the stones and sands, his breast calmed. He reflected that he could easily have asked Mrs Gover to replace his lunch without any rancour at all. His anger had been unnecessary. Yet no one else could know how much he had kept back—how much he had controlled.

He hadn't the worst temper—not these days. Nothing thrown. No one murdered. But that dragged his thoughts back to the sacrifice of Charles Ellis and a familiar deep sense of regret washed over him. The poor wife. So elegant too.

It was a consolation to remember—and it made him smile to think of it—that he had reproached Mrs Gover with the phrase 'had you thought to listen' like a child's matron. Ridiculous expression. As if you might not listen if you did not think to do so.

Giles turned to face the sea and adjusted the knapsack on his shoulder. A fine, offshore breeze was freshening his face and the sea was lit by a brilliant sun, glittering with greens and flashes of blue. Neither Charles Ellis nor his long-dead brother could disturb his enjoyment of it.

It was spectacular. Truly spectacular. And was it worse for being created through something less than a miracle? This was not, apparently, a sea created on the second day and divided on the third; a known sea; a bounded sea—this was a vast, unfathomable sea that was formed over millions of years, made salty by the rivers washing down from the land. This was the one-time domain of creatures that were alien and unimaginably large.

'Uncle!'

He turned and saw Felix striding across the beach towards him.

'I called...' the young man explained, pointing back at the promenade. He seemed to be finding it hard work to walk across the sand and stones. He was out of breath when he finally stopped in front of Giles. Still, he grinned.

'Good morning! How are you, Uncle?'

Giles straightened his back, wondering whether he was equal to a day of walking.

'It's a beautiful sight, isn't it, Felix?'

'Beautiful. Yes... yes, beautiful. Shall we go?'

He gestured east, along the shore towards the end of the

beach and the base of the cliffs. Giles followed his direction and they fell into step together.

'Do we have far to walk?'

'Well... we need to get onto the flats over there, then we can reach the lower strata,' Felix said. He was squinting, looking into the distance and sounding uncertain whether he should consider that 'far to walk'. 'Most important is the timing, Uncle Giles. We want to use our time well before the tide comes in.'

So they walked along the beach at a brisk pace, raising their voices over the noise of the sea and the wind. Felix told him news of his brother—news he had heard already—and explained something of his journey down from London.

'It is very good of you to spend this time with me, Felix.'

'Oh it's my pleasure, Uncle Giles. I'm really very happy to show you what a geologist sees—as you said in your letter. But tell me—what is it exactly that you wanted to learn?'

Giles stepped up onto a plateau of rock, lifting himself from the sandy part of the beach. What was it he wanted to learn? There were so many strands leading back to this question. He wanted to see for himself. Evidence.

'I have read a great deal, Felix. I am knowledgeable enough for the bishop to consult me on the matter. I follow the proceedings of the Royal Society and while they publish plates and illustrations, I have never actually seen anything for myself, nor held it in my own hand. D'you see?'

Going from his expression, Felix did not.

'You want to see for yourself... the...'

'Strata. Stones. Fossils.'

'Ah. Yes of course. Well, this is most definitely the place. Come, we'll start with the rock formations.'

They walked some distance further until they were at the foot of the cliffs and Felix pointed out the lines that ran across the face. He named them with a fluency that was difficult to interrupt. The primary and transition layers were, it seemed, elusive, but there had been investigations into the Devonian.

'These cliffs are most interesting because this is Jura limestone with chalk and greensand above.'

They were still walking as Felix was explaining. 'The Church Cliffs show us layering almost perfectly.'

'*Church* Cliffs?' Giles asked. But Felix nodded without attempting to answer why they might be so named.

There was no denying the appearance of layers. The cliffs presented grey, horizontal lines of rock. They reached the cliff face and Giles reached out to put a hand on the cold damp stone. Ussher had it that God created the world in 4004 BC, from dates in the Bible.

'How old are these rocks thought to be, then, Felix?'

'These? These are Jurassic. About two hundred million years.'

'Two hundred million? How?'

'Ah!'

Felix suddenly looked excited and tapped the stone by their heads. 'The formation of this stone, Uncle. Fascinating. This is limestone. It is sedimentary rock—rock formed from sediment. And the sediment—this is the interesting part—the sediment is actually calcite, tiny fragments of shells from organisms that once lived in the water. The shell segments settle as sediment and the sediment gradually dries out and becomes flatter and harder.'

Giles ran his finger over the rock, then looked up at the towering cliff. 'This is made from seashells?'

'Well, no, not seashells exactly. Much smaller creatures. No larger than a speck.'

Foolishly, he was about to declare it impossible, thinking it would take far too long to dry out sediment, layer upon layer, to make the whole cliff. But then he recalled the number. Two hundred million years. He craned his aching neck back to look up. Such an age. But he could see it. He could imagine the work of a small effect and a lot of time.

The stone steps up to the library in the Minster were worn in the middle. He had once bent down to the step to discover that he could not so much as scratch the stone. It took hundreds of feet hundreds of years to wear it down. So why should not rock form from sediment over millions of years?

He sighed sadly. So it was true. But of course it was true. He had always known it was true. 'And you find creatures in the rock?'

'Fossils? Why yes, we find fossils. It is largely a matter of luck, but we should be able to come upon some. Look, right here.'

Felix bent and straightened up with a circular stone in his fingers. He was grinning delightedly. He handed it across.

'Ichthyosaur,' he said.

'A what?'

'It is a vertebra—part of the backbone—of an ichthyosaur. There are many to be found among the beach pebbles.'

'A dinosaur?'

'Of a type, yes. First identified by none other than Richard Owen.'

'But it is a stone. How is that possible, having once been bone?'

'Ah. For this, you should understand how tiny are the

particles in sediment. They are smaller than the holes of porous bone. So they enter the bone—fill it, if you like—and as the bone decays, it is replaced by sediment which then hardens in its place.'

The vicar stepped away from the cliff. There was so much that required belief. It was too close to faith. You had to believe in these tiny particles that invaded bone.

'This could just be a piece of rock, could it not? Worn into the shape of a vertebra by luck?'

Felix grinned.

'Certainly it could. Although you can find so many of them among the pebbles here that luck is the less likely cause. But never mind. We should find our own fossil, shouldn't we? We'll pull a stone from the cliff so we know where it comes from and find a fossil in it. Come.'

He led the way to an area where the cliff wall was looser, pitted with large stones. Felix produced a hammer from his knapsack and started pulling stones out from the rock. When he had a small pile of such flat slabs, he attacked them with the hammer and a chisel, splitting them open. Stone after stone fell apart without result, but Felix worked on until his brow was sweating. 'We need a little luck for this...' he kept repeating, until at last the enchantment worked. 'Oh! Luck indeed!'

Giles leaned over his shoulder and his eyes fell upon an exquisite impression left in the surface of the stone.

It had once been a fish. Small—no longer than a couple of inches—but its bones and head were so clearly defined, with large holes where the eyes would once have been and fine lines that ran through the rock showing the backbone, the ribs, the dorsal fin and tail.

He stepped back and sat on the stone ledge, feet in the pebbles. The stone was small enough to hold, although two hands were needed for comfort, but still. There it was. Proof. Proof in the form of a fish.

'How old?'

Felix turned to the gap in the rock from where they had pulled this slab.

'From here? Around one hundred and ninety million years.'

Giles shook his head.

'Are you quite all right, Uncle?' Felix asked.

It was peculiar to be assaulted by such a wave of emotion—and emotion so strong that it brought tears to his eyes. The consequence of time. All these years. At last, here it was. Utterly unmistakeable in its intricate detail.

'Oh, my life!' he groaned.

'Uncle Giles?'

'Yes, yes. I'm fine.'

He wiped the tears from his eyes and lifted his head, sucking at his lip. The sea breeze brushed his face.

'When I was studying for the priesthood, Felix, I could not believe that God would not show his hand in the world. In my heart I felt convinced that God would offer some sort of symbolic token to those who were willing or deserving enough. A sign. A vision. After all, the Bible features many such events.'

'And did he?' Felix asked.

'No. He did not. I thought, once, indeed I was convinced, but it proved to be just the behaviour of crows.'

He looked back at the specimen on his lap. 'Is this a rare fossil? Will your academy be interested in it?'

Felix bobbed his head around uncertainly. 'It's a very fine example, but the fish is unremarkable. If you wanted it...'

'Very much.'

'The academy won't miss it.'

Giles ran his fingers over the shape, brushing away fine grains of dirt. Specks. Then he lifted his head and peered down the beach. It was time to move. 'Come. We'll walk up to the grass there and eat our lunch.'

Their feet crunched on the stones as they walked. Giles hooked his hands behind his back and strode slowly, beginning his explanation.

'You can't imagine what it was like when I first obtained a copy of Mr Darwin's book.'

'Very upsetting I should think.'

'Upsetting? No, not at all. It was a relief. An answer at last. After so many years of doubting.'

He shifted the knapsack on his back, feeling the weight of the stone. 'There were too many times, Felix, when God should have done something. Nothing happened. I'll tell you, there was a choirmaster in my church who was the very devil. How I loathed that man. I forgave him every sin imaginable and I prayed and prayed and prayed.'

'Was that the choirmaster we read about in the newspapers—the one that was murdered?'

'It was indeed. God rest his soul, but he was a vile man.'

Ridiculous. There was no God to care for his soul.

'There was something about the choirboys?'

Giles sighed. It was so hard to go over it again. It took so much explaining.

'He was exceptionally harsh on the boys. And unnatural in his relations with them. One young lad was found drowned and Ellis was thought by many to have been the reason for his suicide. Soon after that he disappeared and was never seen again. As I say, I had prayed for redemption. It came to nought.'

Felix was walking beside him, also with his hands behind his back.

'But they just recently hanged the murderers, did they not, Uncle? They came back from being at sea. How were their crimes discovered?'

'Oh, it was all very involved. Strange business. Two fellows ran off to India the night Matthew Ellis disappeared, so suspicion first fell upon them. But some years later another fellow named John Street disappeared and left behind a letter confessing that *he* had murdered Ellis. He was tried *in absentia*, found guilty and was condemned to be hanged but no one knew where he was. All but forgotten until he turned up just before Christmas. He'd been at sea for twenty years and knew nothing of his trial. But the dead man's brother—half-brother—he told the courts that Street was entirely innocent, that he had himself written the letter and that he was the murderer. He said he should be hanged in the place of the sailor. Extremely brave. Astounding sacrifice. Hopelessly wasted.'

'Why? Was he not the murderer?'

'Neither of them were. Both as innocent as babes. But the courts of law, young Felix, do not care for matters of fact. They reasoned that Street had already been convicted, so he should hang. And Ellis had confessed, so he should hang also. And they hanged them both. A grotesque injustice and no amount of prayer was ever going to make any difference.'

'Prayer would make no difference? Why would you think that, Uncle?'

'Why?'

Giles squinted at his nephew to protect his eyes from the sun. It seemed so ridiculous now. All the time. A constant act that he was required to maintain.

'Because, my dear boy, the world was not created in seven days by our Lord, was it? It was formed over millions of years through the actions of tiny seashells. And the creatures on the land and the sea? They *evolved*, Felix. They evolved. God did not put them here. A process of natural selection. And unlike the teachings of the Church, I am not required to trust in blind faith. Not any longer; not since you cracked open this stone to reveal my one-hundred-and-ninety-million-year-old fish. I have the proof. A real, genuine *sign*. Here in my bag. A very simple thing to do. But the Church couldn't manage it. And God Almighty couldn't manage it. Of course He couldn't.'

Felix looked awkward being on the receiving end of this lecture. 'You... um... you sound a little angry.'

'Can you imagine? I have spent my life knocking on the door of a house that is utterly empty—and was always empty. Charles Ellis commits an act worthy of the Lord Jesus—the most Christian act I have ever witnessed—and what happens? The courts hanged them both.'

It was hard to know what was the worst of it—the bitterness or the embarrassment. Against the horror of the loss there was also the sense that everyone else had known for ages.

'Charles Ellis knew there would be no justice for John Street if he did not create it himself. Not in this life or the next, because there was to be no next. So Ellis set out to help the man, knowing he would die. Can you imagine? I may be a priest, but that man was a saint, Felix, a saint.'

'But why did they hang them both?' Felix asked.

'Of that I have no idea. Ignorance? Arrogance? Vanity? I imagine that such mean-minded men could not conceive of another making such a noble sacrifice so, rather than attempting to understand, they decided to have done with the matter and murder the pair of them.'

Clouds were blooming over the inland sky and Giles looked up at the seagulls wheeling in the breeze as he talked.

'I am still consoling the poor man's widow. It is my job to bring God's word, Felix. I might as well have been calling on the clouds, the pixies, the fairies in the grass.'

To go by Felix's frowning expression, he still did not understand.

'There is no God, Felix. You know that, surely, or perhaps you had not realised?'

His nephew looked very young and fresh-faced suddenly. He stammered for an answer. 'I... had remained open-minded on the question, Uncle Giles.'

'Really? And you, a man of science?' He looked about at the sand under his feet and leaned back to sit on a bank. 'Here,' he said, 'let's eat.'

There was still a hint of mustard to his ham. That spiteful landlady had just cleaned the food, cheating him. For a moment, he wanted to spit it onto the ground. Everyone seemed to think him a fool to be cheated.

Then a crow happened to light upon the dune in front of him. It peered at him. He threw it a crust.

'He seems to like you,' Felix said, displaying slightly childish sentimentality.

'He is a scavenger. He knows the easiest route to food. That's all.'

Giles looked across at the crow, chewing his lunch, and Felix asked, 'You know about crows?'

'I do. I know a great deal about crows; rooks too.'

'Rooks? Do they gather around the Minster?'

'No, no. The nearest rookery is a mile outside the town. I watch them in the mornings and the evenings.' *And at the setting of the sun.* 'Do you know how to tell if one of these birds is watching you?'

'He turns his head towards you, surely?'

'Not at all. Eyes on the sides of their heads, you see? When he's in profile, that's when he's looking at you. Like this fellow. And if he's really interested, see there… he'll turn the other way and use the other eye. First the left eye and then the right. They have their own society and their own rules.'

'Their own rules, Uncle? Are you quite sure?'

'As sure as I am sitting here, my boy. And if one of their number should break the rules, they will kill him. Extraordinary creatures.'

Felix stopped his sandwich by his mouth as an expression of his incredulity. 'They kill their own? Over territory or a mate or food, surely? Not over rules.'

Giles shrugged. He had long ago stopped trying to convince others of what he knew.

'I have seen a crow court happen on three separate occasions. Unmistakeable.'

His nephew looked wide-eyed with surprise. He was,

perhaps, more prepared to believe that a wise old man created heaven and earth.

The crow peered at them, watching the food with hungry intensity. They ate for a few minutes in silence.

'So what will you do, Uncle? I mean, if you have proof now, as you say? Will you remain a priest?'

Giles sighed and put his bread to one side. Ellis had chosen to take the drop for another man. Giles could not even make his living honestly.

'I have no other trade, Felix. And I am too old to learn a new one. This is how it is now. I shall be among the last of my kind.'

'Do you think so?'

'Most assuredly. Natural selection created the creatures of the world. Not God. Now we know. Science is revealing the lie. Steam engines are replacing horses, photography is replacing painting, manufactories are taking the places of craftsmen. The academy will replace the Church. It is a new age. The age of your generation. There will be no place for old fools like me. No priests or minsters. You will see.'

He threw the last of his bread to the crow and watched as Felix turned, thoughtfully, to stare out to sea.

As the afternoon grew old, Giles began looking forward to his journey home. He had booked himself on a boat that would go to Poole via Weymouth, and he would travel back to Wimborne from there. Felix, on the other hand, was staying in Lyme Regis for his studies.

The sun was low in the sky when they walked to the Cobb, where the steamer was tied up, waiting.

Felix talked to him along the walk, telling him about his

learned friends at the university, about the brilliance of the professors and the advances they were making. It was hard to follow, but all that was needed was the occasional nod and a murmur of agreement. He maintained the pretence of listening right up until they reached the foot of the gangplank. There they stopped and Giles took up his knapsack and his valise.

'I hope it is a smooth trip,' Felix said.

'Oh, I shan't mind in any case. I rather like the rocking of the waves. Thank you for your time. You have been very helpful.'

'It has been my pleasure, Uncle. But you must tell me the conclusion of the mystery. That murdered choirmaster... you say the sailor was wrongly accused and the other man who was hanged was innocent. But...'

Giles made ready to explain that no one knew the answer to the mystery. The murderer remained unknown. It was a well-rehearsed response, ready at a moment's notice.

'How d'you know they were both innocent?' Felix asked.

No answer. He had no answer and his cheeks began burning before he could think of one. He could feel it. They were glowing in seconds. How had he been so careless?

'How? Why, they told me... Ellis... he... I knew because he told me how he... he was planning to... you understand he went to the authorities to save John Street, knowing that he would be hanged. But he was innocent, and he told me so.'

Felix did not believe him. It was in his eyes. 'I see,' he said, covering for his understanding.

And he repeated, 'I see.' But his eyes whispered, 'Liar!'

*

They shook hands after that, smiling awkwardly. They commended each other to their families and said goodbye. Giles kept his eye on Felix from the ship's gunwales as the Cobb receded into the distance, traced by the wandering trail of smoke from the engine. It didn't matter now.

The sea birds whirled and swooped over the waves. Would he ever tell? On his deathbed, perhaps? If there was someone there to hear him. And how would he explain himself? That he did it to save the children? Or as an unanswered challenge to the Almighty? Could he ever explain that anger?

It was not something he liked to dwell upon. It was too easy to recall the sensation of the knife scraping on the bone of the choirmaster's ribs. The expression of shock and pain on the man's face. And his thoughts, so often echoed with his own words, 'What does God owe you now?'

He'd spoken as if to himself. And then the choirmaster had staggered out of the library into the arms of that most unexpected party of visitors. Ellis, Street, the others.

The salt air was sharp in his nostrils and he suddenly remembered a passage of Darwin. He had to sit. His back was too stiff these days to reach into his bag while standing. The wind tugged at the pages, making it hard to search, but he found it.

As many more individuals of each species are born than can possibly survive; and as, consequently, there is a frequently recurring struggle for existence, it follows that any being, if it vary however slightly in any manner profitable to itself, under the complex and sometimes varying conditions of life, will have a better chance of surviving and thus be *NATURALLY SELECTED*. From the strong principle of inheritance, any selected variety will tend to propagate its new and modified form.

Giles closed the book, replaced it in his bag and leaned back in his seat to accept the sun's rays and the damp sea air. There was really no lesson in those words except the meaning they were given. No signs. Nothing to speak to him. The only candidate was the notion that well-executed perfidy would triumph over naïve noble-mindedness. But Ellis left children and he, Giles, did not. He looked up at the broad white cliffs of St Anselm's point. All chalk. Millions of years' worth of accumulated fossils. Perhaps the fate of us all. In the end, nothing had any meaning at all.

And yet.

A black flicker caught his eye. At the back of the boat there was a crow, perched most incongruously on the stern railing. It stood still, feathers flapping untidily in the breeze, and it looked at him, first with its left eye, and then with its right.

Glossary

Dorset Dialect

The following definitions are taken from the *Glossary of Dorset Dialect* written by William Barnes and first published in 1847.

A-FEARED   'afeärd' and 'afraid' are truly two sundry words; 'afeärd' is only smitten with fear, and 'afraid' is 'frayed' or scared away, driven, it may be in fear.

AGGY   Corner with sharp-looking joints, as a very thin man. *Agg* (Saxon *ecg*) means an edge, point or corner. Dorset readily takes thing-names and uses them as time-words; as they are or with the ending 'y'.

ANY-WHEN   At any time.

AX   (Anglo-Saxon *axian*) To ask. '*Hi ne dorston axian*.' 'They durst not ask.'—Luke 9:45. 'A question wold y axe of you.'— Duke of Orwans' *Poems*.

BALLYWRAG   To scold or accuse in foul language. (Anglo-Saxon *wregan*)

BANGEN   Banging. Used as an intensifer; as a 'bangen girt apple'.

BEENS   Because. 'I can't do it today, beens I must go to town.'

BISSEN   Abbreviation of 'Bist not'; art not, or is not.
[Author's note: Barnes holds that the Dorset verb 'to be' is close
to the Anglo-Saxon. Dorset has 'I be' and 'thou bist' where
Anglo-Saxon has '*ic beo*' and '*thu byst*'.]

BIT AN' DRAP   A bit of food and a drop of drink.

BLEARE   To low as a cow or to cry loud as a fretful child.

BRAGS   Boastings. 'To make one's brags', 'to boast'.

BRUSHEN   An intensifier of size; as, 'a brushen great rat'.

CASSN'T   Can'st not.

CHINE   A chink. (Anglo-Saxon *cyne*) '*Ic ge-séah áne lytle
cynan.*'—King Alfred's *Boethius*. [Author's note: The narrow
valleys cutting the cliffs to Bournemouth's beaches are called
'chines'.]

CLAPPERS   Fox earths. [Author's note: Fox droppings,
hence 'going like the clappers' means 'running like fox-shit'.]

COTHE   An ailing. Illness.

COWHEART   A coward.

CREWEL   (Welsh) A cowslip.

CRIB   To hook in slyly, or little by little; to pilfer.

CRICKET   A low stool for a child.

DE-DA   Simple; foolish; of inactive mind and body.

DEWBIT   The first meal in the morning, not so substantial
as a regular breakfast. The agricultural labourers, in some parts
of Dorsetshire, were accustomed some years since to say that
in harvest time they required seven meals in the day: dewbit,
breakfast, nuncheon, cruncheon, nammit, crammit, and supper.

DOR   (Frisian) Dull, foolish. 'That were dum and dor.' 'That became dumb and dull or foolish.'

DOUGHBEAKED   Of weak or inactive mind; half-witted.

DUMBLEDORE   The bumblebee.

EASEMENT   An easing as from pain.

EM   Them. [Author's note: not a shortening or an abbreviation, but a word derived from Anglo-Saxon]

EN   Him.

FORESHARE   The right to a parcel of the grass of a common meadow, for the 'foreshare of the year, as from February to August, ere the common feeding by cattle.'

GAKE or *GAWK*   To go or stand and gape about idly.

GALLY-BAGGER   Scare-beggar; a bugbear.

GAWK-HAMMER   (Nothern English) A silly gaping fellow (a gawky). Fools formerly had sometimes for a bauble a blown bladder fastened to a stick for a handle. If it was ever called a gawk-hammer or a ninny-hammer, then the word applied to a silly man may mean having a head as empty as a fool's hammer.

GIRT   Great.

GOSSIP   Is still used about Wimborne for a godfather or god-
mother. *Godcib* (gossip) in Anglo-Saxon meant a good kinsman or kinswoman, and in lower meaning a good friend, but we now use gossip for the talk of the good friends, instead of themselves.

HACKLE   A bee-hackle: a sheaf of straw forming a cloak or roof over a beehive.

HANG-GALLIS   Hang-gallows; fit for the gallows; that ought to be, or is likely to be hanged; 'A hang-gallis rogue.'

HARD   A hard boy is a big boy; hard being opposed to tender, in a child of tender years.

HAYMEAKEN   Haymaking formerly consisted of several operations which, with fine weather, commonly followed each other in Dorsetshire thus: The mown grass-in, swath—was thrown abroad—tedded—and afterwards turned once or twice; in the evening it was raked up into little ridges—rollers—single or double, as they might be formed by one raker, or by two raking against each other; and sometimes put up into small cones or heaps, called cocks. On the following morning the rollers or cocks were thrown abroad in passels (parcels), which, after being turned, were in the evening put up into large ridges—weäles; and the wales were sometimes pooked, put up into larger cones— pooks—in which the hay was loaded. In raking grass into double rollers, or pushing hay up into wales, the fore raker or pickman is said to rake in or push in, or row, and the other to close.

HISSELF   Himself.

HOBBLE   A coarsely loud laugh.

HUCKMUCK   Dirty, slovenly.

HUZ-BIRD   Whore's-bird. Bird meaning child, a naughty name by which anger sometimes calls a child.

LEASE   To glean after the reapers (Anglo-Saxon *lesan*, to gather).

LEAZE   Or Zummerleäze. A field stocked through the summer, in distinction from a meadow, which is mown; thence eweleäse, cowleäse. Anglo-Saxon *læsu*—pasture. '*Ic drife mine sceáp to heora læse.*' 'I drive my sheep to their lease.'—Ælfric's *Dialogue*.

LINCEN An intensifier of size; as '*a lincèn girt heare*'.

LUG A pole: a pole in land measure is 5½ yards.

MADDERS The stinking chamomile (*Anthemis cotula*).

NIRRUP A donkey.

OWL To owl about: ramble by night.

POPPY A dog, however old.

RAVES Sides of a waggon. See *WAGGON*.

SKENT Looseness in the bowels. Applied to cattle.

SLACK-TWISTED Inactive; lazy. Applied to a person.

SLOMMOCK A slatternly woman.

SOMEWHAT Some thing.

SOMEWHEN Some time.

STRAPPEN Of great size.

TEWLY Small and weakly, spoken of a child or a plant.

THIK That. (Th soft as in thee.)

TINE To hedge in ground. (Anglo-Saxon *tynan*.) To hedge in, enclosed by a fence. Whence *tún*, a garden, homestead, farm, now a town. In composition '-ton' as Maiden Newton.

TRIMMEN Great of its kind. 'A trimmen crop o' grass.' 'A trimmen girt heâre.'

TRIMMER A great or fine thing of its kind 'That's a trimmer!' 'What now, trimmer?' 'What now, my fine fellow?'

TURK 'A turk of a thing' is an intensitive expression meaning a big or formidable one of its kind. 'There's a turk of a rat.'

VOREFRIEND   Ancestors.

WAGGON   Dorset names of the chief parts of a waggon:
axles are exes; the bottom (bed) of the waggon consists of planks
on strips (shoots), reaching from side to side through mortises
in timbers (summers), lying from end to end over a bearing
pillar on the hinder axle, and on the two pillars (the hanging
pillar and carriage pillar) bearing on the fore-axle. The fore-axle
is connected with the hinder one by a thorough pole, the fore
end of which has a free motion on a pin (the main pin), which
takes it with the two pillars and fore-axle, and its hinder end,
reaching the hinder axle, is connected by a tail bolt with the
shuttle-axle, that takes the hinder end of the summers and tail
board. A parallelogram of timbers is fixed on the fore-axle to
take the shafts (draughts or sharps), the hinder end of which is
the sweep, and the sides of which are called guides, and on them
are set the slides or felloe-pieces (hounds or bussels), which
bear the pillars when the waggon locks. The sides or raves are
propped by brackets, called stouters or stretchers. The sharps
(shafts) have in them three pairs of staples—the dräits or steäples
to draw by with a chain from the collar; the ridge tie steäples, to
take the ridge tie passing over the cart-tree on the thiller's back,
and keeping up the shafts; and the breechen steaple, to take the
breeching.

WILLY-NILLY   Willing or not willing. [Anglo-Saxon:
Willig nillig for ne willig.]

WOPS   A wasp. *Waeps*, with 'ps' for 'sp', is the old Saxon form
of the word, and our brethren of Holstein still call a wasp '*en
weps*'.

Acknowledgements

Crow Court has been a long time coming and has bene-
fited from all kinds of backing during its development.
Throughout, I have always had the support of my wife,
daughter and family, for which I will remain forever grateful.

I would like to thank Rebecca Lloyd and Indira
Chandrasekhar for first publishing 'The World's End',
Rachael Kerr for her crucial interest in the first full manu-
script and John Mitchinson for championing the whole
project. I am deeply indebted to DeAndra Lupu for her
meticulous, patient editing, Leo Nickolls for the sublime
cover design and everyone at Unbound for their enthusiasm,
support and hard work.

I would also like to thank Jessica Kotzer for her pro-
motional support during crowdfunding, and Katie Lodge
for her lively and enthusiastic readings of the later drafts.
Derek B. Scott was kind enough to read through 'The
Peacock Shawl' and point out the more egregious musical
inaccuracies, and his superb text, *The Singing Bourgeois*, was
an inspiration for much of the background to that story—
if there are any remaining bloopers, they are entirely my
own. Many thanks to Alex Freeman for the photography,
coffee and encouragement. Staff and teachers at the Arvon

Foundation helped my development along the way, but on that score, no one has provided more direct support, infectious enthusiasm, wisdom, insight or guidance than Lynne Fairchild, whose company since before the start of this story has been a true inspiration.

~

'The World's End' was first published in *Pangea*, ed. Rebecca Lloyd and Indira Chandrasekhar, Thames River Press, April 2012.

'Mrs Wilkinson's Grave' was shortlisted in the Global Short Story Competition, March 2014.

'Art's Last Laugh' was first published in *Every Day Fiction*, March 2014.

Unbound is the world's first crowdfunding publisher, established in 2011.

We believe that wonderful things can happen when you clear a path for people who share a passion. That's why we've built a platform that brings together readers and authors to crowdfund books they believe in – and give fresh ideas that don't fit the traditional mould the chance they deserve.

This book is in your hands because readers made it possible. Everyone who pledged their support is listed below. Join them by visiting unbound.com and supporting a book today.

Claire Adams

Angela Arnold

David Baillie

Teresa Baraclough

Howard Barlow

Tony Beck

David Bleicher

Masackia Bozumbil

Andrew Bryant

Margie Buchanan-Smith

Melanie Canham

María José Castrillo

Nigel Charman

Nigel & Maggie Charman

Suw Charman-Anderson

Ian Chester

Hilary Cochrane

Alison Cocks

Amelia Coffen

Gina Collia

Jo Davies

Sophia Davies

E R Andrew Davis

Glenn Dietz

Stuart Dillon

Samuel Dodson

Robert Eardley

Kim Evison

Lynne Fairchild

Jeremy Farshore-Swimwell

Jean Forbes

Alex Freeman

Yolanda Garzon

Rick Gekoski

Lynn Genevieve

Chris Gostick

Susan Graham

Tom Grant

Geoffrey Gudgion

Tamara Henriques

Sue Hogben

Roseena Hussain

Sheryl K

Steve Keenan

Rachael Kerr

Dan Kieran

Michaela Knowles

Jessica Kotzer

Nicola Kumar

Annie Lee

Julian Lee

Paul Leigh

Sheila Lennie

Milos Levajac

Will Liddell

Rebecca Lloyd

Katie Lodge

Graham Macken

Philippa Manasseh

Simon Marsh

Lucy McCahon

Jennifer McCollum Schmidt

Alice McVeigh

Lynne McVernon

Rosario Melera

Paul Milner

Noemí Miranda

John Mitchinson

Alex Morrall

Carlo Navato

Michael Paley

Liz Parker

Sophie Parkes-Nield

Mike Pennell

Justin Pollard

Ian Sayer

Derek Scott

Jane Shepherd

Neil Simpson

Justin Sleep

Toni Smerdon

Tom Smith

Martyn Stead

Annemarie Straathof

Helen Sunderland
Daniel Tate
Santiago Tejada
Kathryn Temple
Jacoby Thwaites
Ann Tudor
Nilopar Uddin
Gabriella van Rooij
Joanne Wallis
Andy Way
Andrew Weaver

Wendy
Richard Whitaker
Lloyd Wigglesworth
Gareth Williams
Jenny Williams
Wendy Wilson
Clare Wood
Adam Woollard
Maureen Wright
Nicholas Yeo